D0480937

'I thoroughly enjoyed *Tattletale*, sympathetic characters and neck breaking twists – highly recommended'

Jenny Blackhurst, author of *Before I Let You In*

'A perfect example of how a psychological thriller should be written – intricately plotted and full of shocking surprises'

Lisa Hall, author of *Between You and Me*

'A clever, twisting story of obsession'　　　　*Woman & Home*

'Delivers suspense, twists and sharp writing'

Lisa Jewell, author of *Then She Was Gone*

'Deliciously clever. The characters were massively addictive and more so because they defied traditional convention'

Emma Kavanagh, author of *The Missing Hours*

'Like any great mystery, *Tattletale* would, at every twist, lead me to think I'd almost put the pieces together – only to turn the puzzle upside down'　　　　*Grazia*

'Gripping, electrifying, heartbreaking'

Erin Kelly, author of *He Said/She Said*

'Sarah Naughton expertly creates claustrophobic menace at the heart of the place that's meant to be safest of all – home'

Louise Millar, author of *City of Strangers*

'A compulsive, twisting story about trauma and revenge, delivered with dazzling skill' *Sunday Mirror*

On The Other Couple

'Intelligent. Gripping. Colourful. Great setting. Absorbing characters'
Jane Corry, author of *My Husband's Wife*

'It's so well plotted you're looking out for every detail . . . Compelling and scary' *Evening Standard*

'From the moment Asha and Ollie set off on honeymoon the cracks begin to show, as Naughton skilfully weaves three timelines into a chilling drama . . . As the tension rose, I turned the pages faster and faster – until the denouement hit me like a juggernaut' Alison Belsham, author of *The Tattoo Thief*

'Brilliantly chilling and claustrophobic, the thought of being trapped in paradise yet knowing something wasn't right was such a frightening concept. I didn't guess at any point what was going to happen . . . I loved it!'
Karen Hamilton, author of *The Perfect Girlfriend*

'Naughton's novel is full of twists and flashbacks [with] a truly shocking finale' *The Lady*

the
mothers

Sarah J Naughton

TRAPEZE

First published in Great Britain in 2020 by Trapeze
an imprint of The Orion Publishing Group Ltd
Carmelite House, 50 Victoria Embankment
London EC4Y 0DZ

An Hachette UK Company

1 3 5 7 9 10 8 6 4 2

Copyright © Sarah J Naughton 2020

The moral right of Sarah J Naughton to be identified as
the author of this work has been asserted in accordance
with the Copyright, Designs and Patents Act of 1988.

All rights reserved. No part of this publication may be
reproduced, stored in a retrieval system, or transmitted
in any form or by any means, electronic, mechanical,
photocopying, recording, or otherwise, without the
prior permission of both the copyright owner and the
above publisher of this book.

All the characters in this book are fictitious,
and any resemblance to actual persons, living
or dead, is purely coincidental.

A CIP catalogue record for this book is
available from the British Library.

ISBN (Mass Market Paperback) 978 1 4091 8460 7
ISBN (eBook) 978 1 4091 8461 4

Typeset by Born Group
Printed and bound in Great Britain by Clays Ltd, Elcograf S.p.A

www.orionbooks.co.uk

For Rhian John, Sofia Kapsalis,
Lynne Mark and Betina Scanlon.

Mothers are all slightly insane.

JD Salinger, *The Catcher in the Rye*

The only thing to do was to kill him.

Otherwise something else certainly would.

The junkies she saw shambling along the pavement as she sat listlessly by the window would stab him with their needles as they passed the pram.

The germs that polluted every surface would drift into his nostrils, taking root in his tiny lungs, percolating through his bloodstream, poisoning him.

His very birth had almost killed him. Her pre-eclampsia had led to multiple organ failure. He had been delivered blue and life-less, revived by desperate doctors. Her milk hadn't come through because there was still placenta left in her body. She had to go back to hospital for a D&C, during which she lost three pints of blood, and afterwards an infection meant she still couldn't breastfeed. He became jaundiced and skeletal and had to be put on a drip.

It was all a sign that the world was too dangerous for him.

But they had made her take him home, and her husband had gone back to work, and now they were alone, just the two of them against the vast savagery of the world.

A month after his birth, her consciousness had shrunk down to a single point of pure terror.

She forced herself to stay awake all night, checking that he was breathing, taking his temperature, roaming the darkened house looking for intruders just waiting for a gap in her vigilance.

She didn't dare eat in case some toxin passed into him.

People were lying to her all the time. Even her husband. He was making plans, she knew, to take the baby away from her. To give him to someone who would not love him, who would neglect and abuse and finally murder him.

Then came the revelation.

There was a way to keep him safe forever.

It was late afternoon, the sky already darkening. Winter was coming, full of bitter cold and disease. He napped upstairs as she kept vigil at the window in her pyjamas, staring out at the threatening sky and the angry cars.

Her phone rang. One of her so-called 'friends' checking up on her. Spying on her, to report back to her husband.

He would be home soon. She had to act now.

She got up and went into the hall.

Faces grinned down at her from the walls, all teeth and eyes. Were there cameras behind those glittering black pupils?

Grunting with effort, the fresh scars straining and burning, she climbed the stairs and went into her bedroom. Then she came out again and walked down the landing.

He was still napping. He would never even know.

Animals danced on his walls, a hare, a stag and an owl. Wild beasts of ancient magic. They knew what she had to do. They would protect him, stay by his side as his spirit animals, carry him to peace and safety.

She bent to kiss his warm forehead.

From downstairs she heard the front door close. Someone was calling her name.

She didn't reply. Time was running out.

She raised the pillow.

Footsteps drummed on the stairs like the prelude to an execution. Her baby opened his eyes. She lowered the pillow.

1

Iona

Present

It had been raining since dawn. She knew because she never slept past five these days. The floor of the ticket hall was awash with filthy water, and the yellow A-frame warning signs were out. Touching out of the barrier, she emerged onto Sloane Square. For once it was as grim and overcast in the centre of town as it was out east. The rainy pavements had none of the sparkle they possessed in the movies, just a greasy sheen, spattered with leaves that had been pounded by commuter feet to lethal slime.

Putting up her umbrella, she set off in the direction of the police station but decided to detour from her usual residential route to the shopping street of Pimlico Road.

The Secret Santa names had been assigned and, while normally she paid the whole thing very little attention, opting for a box of Quality Street for her recipient and giving her own gift – usually penis-based – straight to charity, this year she would have to make more of an effort. Because this year she had picked Maya.

She walked slowly past the windows of the pricey shops. There was a nice silver leather purse with a neon pink M, but the price tag made her wince. Slightly more affordable was a scented candle in a little glass tumbler, but the brand name was famous enough that it would be obvious she had overspent. The budget was a tenner and woe betide anyone who went over – they would have to answer to Darcy. Their control room manager took the annual Secret Santa nightmare as seriously as she did every other aspect of her job.

A passing car threw up an arc of dirty water that soaked Iona's black trousers and she was tempted, when the guy stopped at the lights, to rap on his window. But on catching up with the car she saw it was being driven by a harassed woman with two squabbling kids in the back. The lights turned green and the car pulled away.

In sight of the station she paused to check her appearance in a window, this one had a darkened interior, as shop after shop on the high street gave up the ghost.

She looked old. A decade past her thirty-one years. Make-up had always been too much faff as far as she was concerned, but perhaps it was time to consider a bit of foundation. At least she'd covered up the scar. She never used to bother, but then Maya arrived.

Someone called her name. Looking round self-consciously she saw Darcy, soaked to the skin, with a free newspaper turning to pulp over her head. Extending her umbrella, Iona walked with the older woman the rest of the way to the station.

Yannis was waiting outside her office.

'Tell me you've got a grisly murder for me,' Iona said, shaking out the umbrella and hanging her jacket on the back of the chair. 'I need something to warm me up.'

'Sorry.' The detective sergeant grimaced. 'Missing person.'

'Yippee.'

'And not even a juicy one, I'm afraid.' By which she knew he meant prostitute or child. 'Banker, 42, didn't come home from work yesterday and the company says he wasn't in all day. Phone's off. Wife called it in this morning.'

Iona groaned and rubbed her face, then stopped when she realised she might rub off the concealer covering the scar. Maya was standing at the water cooler outside. She'd had her ponytail cut into a neat black bob that fell like a curtain across her face so that you could no longer see her cheekbones and long eyelashes. They'd hired Maya three months ago as Logistics and Resource Planning Manager but, whatever the hell one of those was, Maya didn't look like one. She looked like a DJ or an artist. Intelligent and quirky and completely stunning. And probably straight.

Iona pulled on the jacket she had just taken off.

'Might as well get it over with.'

'If we have to,' Yannis grumbled, and the two of them headed out of the office.

The streets were choked with traffic as rain-shy commuters hailed taxis instead of walking. Yannis drove, humming to himself. His caramel skin was the exact same tone as his hair, which was shorn to tight whorls across his scalp. The slew of freckles and light blue eyes alongside his black features would make him a shoe-in for international advertising campaigns, but he was a detective through and through. Serious and focused, to the frustration of some of the young women back at the station. But not all of them. And maybe not Maya. She hoped.

The Uptons lived in a three-storey Georgian townhouse at the wrong end of the Kings Road. It was the only house in the terrace without a thick coating of grime on the stucco and gaps in the cornicing like knocked-out teeth: the only basement not a dumping ground for litter. Most of the houses on this street were divided into flats, their windows opaque with filth, cracks in the glass repaired by parcel tape. Still, Iona thought, the Uptons' place was probably worth a cool one and a half mill. Perhaps they were hoping the area was up and coming. But anything that was going to up-and-come in Chelsea had probably done so already.

'That's his car,' Yannis said as they parked and got out into the rain.

The black Audi stood out among the Ford Focuses and ancient Vauxhalls. Iona walked around it, peering through the windows.

Surprisingly spick and span for a family car: a bag of boiled sweets in the compartment between the seats, a sports drink bottle in the footwell, a gap for the stereo to go. Only sensible to take it out in an area like this.

'So, either he wants to make it hard for us to trace him,' she said, almost to herself, 'or something's happened to him.'

'But if that's the case,' Yannis said, his reflection swimming up beside her in the car window, 'a mugging gone wrong, a sudden heart attack, then surely a body would have turned up by now.'

She looked around her. This was perhaps the worst part of Chelsea: worse than the sprawling council estate by the river. These flats were bedsits let out to the desperate who had no chance of even making it onto council lists.

Desperate enough to mug Upton and leave him bleeding in the gutter? Or to murder him and dump the body somewhere? That suggested a degree of organisation not generally displayed by those existing at society's margins.

A junkie Iona vaguely recognised was shuffling up the pavement towards them. Raising her head at the last moment, a look of consternation flashed across her ravaged features and she turned and scuttled back the way she had come.

'Not this time, Marta,' Yannis called after her. 'You're all right!'

As she tottered away they climbed the steps and rang the bell.

Bella Upton looked as bad as might be expected for a woman whose husband was missing. On a good day, with washed hair and a decent night's sleep, she would be pretty. She was about thirty-five, with a round face framed by long, chestnut hair and large, expressive brown eyes. She blinked slowly when she opened the door and seemed to take long moments to register their badges.

'Good morning, Mrs Upton. I'm Detective Inspector Iona Chatwin, and this is Detective Sergeant Yannis Mohamud. May we come in?'

As they followed her down the hall, Iona looked at the photographs lining the walls. It was standard middle-class stuff: silver frames, a couple of professional studio shots, fancy holiday destinations. But the shuffling woman in front of them, shrouded in a long cardigan, was a far cry from the sparky, attractive girl in the photographs.

Iona paused at a posed black and white image of a man holding the child.

'Is this your husband?'

'Yes. I've got some clearer ones that you can use.'

'I don't think we need to worry about that just yet,' Yannis said. 'Most missing persons return within—'

'Forty-eight hours. Yes, I know.'

The man was plump-faced with light brown hair and one of those beards that used to be called *hipster* but were now pretty ubiquitous. Yannis had tried to grow one but it had come out carrot-orange. The beard and conventional style of dress – Upton seemed to favour jeans, T-shirts and hoodies – would make him difficult to pick out on CCTV.

They followed his wife through to an open-plan area: kitchen at the back, morphing into a dining room in the middle, then a living room at the front, looking out on the traffic-choked A-road. Iona wouldn't want to live that way – there was nowhere to hide.

It was, for instance, quite hard to carry on a conversation about a missing father when his son was watching cartoons a few feet away. When they arrived he had got down from the kitchen table and gone to sit in front of the TV without protest. He looked like a mini banker to Iona: short back and sides, blue checked shirt tucked into beige cords, tiny deck shoes. Stocky and strong-looking.

They sat down at the kitchen table. The sun pouring through the grimy windows had warmed its surface, releasing a sweet, woody scent.

As Bella Upton filled the kettle she slopped water over her hand and the floor, though she didn't seem to notice, and as she waited for it to boil she simply stood staring at the blank white face of a kitchen cabinet. Her eyes were unfocused, her hands hung limp at her sides. Had she been prescribed some kind of tranquilliser to deal with the situation? Iona wondered.

The kettle boiled and she seemed to shake herself from her trance, opening the cupboard and taking out two mugs. Iona winced as the woman poured out the boiling water, but there were no spillages this time.

'Sugar?'

They gave the familiar orders. One for herself, three for Yannis. People expected the police to have too much sugar in their tea, it was a comforting tradition. Iona could hear the trilling of the spoon against the mugs as the woman stirred, like a very quiet alarm clock. Her hands were shaking.

Removing the teabags Bella laid them on the draining board beside the knife she had used to cut the child's fruit. Instinct made Iona glance at the knife block – the remaining slots were full. Bella brought the tea over, sat down opposite them and extracted a raggedy tissue from her pocket.

Iona took a sip, suspecting from the slightly sour smell that the milk was on the turn, then laid the mug quietly on the table.

'We understand that Ewan's been missing since yesterday, Friday?'

Bella nodded. 'I got a phone call from the office to say that he hadn't turned up for work.'

'So, he left as usual on the Friday morning but didn't actually make it into work. And you haven't heard from him at all. No text messages, nothing?'

'No. I've been trying to call his phone but it goes straight to voicemail.'

'And what about emails and social media. Has there been any activity as far as you could tell?'

'I don't have access to all that,' she said.

'No problem,' Yannis said. 'We can get into his computer if it becomes necessary.'

'Which we hope it won't,' Iona cut in. 'We have no reason to believe he's come to any harm. How has he been in himself recently?'

'A bit stressed at work, I suppose.'

'Any mental health problems, as far as you know?'

'No, not at all. But if he did it as a spur-of-the-moment thing because he was stressed or something, he wouldn't have taken his passport, would he?'

'He took his passport?' Yannis returned Iona's glance.

'And a suitcase. We keep the passports in the drawer with the address book. When he didn't come home I started trying his family and I saw that it was gone.'

So, he had left of his own accord, and he had planned it in advance. An affair?

'Okay.' This put things in a rather different light. If a man chose to leave his wife and child, that was his business. It was not a police matter.

'Have any of his family heard from him?' Yannis continued seamlessly. It was the only thing to do now. Make reassuring noises and leave as quickly as possible.

'No. No one. I told him he shouldn't have taken the promotion. It was obvious Juliet – she's the other senior manager – was going to get pregnant. She'd got married a few years before, so of course she does and they don't replace her. It doubled his workload. It's not fair, is it? When women do that. They'd literally just trained her, spent all that money, and now she probably won't be back.'

Iona pressed her lips together in a sympathetic smile. Yannis looked away. One of the lads had suggested as much about her, when she was promoted to DI. Before they realised.

'He was working later and later,' Bella continued, 'and then when he came home he had to carry on in the study.' She nodded towards a door leading from the kitchen back into the hall.

'But the stress wasn't serious enough for him to have seen a doctor and he wasn't taking any medication?'

Bella shook her head quickly, as if that was a good thing. But untreated depression was by far the most dangerous kind. Still, if he'd packed a suitcase he probably intended to stay alive at least for the near future.

'Okay, well that all sounds very positive. He might have just needed to get away for a while. It happens to the best of us. Now, unless there's anything else you think we should know?'

Bella blinked at her and Iona felt a moment's guilt, knowing that this would be slipped in right at the very bottom of the pile of matters to attend to.

'At least he took his mobile,' Iona continued gently, 'so there's every chance he'll get in touch with you.'

'It's been off the whole time, but you can still trace it, right?'

'Yes, if the battery is still inside, we should be able to track it.' She looked at Yannis, who nodded professionally. They would not, of course, waste time and resources attempting this.

'Until then, try not to worry. There's no reason to believe that anything untoward has happened to him. I'm sure he'll turn up safe and well within the next couple of days.'

Taking her cue from them, Bella got to her feet and led them back out into the hall.

Ewan Upton's face beamed down at them from the walls. A good guy who had reached the end of his tether, perhaps. Iona hoped he would come to his senses and return home again. He had a little boy, who was probably as confused and upset as his mother.

They reached the door. Yannis opened it and they stepped outside into the drizzle. After the warmth of the family home the run-down street felt colder and more depressing. It had been raining for weeks now and at high tide the river was threatening to overtop the embankment. Sometimes a bit of bad weather, added to the ever-shortening days, was enough to send people over the edge.

'Thanks, Mrs Upton. We'll be in touch.' Iona shook the woman's hand. It was limp and very soft.

'Mummy?' The little boy had wandered out into the hall.

'It's all right, Teddy,' Bella said. 'We can go do the jigsaw now.'

He wandered up and took his mother's hand.

'What happened to your face?' he said, squinting up at Iona.

She automatically raised her hand to the scar on her jaw. Even after seven months it was still livid purple and the concealer must have rubbed off in the rain.

'A man wasn't too happy about me trying to arrest him, so he got very cross and hit me,' Iona said, smiling. The truth was, he had slashed her with a hunting knife, missing her carotid artery by two inches.

'Always men, isn't it?' Bella said, and quietly shut the door.

2

Mothers Club

3 Years Previously

Bella opened the door with a beaming smile that had been somewhat helped along by a large glass of Chardonnay.

At least the house looked nice. She had put up the Christmas decorations early, just for tonight, and with the snow falling, and candlelight sparkling in the windows, the effect made her proud. She could still make things pretty.

Her heart sank a little when she saw who stood there, flowers in one hand, a bottle of something that was bound to be expensive in the other.

Tall, slim, glamorous, with a high-flying career as a lawyer, a huge house in the best part of Chelsea and a handsome husband, nothing ever went wrong for Chrissy. Her daughter had been born by elective caesarean section in a private hospital and her only birth horror story was about how a last-minute change of consultant meant Chloe was delivered by someone she went to university with.

One of the other mums had asked Chrissy once why she chose to have antenatal classes with the hoi polloi when she could have gone privately with the cast of *Made In Chelsea*, but Chrissy had just laughed and said she was hoi polloi herself. Which was bollocks, of course. Tonight she was in beige cashmere and white jeans and a pair of jewel-encrusted loafers that probably cost more than Ewan's car.

'Hello, darling.' Chrissy enclosed her in a bubble of expensive perfume. 'How are you?' She pulled away and held Bella at arm's length.

'Good. Really good.' Bella smiled, feeling sweat prickle under her hair.

'And how's that gorgeous boy?'

'I'm fine, thank you.' Ewan had come out into the hall.

'Not *you*,' Chrissy laughed. 'Teddy!'

'Oh.' Ewan put on a pretend pout.

'Teddy's fine,' Bella said. 'Sleeping like a—'

'Baby?' Ewan completed, and they all laughed. Bella's face was starting to hurt.

'Close the door, Bells, you're letting all the heat out.'

Ewan poured the drinks and they chatted inconsequentially about the babies' sleeping patterns. Chrissy's announcement that Chloe had been sleeping through the night from a month old made something akin to panic close around Bella's throat. Was there something wrong with Teddy? Was she not feeding him enough during the day? He seemed to be latched on for hours.

'Are you still breastfeeding?' Bella said lightly.

'No. I did it for a couple weeks, which is hopefully enough to have some benefit for her immune system. How about you?'

'Still going. I'm going to try and carry on for six months. Only another quarter of a year of bleeding nipples and crushing exhaustion to go.' She laughed awkwardly, wondering if she'd made a vulgar faux pas.

'Well done you,' Chrissy said.

Bella glanced at Ewan to see if he had been listening, but he was fiddling with the iPod speakers and when he'd finished he went off to the kitchen. The conversation dried up. Had her comment sounded bragging? Had she annoyed Chrissy?

'I love your shoes,' Bella said desperately.

'Thanks. I've had them years. I like your dress.'

'I haven't worn it since I gave up work. It's a bit tight, to be honest.'

'It's so hard to lose weight when you're breastfeeding,' Chrissy said.

Bella bit her tongue. Chrissy had been back in her size 10 jeans the day after she gave birth while, nine weeks down the line, Bella still looked pregnant.

The doorbell rang.

'I'll get it!' Bella trilled.

Pausing a moment in the darkened hallway she took some deep breaths. She could tell by the silhouette that this was Electra. While Chrissy was far too polite to bring up the state Bella had been in when they last saw her, Electra might mention it, especially after a glass of wine. A wave of mortification took Bella's breath away, followed swiftly by the dread that had become habitual. Once he'd said hello to them all Ewan was going out. What if she said something wrong?

She opened the door.

'Hi!' Electra said. 'Am I the first?'

'No. Chrissy's here.'

'Oh, good. She'll have brought something decent that we can guzzle down before the others arrive. Here you go.' She thrust a bottle into Bella's hand. 'It's from Zack's bar. Quite a good one, apparently. Now lemme in, I'm fecking freezing.'

It was only early December, but winter had bitten early. Glancing down the street to see if any of the others were in sight Bella saw the junkie from the bedsit next door fighting with her boyfriend on the pavement. The man was trying to hold her off from scratching his face. Perhaps sensing Bella's attention they paused and their heads began to turn in her direction. She shut the door quickly.

All in black, with a severe black crop Bella would never have the courage to sport and the sort of heels she gave up when she was pregnant, Electra strode through the door to the living room as if the place were her own.

'Give me a drink, I feel like a zombie. Got about two hours' sleep last night.'

From the hall Bella heard Chrissy commiserating.

'Pearl's fine, sleeps about seven hours straight, but Ozzy's up every two hours without fail.'

Seven hours! Bella's heart sank and she leaned against the wall for support. She was so tired. The doctor said she mustn't get too tired, but she had to do the night-time feeds. Ewan didn't like the idea of giving Teddy a bottle to see him through, and he was right. Breast was best. Even with her medication. It was such a low dose, and anyway, they'd proved it didn't affect nursing babies.

The cold air had tumbled into the hall and now wrapped itself around her ankles. She was wearing her sheepskin slippers. Why on earth hadn't she put shoes on?

For a moment she couldn't face going back in. She should never have offered to host the first mums gathering. Ewan had said she was in no fit state. She should have listened. When the doorbell rang again she jumped.

'Am I late?' Skye said.

'No, not at all,' Bella exhaled with relief. Of all the mums, Skye was the least intimidating. It was a slightly shameful observation, but in the hierarchy Skye definitely came below her. She had bleached dreadlocks and tattoos. Her tiny houseboat must be freezing and damp in this weather. Jen only had a council flat, but her unshakeable confidence won out against her poverty every time.

'I didn't bring anything,' Skye said. 'Was I supposed to?'

'Oh, not at all,' Bella said breezily. 'Just yourself! Come and say hello to Ewan before he goes out.'

But Ewan was deep in conversation with Chrissy, his eyebrows tilted earnestly as he spoke, in a way that suggested to Bella that he was trying to impress her. Chrissy was nodding politely.

'Skye's here!' Bella called, and Ewan gave a twitch of irritation when Chrissy broke away from the conversation to greet the new arrival.

'Hello, Skye.' Ewan reached to shake her hand and Bella hoped she hadn't noticed his sidelong glance at Skye's inked arms. Under the silver Puffa she deposited on the sofa Skye was wearing baggy harem trousers and a vest featuring an image of some many-limbed god.

'How's Juniper?' Chrissy said.

'Stinking cold,' Skye replied. 'She could barely breathe last night. I actually had to suck the snot out of her nose.'

'What with?' Bella said.

'My mouth!'

'Euw.' Electra screwed up her face.

Skye smiled. 'A mother will do anything for love.'

'Ah, holiest of holy. The sacred mother.' Ewan grinned. 'The rest of us are not worthy.'

'He calls us the Mothers Club,' Bella said, smiling.

Ewan looked at her sharply. But the mums weren't offended. They were laughing.

Now that everyone was here Bella went to the kitchen and took the cling film off the plates of nibbles she'd prepared during Teddy's afternoon nap. She was gratified to hear the conversation flowing smoothly in the living room. She brought the plates in and was pleased again when the women tucked in with enthusiasm. She liked looking after people. Ewan always said she was a natural mother. That was partly why he suggested her giving up work. She'd wanted to anyway, of course, what woman could stand to be apart from her baby?

'Has anyone heard from Jen?' Electra said with her mouth full.

'I invited her on the group chat,' Bella said, 'but I guessed she wouldn't come.'

'Poor thing,' said Skye. 'I wonder how they're doing.'

Panic gripped Bella's throat again. She couldn't think about that horrible thing that had happened, she just couldn't. Feeling Chrissy's eyes on her she went to the window and relit one of the candles that had gone out.

'Anyone recommend a good builder?' Chrissy asked. 'We're thinking of lowering our basement.'

The conversation changed direction, to the difficulty of finding decent tradesmen in London, and then on to whether or not it was PC-gone-mad to refer to them as *tradespeople*.

The second bottle was soon empty, so Bella went to the kitchen for Chrissy's, hoping it would be chilled enough. It had an actual cork, and while she was riffling through the drawer looking for a corkscrew the doorbell rang again.

They all stopped talking.

'Might be people canvassing,' Bella said. 'Isn't there a local election soon?'

Ewan made no move to answer it, so she went out to the hall. A woman's silhouette filled the glass pane of the door, hair tied in a topknot. Bella froze, her fingers on the latch. She had the urge to drop down to a crouch in the darkness and pretend they weren't here. But her figure would be clear enough through the patterned glass. She opened the door.

'Hi!' Her jollity was wincingly overdone. 'Great to see you! I wasn't sure you'd make it!'

'Ah, I'm always late for everything.' Jen stood on the step, the snow falling on her dark hair.

'Come in, come in, you must be freezing!'

Jen was wearing leggings that looked like they were made of spandex and a tiny leather jacket. She had got so thin since Bella last saw her, losing the baby weight and more. Bella led her down the hall to the living room.

Somehow the conversation was flowing again and seamlessly segued into expressions of delight that Jen had decided to come.

Bella was surprised to see Ewan go in for a hug too, and hoped Skye wasn't offended that she had only been offered a handshake. Perhaps she would think he was only doing it out of pity.

'Looking fantastic as always,' he said into Jen's hair.

He was wrong. Jen was too thin and her hair and eyes had lost their lustre, but the tone was spot on. Like Bella, Jen needed to be around plenty of positivity. She thanked him and said he didn't look too bad himself. He pretended to preen.

'Right, ladies,' he said. 'I think I may have outstayed my welcome, so I shall get out of your hair.'

The women cooed that of course he must stay.

'Where will you go?' Bella said.

'Clubbing,' Ewan grinned, but he didn't elaborate.

'How late will you be?' she said.

'It depends how long you ladies plan to carouse.'

'All night,' Jen said.

After he left Bella felt a little of the tension drain out of her. Now that she was alone with them she felt okay. The shame that they had seen her at her lowest had been replaced by something else. It was almost comforting. They had *all* seen one another at their lowest. Constipated, stomachs swollen to bursting, breasts leaking. Even Chrissy had got mastitis. It was okay.

'We should get a picture of all of us,' Jen said, taking out her phone.

'Oh, no!' Electra cried. 'I always look totally chinless in selfies.'

'We've still got a proper camera,' Bella said. 'I can set it up on a timer.'

It took a while to fiddle about with the thing, but finally the little red light started winking. No one was sure if you had to press another button, so when it flashed they hadn't had a chance to pose properly. Smiles were half-formed, faces were shadowed. And yet there was something about the picture that they all liked.

'Email me a copy,' Chrissy said, and the others agreed.

Another bottle gone, Bella went back to the kitchen.

'A toast!' Chrissy announced on her return. 'To the Mothers Club!'

'And all who sail in her!' added Electra.

They laughed and clinked glasses. The candlelight was flattering. Chrissy, all white and gold and sparkling jewels, looked like a goddess. Electra was a dark angel, her eyes flashing. Jen was Kardashian-sexy. Even Skye looked lovely, the tattoos that seemed dull and grubby in the daylight had taken on a serpentine beauty.

Bella caught a glimpse of herself in the mirror above the fire. All that smiling, even if some of it was forced, had made her eyes bright and her cheeks pink, and the flesh bulging above the tight bodice of her cocktail dress was peachy and glowing. Cherubic. She smiled to herself. Something in her released and she took a large slug of the wine. She had promised Ewan she'd only have two glasses, but one extra wouldn't hurt the baby. Perhaps it wouldn't be such a bad night after all.

3

Iona

Present

More rain, turning the Monday morning dusk-dark, hissing against the windows, shattering the lights of the cars in the street outside into shards of red and white. Her roof had started to leak, painting brownish swirls across the bathroom ceiling, shorting the lights so she couldn't see to apply the concealer. The scar was uncovered today and so it was just her luck to bump into Maya in the unforgiving lights of the tube station.

'I'm getting fed up of this,' Maya said behind her, making her jump. 'I got fed up of the sun in the summer and now I'm fed up of the rain. Guess I'm just a miserable bitch.'

Unable to think of a better response, Iona said, 'Have you had your hair cut?'

'Yeah. Some wanker grabbed it outside a bar last month, so that put me off having big hair a bit. Can I come under your brolly?'

'Sure.'

Maya came to stand so close to her that Iona could smell her deodorant, activated by the sweaty fug of the tube train. It was a deliciously human smell. She'd always hated perfume. They stepped out into the rain.

'Did you nick him?'

'Ha. No. I just stuck my foot out when he was passing me later on with a tray of drinks and he chucked them all over the floor. Classy, eh?'

Iona smiled. 'Perfect.' Then she blushed. Did Maya think she was referring to her, as opposed to the act itself. 'What bar was it?' she gabbled.

'One in Soho.'

Simultaneously they jumped over a puddle. It was like being a little girl again, playing in the rain with your best friend. Iona resisted the urge to link arms with Maya, though it would have been much more comfortable.

'It was a dive really. But some mates wanted to go.'

Again Iona was stumped for a response that wouldn't look too keen.

'Anything interesting on at the mo— woah!' Maya grabbed Iona by the jacket just in time to stop her walking straight out in front of a bus.

'Shit, thanks,' Iona panted.

'That's the thing about detective inspectors,' Maya said. 'Amazing observational skills.' Reaching for Iona's shoulders she tugged the jacket back into place. 'There you go.'

'Thanks,' Iona repeated.

They crossed the road, Iona following dumbly in Maya's wake.

'So, what have you got on?' Iona said.

'I just asked you that.'

'Oh right. Um, nothing much. Missing banker. Probably just run off with someone.'

'Sounds thrilling. Well, here we are.'

They went into the station, Iona pausing in the doorway to shake out the umbrella. When she turned back Maya was gone.

Upstairs, Yannis was waiting for her. It must be something interesting. The curls of his hair were jewelled with rain, so he'd only just come in himself. Her pulse quickened with the usual thrill at the prospect of a meaty case.

'So that missing guy, Ewan Upton? Looks like he's been skimming from his firm.'

'Oh.'

Fraud was infinitely duller than abduction, but they couldn't hand it straight over to the fraud department without doing due diligence trying to locate him.

'They called just now. Three hundred k over the past six months. They were about to have an audit, so it would probably have shown up.'

'So that's why he legged it.'

'Looks like it.'

'I guess that's why he was so stressed at work, like the wife said.'

Yannis leaned on the door frame, sipping the protein shake that was his usual breakfast choice. 'Do you reckon she knew?'

'Maybe. Maybe it was just too difficult to up sticks with the kid before the audit.'

'I guess there could be a plan to join him later.'

'So why report him missing?' Iona said. 'We should take a closer look into their finances, though. Find out where the money's gone.'

'Should I get a search warrant?'

'Not yet. We don't want to alert her if she is involved. Just get the account records from the bank. If we don't have any luck there we seize his computer.'

'Okay.'

'Oh, and alert the border police. Then I think we should pay her another visit.'

Bella Upton looked worse than ever when she answered the door the second time. Still in her pyjamas, she had spilt milk or similar down her front and it had dried stiffly, rucking the soft flannel, opening up a gap between the buttons that revealed the edge of one heavy breast. Iona had the urge to do it up for her before Yannis noticed.

Bella's eyes widened when she saw them.

'Have you found him?'

'No news at the moment, Mrs Upton, I'm afraid, but we wanted to clarify a few things from our last meeting. Could we come in?'

The house smelled of bins that should have been put out and laundry that should have been done. Teddy was sitting on his potty in front of the TV, eating toast, and when he got up, in just a vest, the tang of excrement added to the foetid mix.

This time they weren't offered tea.

'Have you heard from him?' Iona asked, sitting down.

Bella shook her head.

'Well, it's still early days.' Iona smiled. 'I thought we could just go over exactly what happened on the Thursday evening before he disappeared.'

'I was out with friends that night.'

'How did he seem when you left the house?'

'I didn't really say much to him. He was working in the study.'

'But he was okay when he got home from work? No more stressed than usual? The two of you got on all right?'

'Yes, fine. I cooked for him and Teddy because I was going to eat at Chrissy's, but Ewan doesn't like eating before eight thirty, so I left a meal in the microwave for him. Then I fed and bathed Teddy and put him to bed. Then I got ready and went out at about seven.'

'You said goodbye to Ewan?'

'He was working.'

'But you're sure he was definitely at home?'

'Yes, he was in his office.'

'So, next morning when he left for work, did he seem okay?'

It took a moment for Bella to answer. 'I never actually said goodbye to him on the Friday.'

'No?'

'I didn't actually hear him go.'

Actually, actually.

'I'd got quite drunk at Chrissy's and then fell asleep on the sofa when I got home.'

Ah, hence the *actually*. She was ashamed.

'I only woke up when Teddy started calling to get out of his cot. Ewan was already gone.'

'But was he definitely still here when you got back on the Thursday night?'

'I'm sorry,' Bella said softly. 'I just can't remember. I . . . I just assumed he was.'

'And you didn't get up at all in the night? To use the bathroom, or get a glass of water?' Yannis said.

As she shook her head her auburn lowlights flashed in the overhead light. The roots were growing out the same dark brown that she had in the photograph on the radiator cabinet. A slightly younger Bella Upton stood in this very room, with four other women. She was smiling, but there were dark rings around her eyes that the party make-up didn't quite cover.

'Is there any chance,' Yannis said, 'that Ewan might have gone the night before and you didn't notice when you came in?'

'I suppose it's possible, but then Teddy would have been alone in the house. He wouldn't do that . . . surely . . .' She tailed off and silence descended but for the kettledrum sound effects of the cartoon in the front room. It seemed to Iona that Bella Upton was starting to realise that she didn't know her husband quite as well as she thought.

'Wait.'

Bella went to the microwave and opened it, then stood back to show them that it was empty. 'He must have had his dinner, and he must have put the plate in the dishwasher and run it because it was all clean on Friday morning. I know because my childminder didn't turn up – she normally clears it – so I had to put everything away myself. There was definitely a big plate there.'

'Okay,' Iona said. 'So either he left late Thursday night, while you were out, or on the Friday morning, before you woke up. Let's go back to Thursday night. You arrived at your friend's house. What did you say her name was?'

'Chrissy Welch.' Bella nodded towards the picture on the cabinet. 'She's the blonde one at the end. She has a daughter, Chloe, the same age as Teddy.'

'Anyone else there?'

'Electra – with the short black hair – Skye with the dreadlocks and Jen at the other end.'

Iona studied the faces in the picture. The one at the end was younger than the others: attractive, in the unsubtle way that was considered the height of desirability these days. Not Iona's type at all.

'We all met at antenatal classes when we were pregnant. We've kept in touch because of the children really. We haven't got much in common.'

'And where was this?'

'Chrissy lives in Cheyne Walk. One of the big houses. She's a divorce lawyer.'

'And you arrived there at what time?'

'Seven thirtyish.'

'And what time did you leave?'

'Hang on, let me check my phone.' Her voice was trembling and tears had sprung to her eyes. 'We have a WhatsApp group.' She swiped through the screens. 'Yes, here. Chrissy sent a message to the others around eleven to say I was home.'

Yannis shifted in his seat. Was he judging this woman? If so, that wasn't fair. Why shouldn't she get blind drunk on the rare occasions she wasn't looking after a toddler?

'We really need to clarify when exactly Ewan left,' Iona said gently. 'So we can check CCTV footage, et cetera. You yourself have admitted you'd had a bit to drink on the Thursday night. Perhaps your friends are clearer about the events of that evening. Didn't you say Chrissy brought you home? She might have noticed something that could help.'

Yannis added, 'And at least she can confirm your movements.'

Bella Upton gave a physical jolt and her eyes widened. 'This is nothing to do with me,' she said. 'I had no idea what he was planning. Don't you . . . don't you think I'd have tried to talk him out of it?'

She seemed genuinely shocked by Yannis's implication. Or perhaps it had just confirmed her worst fear – that she was a suspect in the embezzlement. If Ewan Upton had left her here to deal with the aftermath of his crime, he really was an arsehole.

'Thank you, Mrs Upton,' Iona said, getting up. 'That's been very helpful. We'll be in touch when we have anything to tell you.'

Clearly sensing that the mood of the investigation had changed, Bella Upton did not speak as she led them back down the hall.

They walked down the steps and out to the car, dodging the detritus from the weekend's exertions: nitrous oxide canisters, takeaway cartons, lager cans. A single leopard-print stiletto lay abandoned on the first step of the house next door.

As Yannis pulled away Iona glanced back to see Bella Upton watching them from the window. A guilty woman? Or just a tense, scared, bewildered one?

Chrissy Welch had clearly made a lot of money from the misery of others. Her house was huge, and slap bang in the middle of the best part of Chelsea, right by the river but just a stone's throw from the boutiques and juice bars. Four storeys of yellow-grey London brick, fenced off by a tall black railing woven with wisteria. In the summer it would be a glorious explosion of mauve or pink but was now a tangle of sorry-looking twigs.

Taking up two reserved parking spaces in front of a house along the street was a skip filled with earth and rubble. Another basement being dug out. People in Chelsea didn't seem to place much value on their gardens. They took great bites out of them with extended basements, or conservatories, and any patch of grass that managed to sneak through was mercilessly paved. Iona herself couldn't think of a nicer way to while away a sunny afternoon than lying on her back on her postage-stamp-sized lawn with a good book, but perhaps these people led more exciting lives.

They pulled in behind a black Range Rover. Presumably the car that transported Bella home. Unless it was the husband's. Iona got out and walked around the car. Peering through the windows at the immaculate interior she thought that if the car was hers there was no way she'd risk a drunken friend vomiting on her leather seats. But that was the benefit of owning a five-year-old Mazda. You didn't have to care.

Walking with Yannis up to the gate she buzzed the intercom and a moment later the gate swung open.

The front door was answered by an elegant black woman who looked them up and down with barely concealed contempt before disappearing down the stairs at the end of the hall, leaving them standing there like lemons.

A few minutes later they were called down.

The open-plan space was huge and bright thanks to a ceiling bristling with LEDs. The Welches had extended their basement too, it seemed. The paintwork looked fresh and the French doors at the end still had their covering of blue protective film. On a brighter day it would be like being underwater.

Chrissy Welch did not get up from the large L-shaped sofa to greet them, nor did she look up, just carried on scrolling down her phone screen, evidently waiting for them to step into her field of vision. Iona bristled immediately, but from Yannis's intake of breath she guessed a male, straight cop would forgive this woman a great deal.

It was hard to tell how tall she was, but her legs, clad in tight leather trousers, stretched far beneath the coffee table, a glass and brass thing liberally scattered with candles and photography books. There was not a fingerprint or coffee-cup stain to be seen – but that was what the help was for. The black lady brought over a tray of coffees, complete with sugar in a silver dish and a jug of cream.

'Thank you, Haniah,' Chrissy Welch said. 'Could you make sure Chloe takes her minibeast project to nursery this morning?'

'She worked so hard on that,' the older woman said in a Ghanaian accent.

'I know. I think she's got a bit of a crush on Mr Lucas. You know, the one with the freckles? She wants to get him a furry onesie for Christmas!'

Iona cleared her throat.

When Chrissy turned back to them her expression had returned to its former coldness.

It was immediately obvious as they sat down, uncomfortably wedged together on the short arm of the L, that they were talking to a lawyer. Chrissy Welch regarded them with cool disdain, alert but not tense, sipping a coffee that had been bought outside, though theirs must have been made with the huge and gleaming Gaggia machine on the kitchen counter.

Their professions made them arch-enemies from the get-go, Iona thought. Lawyers considered the police corrupt, incompetent and thick, and cops considered lawyers amoral bottom feeders who kept murderers and child abusers on the streets.

'So,' Chrissy said, after the introductions were made. 'Have you found him yet?'

'We're working on it,' Iona said.

'Any sign at the borders?'

'Not so far.'

'So he's still in the country. What about his mobile phone? Have you tracked it?'

'We're working on it.' Who was interviewing whom, exactly?

Chrissy sighed. 'Poor Bella.' She didn't sound sorry.

'It's Mrs Upton we want to talk to you about. Specifically her movements the night before her husband vanished.'

Chrissy Welch held Iona's gaze, trained to wait for an actual question.

'You dropped her home after the drinks at your house. She claims not to remember whether or not she saw her husband, but we thought you might have noticed something.'

'His car was there, if that's what you mean.'

'What time was this?'

'Well, I was back in time for the end of *Question Time*, so I would say around eleven.'

'Were there lights on in the house?'

'I don't remember.'

'Did you see her into the house?'

'No.'

'Did you catch a glimpse of Ewan Upton? Did he come out to meet his wife, check she was okay?'

'No.'

The silence stretched.

'Would you say that their marriage was a happy one?'

'I don't know.' Her eyes were hard. Despite her looks this was a woman Iona could never fall in love with.

'If you had to conjecture?'

'Well, Bella is overweight and drinks heavily, so that would suggest a degree of unhappiness, I would say, wouldn't you?'

'Do you think Ewan Upton was having an affair?'

'I have no idea, but it wouldn't surprise me.'

'Who with?'

'Like I said, I have no idea.'

They waited. This wasn't going well. The lawyer was unlikely to let anything slip that she didn't want to.

'She didn't confide in you about any financial problems, ask your advice from a legal standpoint?'

'No.'

'And how did she seem that night? Her state of mind?'

'Same as usual. Complaining, drunk by eight.'

'Did she seem stressed? Did she take any calls while you were together?'

'No.'

'On both counts?'

'Yes.'

Well, she'd achieved what they came here for and corroborated the wife's story.

'Thank you for your time,' Iona said. 'We'll be in touch if we have any other questions.' She got up and shuffled around the coffee table.

'Of course, I wasn't the last one to see her.'

Iona stopped.

'It was Jen who got her into the house.'

'Jen?'

'Jennifer Baptiste. She knows the alarm code, so could get Bella inside.'

'Why does she know the alarm code?' Yannis said.

Chrissy blinked at him as if he was stupid. 'She childminds for Teddy. Didn't you know that?'

'No.'

There was a flicker of a smile on the woman's perfectly painted lips. 'Personally if I was Bella I'd be slightly nervous inviting a woman like that into my house, but hey ho, some people are very trusting.'

'A woman like what?'

Chrissy glanced over to a side table by the window. Amongst the crowd of framed family photographs of impossibly beautiful people was the same picture of the five women that had been in Bella Upton's house. It was tucked in at the back, framed simply in wood. Under the bright lights Iona could see their faces better: they were smiling faintly at her.

'Well, she's attractive, if you're into that sort of thing. And I don't imagine she'd have any scruples at all in getting what she wants.'

'And what *does* she want?'

'How should I know?' Chrissy laughed. 'Money? She lives in a council flat on the Cambourne estate after all.'

'Are you implying she might have had an agenda while working for the Uptons? An affair perhaps, with a well-off man?'

The laugh shut off like the flick of a switch. 'I don't believe I implied anything. You asked me to conjecture and I don't think it's news to anyone to suggest that most people want more money.'

'Do you?' It was desperately unprofessional but Iona just couldn't help herself.

Chrissy's smile spread up to her perfect cheekbones. 'We're just fine, thank you.'

They stared at one another a moment, then fortunately Yannis stepped in. 'So, did you wait for Jen to come back out?'

'No, actually. She said she'd get Bella to bed. She knows where everything is, bowls and towels for if she was sick. Besides, she only lives round the corner, so I left her there. She texted afterwards to say that Bella was fine.'

'So if Ewan Upton had been there at the time, Jen might have seen him?'

'I suppose so. Now, if you don't mind, I have to get to work. Let me see you out.'

They allowed themselves to be escorted back up the stairs and out of the door.

From the squad car they watched Chrissy Welch fold herself into the black Range Rover and drive away, accompanied by the stares of a group of labourers digging at the corner of the street. Gone were the days when workmen whistled at women – these guys were almost pitiful in their admiration.

'Doesn't seem to like her friends much, does she?' Yannis said. 'You wouldn't catch me slagging my mates off like that. They're my mates because I like them. But I suppose that's women for you. No offence.'

Iona smiled and turned her face to the window, watching the river scroll past. There was Grosvenor Pier, stretching out into the grey water, boats rocking in the swell, the little ones dwarfed by huge glamorous vessels that were more like hotels than homes. The glowing portholes of the few occupied boats looked cosy on a dull day like this, but, realistically, river life was probably cold and damp and, in rough weather, thoroughly nauseating.

Back at the station they tried to get in touch with Jennifer Baptiste but her phone was off.

At lunchtime the finance checks came back: clean. The missing money hadn't been transferred to any of Upton's personal accounts. But, Iona thought, he would want to access it from wherever he had fled to, so perhaps he had put the funds into an account in his wife's name. After ordering checks on Bella's accounts, and instructing Yannis to speak to the Uptons' neighbours, Iona went out to look for Maya's Secret Santa present.

Forty-five minutes later she returned, unsuccessful, to find Yannis waiting for her.

'So, the neighbours,' he said. 'One lives abroad and the house isn't rented out, the other side has been divided into flats. The ground and first floor are let out to a couple of Somalian guys. They work nights. Didn't see anything. The basement flat is rented to . . . wait for it . . . Marta Hughes.'

Iona rolled her eyes. The belligerent junkie had caused them endless problems over the years, attacking innocent members of the public on buses or in the street. She had tried to set fire to a Costa Coffee on the Kings Road when they accused her of stealing a sandwich.

'Was she helpful?' Iona said, dryly.

'Miraculously, she claims to have seen Bella being escorted home the night of the fourth. She remembers it, she claims, because it was her friend's birthday and she was off out to meet him when she saw the mums arrive in Chrissy's Range Rover.'

'That's remarkably lucid of her.'

Yannis grimaced. 'Not really. She claimed she saw them *twice*. Exactly the same scenario: them helping Bella into the house, only a few hours later, when she came back from the birthday celebrations under the railway bridge.' He rolled his eyes. It was where the local homeless congregated to smoke crack, once they'd made enough to buy some.

'How much later?'

'Funnily enough she couldn't be sure.'

'Interesting. So Bella may have gone out again and then come back.'

'She was comatose drunk. Why would she go out again? Marta's junkie brain is playing tricks on her.'

'You're probably right,' Iona said.

4

Mothers Club

2 Years Previously

Haniah had done a wonderful job, as usual. There was truffled goat's cheese on filo pastry, asparagus spears wrapped in prosciutto, salads topped with crimson jewels of pomegranate seeds, and a bean dish called *waakye* that was a Ghanaian speciality. The last two were for vegan Skye. Russell was sneering about this, saying Skye could just make do with bread and oil, but Chrissy had some sympathy. Vigilant for any hint of middle-aged thickness developing around her waist, meat and dairy would be the first two things she cut out.

It had become a regular thing, these Mothers Club meetings, as Bella's husband had dubbed them (suspecting he meant to mock them, Chrissy had made sure they fully embraced the moniker). Every six months was now nearer to every three months, each mum – and Jen – taking turns to host. Weirdly, considering she had zero in common with this motley bunch, Chrissy had come to look forward to seeing them all.

Russell wandered in and picked a pomegranate seed from the bowl.

'Stop that,' she said, more sharply than she intended.

'Wooo-ooh,' he sing-songed, eyes theatrically wide. 'What's the matter with you?'

'Nothing.'

As the end of her year's maternity leave approached, she found herself becoming more and more tense. Her boss had made the fatal error of telling her what a wonderful job her subordinate had done in her absence, how well he had got along with her clients. She'd pretended to be pleased things were ticking on so well without her, even to Russell, but so many talented and powerful women had fallen on the sword of motherhood before her, her position felt fragile.

Russell gave an exaggerated sigh and her irritation level snapped right back up.

'I'm worried about work, actually.'

The amusement vanished from his expression. 'It was your choice to go back full-time.'

He was right. They'd offered her four days a week, but she'd refused.

'Yeah, well, I don't have much choice, do I?'

The truth was, she was itching to get back, but to admit it would make her sound like a freak, not wanting to spend all her time with her precious baby.

'Jesus,' Russell snapped. 'Do you have to throw this in my face the whole time?'

'Throw what in your face?'

'*Oh, poor me,*' he minced, '*having to leave my poor baby at home with a nanny because my crappy husband doesn't earn enough to support me.* If you'd wanted an alpha male, you should have gone out and got one instead of just being resentful you're stuck with me.'

This was the moment she should have said, *But I want you, silly.* But she couldn't bring herself to be reassuring when he was being so vile.

'Is this about the promotion?' she said. It was dangerously provocative, but she didn't care.

'What?'

'Don't take it out on me because you couldn't get the job you wanted.'

'Couldn't? In any other company I'd have walked it. But if there's a black guy or a woman or some other minority I don't have a chance.'

'Women aren't a minority.'

'Tell me about it. Oh, wait, you always do.'

She stared at him with something akin to hatred. Maybe she did resent him. Maybe life would be a whole lot easier if everything – the mortgage, the private health, the staff, the nursery fees, the holidays, the food, the fucking gas bill – didn't fall on her shoulders.

But, Christ, she didn't want a fight. Not with everything else on her mind. Not with Chloe awake upstairs and her friends about to arrive.

'Hey,' she said gently. 'I'm sorry. I'm just tired and grumpy.'

Swallowing the sense of injustice that was a crab apple in her throat, she went behind him and slipped her arms about his waist.

Something in the way he held himself – stiff and erect – told her that he was pleased she'd capitulated. That it made him feel like he was the boss. She'd seen it before, with certain men that she worked with. Make the mistake of giving in on the small things, to meet them in the middle, and it just made them think they'd won. Men like that lost respect for you when they saw what they interpreted as weakness.

She struck the thought from her mind, angrily. This was her husband. He was a decent man.

She kissed the back of his neck where the soft blond hair began. Back at uni, they'd been equally good-looking – a no-brainer when they finally got together – but she was ageing now, her features coarsening while his became rugged. That, at least, should please him.

The warmth and scent of him, and the pressure of his body against hers, was a turn-on and she slipped her hand down the front of his jeans. Their sex life had stuttered after Chloe was born and was taking a while to get back on track.

He stepped away from her. 'Your friends will be here soon.'

She held her wrist as if the hand had been burned. This was the third time in as many months that he had spurned her advances. No man had ever rejected her before Russell. It had been part of the mystery at the beginning, but now, when she was feeling fragile anyway, it hurt.

'I've asked Haniah to step up her hours when I go back,' she said, to punish him. 'She'll prepare the evening meal so that when I get home I'll be able to spend some time with Chloe.'

'Fine,' he said coldly. 'It's your money.' Then, slinging on his jacket, he went upstairs and left the house.

Electra was the first to arrive and as she reached for her drink Chrissy noticed a large bruise on her forearm. Could it be Zack? One child put enough strain on a relationship, let alone two. Or was she just predisposed to see marital disharmony everywhere?

'Is it too cold to sit outside?' she said. 'The summerhouse has heaters.'

'Bring it on,' Electra said. 'As long as I can smoke I'll be happy as a sandgirl.'

They walked across the lawn to the summerhouse tucked into the far wall.

Electra only smoked when she drank, but when she did, it suited her. She looked like some 1920s film idol, brooding at the gathering dusk, the patio heaters casting a red sheen on her hair.

'So,' Chrissy said. 'How's it going?'

Electra took a gulp of wine. 'Don't ask.'

'That bad?'

'Pearl's a ray of sunshine. Seriously. She's always smiling. She's just started walking.'

'Wow, that's early!'

'Yeah. Well, Ozzy can't even roll over. Or he won't. He just lies on his back and bawls until I pick him up. I took him to the GP to see if he had colic or something, but they said he's fine. Zack's got endless patience, but when Ozzy's got me up in the middle of the night for the tenth time I feel like I might actually kill him.' Electra closed her eyes and tipped her head back, smoke coiling from her nostrils.

Chrissy laughed. 'I might do the same to Russell.'

Electra groaned. 'It's a nightmare, isn't it? The poor sods don't realise that *everyfuckingthing* –' she swooped her arm around, drawing a circle with the glowing tip of the cigarette '– has changed. They think you're going to be hot for them again as soon as the stitches heal, but most nights I'd rather go to sleep.'

Chrissy laughed again, hoping it sounded natural.

'How do you feel about going back to work?'

'I was looking forward to it, until I found out they hadn't missed me in the slightest and my clients are all thrilled to be working with my junior.'

'Ouch.'

'Exactly. And the case I thought might actually have gone to court is still dragging on, so I have to deal with this nutty former prostitute who now claims she can't live on less than nine thousand a month.'

'Jesus. We manage on two and half!'

Chrissy was careful not to react.

'I wanted Zack to go back to uni but we can't afford it now.'

'Is he still working at the bar?'

'They've promoted him to manager but it's still shit.'

Haniah came out, leading Bella. In the fading light the shadows were deep around her eyes. Chrissy thought again how pretty she would be when she lost the baby weight. Was that horribly shallow of her?

As another bottle went down, the sun dipped behind the house. From hers and Russell's bedroom on the second floor the river would be a crimson ribbon snaking east to west. Many times they had made love in the glow of that London sunset. But she couldn't remember the last.

Bella was telling Electra that she was sure Teddy had said the word 'book' when she put him to bed recently.

'God, really?' Electra said. 'Pearl babbles all the time, especially when I sing them nursery rhymes, but Ozzy doesn't make a sound. Maybe he's depressed.' She laughed grimly.

'Oh,' Chrissy said loudly. 'Here's Jen.'

All three women took their cue to stop talking about babies immediately as Jen strode across the patio in over-the-knee boots with killer heels.

'Hello, ladies! God, am I glad to see you lot.' She slumped into a chair and Chrissy filled the glass she waggled. She looked better than at their last gathering. She'd put on weight and some of the old spark had returned to her eyes.

'Is everything all right?' Bella said.

'Me and Eliot have split up.'

'Oh, I'm so sorry,' Bella said.

'Don't be. He's being a cock, so I kicked him out. Sent him back to his mum's. After all, it's my bloody flat.'

Orphaned at twenty-three when her mum died of breast cancer, Jen had inherited the council flat. It must have been so hard for her, after what happened, to have no one to turn to for comfort. Although Chrissy had had to literally send her mother packing after three weeks of the *Granny knows best* routine.

Jen began laying into Eliot – he was a wanker, he was immature, he was thick – while the others nodded and hmmed uneasily. They'd all quite liked Jen's quiet boyfriend when he'd attended the antenatal classes. He was sweet and nervous and so young.

Skye arrived then, liberating them from the conversation.

'Sorry I'm late. Almost didn't make it. Juniper had an asthma attack yesterday.'

Bella gasped. 'Is she okay?'

'It wasn't a serious one, but they kept her in hospital overnight to make sure. Now she's got the medication it should all be okay.'

'Do you think it's the boat?' Electra said.

Skye sighed. 'I don't know. Maybe. Even in the summer it's damp, and at the moment I just can't keep it warm overnight.'

Haniah moved soundlessly among them, laying down plates and bowls and napkins.

'I think I'll have to sell it, rent a flat somewhere.'

'Sell the *Emmeline*?' Bella said. 'That's such a shame. It's so lovely.'

Skye sighed. 'Trouble is, who's going to buy her with winter coming? Anyway, let's not start with a downer. Chris, this beany thing is lovely.'

Chrissy held up her hands. 'Not my doing. Haniah's the gourmet chef.'

'Chloe's asleep so I'll be off now,' the housekeeper said. 'See you tomorrow.'

They drank and chatted and somebody asked for music. Normally Chrissy would have taken them all inside at that point, for the sake of the neighbours, but tonight she felt rebellious, and turned the stereo in the kitchen loud enough for them to hear at the bottom of the garden.

Soon four bottles had gone down. At least one of them drunk almost entirely by Bella, who filled her glass far more frequently – and somewhat furtively – than everyone else. Chrissy didn't blame her, though. She'd been through so much.

There was a gap in the conversation, but it wasn't an awkward one. They were all pleasantly tipsy now. Bella was humming to herself.

It was Jen that broke the silence. 'So, we saw the specialist, me and Eliot. This guy up in Harley Street.'

All eyes turned to her.

'We both have this gene. It's got a name but I can't remember it. It causes this thing called . . . foetal akinesia. Which makes the baby stop growing properly. There's other stuff too. Their lungs don't develop and they have facial abnormalities. Even if they survive the birth they die soon afterwards.'

Bella made a high-pitched sound in her throat. Electra swore and lit a cigarette. Skye lowered her gaze.

'Basically, Zoe didn't have a chance.'

'Oh, Jen, I'm so sorry,' Chrissy said. This was the first time, in the six months since Jen and Eliot's daughter was stillborn at full term, that Jen had uttered her name. The day after her return from hospital she had made Eliot hire a van to get rid of all the things she had purchased: the expensive cot, the cashmere blankets, the Silver Cross pram – only the best for Jen's daughter. All of it had gone to the charity shop and the following week the bedroom had been repainted white and returned to its former use as a box room.

The others, particularly Bella, had considered this behaviour bewilderingly callous, but Chrissy understood. Jen was trying to protect herself. She had kicked and scratched and bitten her way through a difficult upbringing. She was a survivor. If she allowed herself to grieve she might fall apart completely, and the myth of her own invincibility would shatter. And then she might end up like Bella.

'Eliot behaved like a total twat with the doctor, shouting about *how could they have missed it*. He swung a punch at the guy in the end and they called security. Now he's been banned from going back, and that guy was supposed to be the best in the country for genetic things. That's why I finished it. If I'm gonna have a baby, it'll be with a grown-up, not some . . . stupid little boy.' Her mouth twisted cruelly, but Chrissy could see the emotion shining in her eyes. 'Anyway,' Jen went on briskly, 'turn the music up. I feel like partying.'

They were dancing as the moon rose, to the nineties tracks they had all – except Jen – grown up with. Jen made them all laugh with a complicated dance move from a video game, Bella jiggled unselfconsciously, Electra strutted and posed and ruffled her hair like a young Madonna and Skye waved her arms like she was at a rave. Chrissy hadn't laughed so much in months. It took ages for her to hear the doorbell.

When she finally got up to the front door she expected the caller to have given up and gone away.

'Hello?' she giggled down the intercom.

40

'Do you know what time it is?' a man's voice barked.

'Erm, almost eleven?' She recognised the gruff voice of Admiral Mogg.

'Eleven forty-five, and my wife has been trying to sleep since ten. We're not stick-in-the-muds by any means, but this is just intolerable.'

She gave a quiet snort. It was unlike her to be provocative, but she was pretty drunk now.

'I'll thank you not to laugh at me, young lady! If that music isn't turned down in the next ten minutes I'll be calling the police. And another thing, we will also be objecting to your building work. If you think we'll put up with drilling and banging for the next six months, you can think again.'

A moment later she heard the clang of his gate and the intercom fell silent.

'Oh, fuck off you pompous twat,' she muttered, then made her way back down the hall to turn the music down. It was probably time to wind things up anyway. Russell would be back any minute – the Cross Keys shut at midnight.

The others, it would seem, had had the same idea. Bella and Jen were in the kitchen holding their jackets. Chrissy was about to start bemoaning her dreadful neighbour, but then she caught what Bella was saying.

'If it would help, I'd be happy to donate you some of my eggs.'

Chrissy backed out into the hall again.

'I don't know if there's anything they can do with them these days, like take out my DNA and put yours in or something?'

Chrissy held her breath in the shadows, her eyes fixed on Jen's face. Would she see this as some kind of charity and be mortally offended? Would it affect the dynamic of the group? Chrissy hoped not. She was starting to like this oddball bunch, so unlike the slick lawyers she spent most of her time with.

The flurry of movement made her jump. Jen had flung her arms around Bella.

'Thank you so much,' Jen said into Bella's hair. 'Seriously. That is so kind of you. You don't even know.' Pulling away she held Bella's hands. 'But maybe I'll meet someone with the *right* genes. There's still time.'

'Of course there is. You're so young. And so gorgeous.'

'Shut up!'

'Right, ladies.' Chrissy stepped into the kitchen. 'That was our friendly neighbourhood dictator. He says it's curfew time.'

Skye came in with Electra, their pale faces warmed pink with drink and patio heater and dancing. Belongings were collected, dregs were knocked back, embraces were received, and then one by one the women stepped out into the night.

Standing by the gate, watching them totter away, Chrissy felt a moment's anxiety for them, alone and defenceless in the London night. If she'd drunk a glass or two less she could have run them all back.

The light sensor on the outside lantern went out and the street was plunged into a gloom unnatural in the rest of London. It was the river that did it, that smear of darkness amidst the sea of lights. But there were no lights here. Nobody walked down this street unless they lived here or were visiting.

And yet, late as it was, footsteps were coming the other way, following along behind her friends. Chrissy turned sharply. A man's figure, made anonymous by the shadows of the trees that separated the terrace of houses from the river. There had been a murder here, a few years ago. A banker had innocently opened his door to what he thought was the postman and been stabbed through the heart. Plain old jealousy and spite because he was rich.

Were there envious eyes on her family? People not so lucky, who meant them harm?

She shrank back and began to close the gate, but the figure burst into a sprint and caught and held it. The sudden movement triggered the sensor and the patio was flooded in light.

She laughed.

Russell laughed.

'Oh my god, I thought—'

'That I was an axe murderer?'

'Yes! Come in quick, before a real one comes along!'

Absurdly, her heart was beating faster as they tumbled into the hall, laughing. They stood facing one another. Moonlight flooded in through the back window. Russell was as drunk as she was, his shirt unbuttoned, his hair tousled. In the gloom he might have been twenty-five again.

An ache started up between her legs.

She kissed him. For once he responded immediately and strongly, pushing her up against the wall, thrusting his tongue into her mouth. Then he grasped her thigh and lifted it onto his hip. Unwilling to miss what was clearly *the* moment, she pulled her knickers aside.

He was doing something with his own crotch. Was he masturbating?

She reached down and tried to take over, but he wouldn't let her. He was still soft. Was he too pissed? But no, something was happening now. He yanked her thigh, outwards and impossibly high, and one of her tendons twanged. Squeezing her eyes shut to stop herself crying out, she felt him enter her, roughly enough that her head banged against the wall. Then he was fucking her, grunting at every thrust. She made some appreciative noises, but the truth was, it had been so long she'd forgotten how it was supposed to feel. She thought she remembered that the first moment of penetration always made her gasp, as much in pain as pleasure, but now she could barely feel anything.

Had something happened to her, down there, during Chloe's birth? Some numbing or stretching? Even though she'd had a caesarean?

She shifted, trying to get a better angle, and promptly overbalanced. Stumbling sideways she had to catch the banisters to stop herself falling.

Russell stayed where he was and there was no ignoring the way his penis dangled, flaccid, between his thighs.

Okay.

Well, this wasn't the most comfortable spot for starters, and they were both drunk. Perhaps she should use her mouth on him for a while, until he was properly hard. But when she went back over to him, he pushed her away.

'You're drunk,' he said.

'I had friends over!'

'There's always some excuse. You didn't have friends over yesterday and you still sank half a bottle.'

Chrissy snorted. 'So does half the civilised world.'

'It's just not particularly attractive, that's all.'

'Oh right.' She folded her arms defensively. 'So, this is my fault.'

Anger flashed in Russell's eyes, but he didn't say anything. Just shook his head, then pulled up his trousers and went upstairs.

Chrissy went down to the basement and put the kettle on. Maybe she *was* drinking too much. It wasn't as if she had a problem. She could stop right now and still enjoy herself at gatherings like tonight's. Hadn't she done so for nine months when she was pregnant, after all? It was unpleasant to think that she had become unattractive to Russell when she fancied him, physically, as much as she'd ever done. Was she becoming a raddled, perimenopausal drunk, a few short years away from Patsy from *Ab Fab*? Well, she would stop, then. Knock it on the head completely. It would be a treat to seduce him sober, like she did when they were young and full of energy, not half drunk or half asleep.

The kettle boiled. She poured herself a coffee and turned on the TV. A vampire film was playing, decades old. Sitting down on the sofa she was about to turn over to CNN when she paused. She remembered this scene: the sexy female vampires seducing the hapless lawyer. It was silly, melodramatic, the actor wooden and gormless. And yet, as they opened his shirt and ran their fingernails across his chest the ache between her legs became so strong she had to press her hand to her groin to relieve it.

The scene changed and she turned the TV off, then she told the machine to turn off the lights. Moonlight shafted in through the patio doors. Unbuttoning her dress, she let it fall on her breasts, like a caress of cool fingers. She pressed her pelvis forward, pushing against her own hand as if it were a door she was demanding be opened.

She came quickly, calling out harshly to the silence.

5

Iona

Present

Tuesday morning Maya wasn't in. Iona closed the door to her office so no one would notice her subdued mood.

There was something addictive about the little spikes of adrenaline or dopamine or whatever it was that surged through her whenever she had any contact with Maya. Somehow her normal Sunday routine – a jog in the park, reading the papers over a pint, a takeaway curry with a Netflix box set – hadn't seemed so much fun. She'd been counting the hours until Monday morning and now she would be counting the hours until Maya returned, from being off sick or wherever she was. Please, not relocated to another station.

There was a knock on the door.

It was Yannis. 'Phone records are back.' He laid a sheaf of papers on the table. 'There are the usual numbers.' Yannis pointed at the columns of data. 'Home, Bella's mobile, work. His parents. And then there's this one.'

He pushed the sheet of paper towards her. It was a list of all the calls made to and from Ewan Upton's mobile over the past three months. The number Yannis was pointing to only started appearing in August.

'So, do we know who it is?'

'Jennifer Baptiste,' Yannis said.

'Oka-ay,' Iona said. 'Well, she was their childminder, right?'

'Yeah, but it's still usually mum who deals with the childcare, isn't it? That's a lot of calls to dad.'

They looked at one another.

'Her phone's still off,' he added.

Iona got up and pulled on her jacket. 'Then I'd say it's time we paid Miss Baptiste a visit.'

They didn't speak much as they crawled through the snarl of London traffic, past the ornate mansion blocks and Georgian townhouses of well-to-do Chelsea, where a single bed would get you no change from a million, past gastropubs, boutiques specialising in baby clothes, yoga studios and beauty therapists, to a kink in the road that separated the two Chelseas as definitively as a rail track.

The original Victorian terraces had been replaced by this seventies monstrosity: stubby fingers of red brick jabbing at the sky. The kind of Brutalist architecture that was becoming fashionable again but was no fun to come home to. It wasn't fair, Iona thought as they rose like an insult on the horizon, that the poor should be experimented upon by young architects who wanted to make a name for themselves. A house was a thing of substance and dignity, you opened your front door and you could see your neighbours. You were a member of a community, not just the contents of a little box slotted on top of the one below. And after Grenfell there was fear too.

Pulling into a space behind a clapped-out Vauxhall minivan, they got out to the sudden hush that always accompanied the arrival of a police car, even an unmarked one. It was high time the police made their cars less conspicuous: a few old bangers wouldn't go amiss, instead of the predictable dark-coloured saloon, always spotlessly clean. Iona's neck prickled under the scrutiny of unseen eyes. Hostile. They were always hostile. Always thought you were trying to set them up, even when you were trying to help: most of the time senior officers like herself cut these people more slack than they ever would a white-collar criminal.

As they walked between the towers, something landed on the pavement directly in front of Yannis. They both jumped and Iona spun round. Insolent windows stared down at them. It was only an apple core, but it hadn't been accompanied by the cheeky giggles of a tearaway truant. These days children knew full well how simple it was to terrorise, and how powerful it made them feel.

Annoyed with herself for the pounding of her heart, she strode up the path to the entrance of Atreus Tower. The flats were accessed via a communal door, whose code they'd obtained from the building manager, into an unmanned foyer. Once it had banged shut behind them her eyes took a moment to adjust to the dim fluorescent lighting.

This was not a place to linger. Apart from a wall of metal postboxes, some of the locks broken, the room was empty. A resident would move swiftly through to the lift, or the door at the end that led to flats 1 to 4.

As they approached the door their footsteps echoed across the chequerboard tiles. Unless the tenants had put in some kind of soundproofing you would hear every word of a quarrel in one of the surrounding flats.

On the other side was a passageway studded with more doors, the darkness only relieved by a small window at the end. The brass number of Flat 4 gleamed in the shadows.

Iona walked up and knocked. The sound echoed and died away.

She knocked again, louder. 'Miss Baptiste?'

A door opened further down the corridor.

'She's not in,' said an elderly woman from behind a chain, shutting the door before they had the chance to question her further.

'Go round and see what you can through the windows,' Iona told Yannis.

As she waited the window at the end darkened and then blurred with rain. Normally she liked a bit of weather, the variety that the English climate offered, but this had been going on relentlessly for weeks. Anyone prone to depression must want to slash their wrists. She'd take nice crisp freezing cold over this any day.

Yannis came back, jogging breathlessly up the hall.

'The curtains were drawn so I shone my torch in. Look.' He held out his mobile phone. He had taken a picture through the curtains. In the centre of the screen was a coffee table, rather blurred where he'd tried to close in on it. In the middle of its glass top, too pixelated to see clearly, was a dark smudge.

'Could that be blood, do you think?' he said.

'Or coffee. Only one way to find out. Do the honours, Yan.'

Striding up to the door, Yannis pivoted on his left leg, then kicked with perfect precision at the lock of number four.

Nothing happened. Iona snorted.

The second attempt, however, was more successful and the door banged open. It led straight into a small lounge with high narrow windows. Yannis hit the lights.

The place had been decorated with care and the sort of universal good taste that featured in every hotel and interior design website these days: beige walls, wooden floors (presumably laminate), neutral furniture, a bit of glass and chrome. A brown leather sofa was directed towards a TV. Before it was the glass-topped table from the photograph.

Iona walked up to it and stopped.

Something had been dropped or thrown onto the glass, splintering it into a spiderweb of cracks. In the middle of this web was a single black hair coiled into a puddle of fluid. The puddle was brown at the edges, where it had started to dry, but the centre was pillar-box red. Blood.

'Boss.' Yannis had walked into the adjoining galley kitchen. On the white laminate floor was another bloodstain, around the size of a ten pence piece.

'That's why she's not been answering calls,' Yannis said quietly, pointing at a pink mobile phone sitting on the kitchen counter. Beside it lay a silver wallet and a bunch of keys with a plastic key ring in the shape of the letter J.

'Doesn't look like she was planning to take a trip,' Iona said.

A half-full cup of cold tea sat on the draining board and a bowl and spoon in the sink were grouted with Weetabix. No one with any sense did this. The dried-on sludge would take a hydraulic drill to remove.

A door beside the kitchen led to a tiny bedroom. The room smelled foetid, as if the sheets hadn't been cleaned for a while. She walked over to the bed. The duvet was bunched in the middle, as if a wayward teenager had arranged it to fool his parents that he was sleeping peacefully. Or as if to conceal the body of a diminutive young woman. Glancing at Yannis, she yanked it back.

They both exhaled. The bed was empty. There didn't seem to be any blood, though forensics would have to confirm that.

On the dressing table sat an open pot of moisturiser and a set of hair straighteners. This, to Iona, was more concerning than anything else. In her experience women who used hair straighteners never went anywhere without them. On the wall above was the same photograph of the five friends that Bella Upton and Chrissy Welch possessed. It had been framed in metal with a machine-cut word top and bottom: *forever friends*.

'An accident?' Yannis said, after they'd checked the bathroom and fitted wardrobes and the tiny box room next door. 'She hits her head on the table and takes herself off to A&E?'

'No sign at the hospitals though, right?'

'And unless it was a serious injury she'd have been home by now.'

'The way the table's positioned, though. You're not going to get a serious injury by falling on it.'

'Unless someone slams your head into it.'

'Are we looking at a potential serious assault?' Iona said.

'If so –' Yannis's voice was soft '– where is she?'

'There's so little blood.'

'He could have knocked her out on the table and then . . .' He tailed off. 'I don't know, suffocated or strangled her and dumped the body somewhere.'

'He?' Iona said.

'Well, there's no evidence of a break-in so it does point to someone she knew. A boyfriend?'

'Except that we've got two missing people. Ewan Upton and now Jennifer Baptiste. What if they're linked? Upton may have had another reason for fleeing when he did.'

'So, what? He has an affair with his childminder, it goes sour, so he murders her, then legs it?'

Iona wrinkled her nose. It did sound tenuous. 'What about the money?'

'Unless they intended to go together, and then something went wrong?'

'First things first,' Iona said. 'Call in forensics, let's see if there's any DNA aside from hers.'

'Okay. I'll get some tape from the car.'

He left her in the gloomy hallway.

If one of these men, Iona thought, Ewan Upton or some boyfriend, had had the presence of mind to dispose of a body, why not take Baptiste's phone and wallet, to make it look like she had gone of her own accord?

She knocked on the old lady's door, showing her badge when the old woman answered.

The woman closed it and opened it without the chain. 'What's going on?'

She must have been eighty, but her clothes were those of a much younger woman.

'Do you know the resident of number four?'

'Jennifer? Yes. And her parents before that.'

'Could I come in for a moment?'

'Well, it's a bit of a mess. I wasn't expecting—'

51

'Thank you.'

Her name was Mrs Kale and her flat smelled strongly of talcum powder. It was immaculately tidy, though probably not as clean as when the woman had better eyesight. A tabby cat sat on the back of a brown sofa felted with hair, flicking the tip of its tail malevolently. Iona's eyes started to prickle. She declined tea when she saw the woman's own drink, swimming with flakes of limescale.

'Have you heard any disturbance coming from number four recently?'

'Why? Has something happened?'

'Jennifer is missing.'

'Oh no.' Mrs Kale's drawn-on eyebrows lifted. 'That poor family has had nothing but bad luck.'

'Oh?'

'They used to live up on twelve. Then the father falls down the stairs going down to the laundry room. Cracked his head open, poor man. Though it was always going to happen, the amount he drank. Jennifer and her mother moved down here. Then the mother died in her forties. And then those two young people lose their baby.'

She sipped her tea and a flake of limescale disappeared between her wrinkled lips.

'Jennifer?'

'And Eliot, her young man. Nice boy.'

'Does he live here too?'

'Oh he moved out a week or so ago. Now *then* I heard a disturbance. They were at it hammer and tongs that night, but I didn't think much of it. They're always breaking up and getting back together.'

'But you saw Jennifer afterwards? Did she seem okay? Was she scared of him?'

The old lady chuckled ruefully. 'That girl's not scared of anything. She looked very well the last time I saw her. Blooming. I wondered if she'd got a new man.'

'Right.'

From the point of view of domestic violence, ending one relationship and starting another was the most dangerous time for a woman.

'So, when was the last time you saw her?' Iona said.

'Oh, I've not been well, darling. Flu. And we're only just in December. I tell you, those jabs do nothing. Every year I get one, and every year I get ill. I wouldn't be surprised if it's the bloody thing that brings it on.'

Iona's eyes were starting to smart properly now and her sinuses were swelling.

'Oh, hang on, she did come round on the third, to collect the keys Eliot left with me when he came to pick up some stuff. I remember because it was Thomas's birthday.' She leaned back and stroked the bony back of the malevolent cat.

The third was the day before Ewan Upton's disappearance.

'Well, thank you for your time, Mrs Kale, and please do get in touch if you remember anything else.'

'Righto.'

When she emerged from the flat, Yannis was waiting for her. He had already sealed the door with police tape. 'Forensics are on their way.'

'So,' she said as they walked back to the car, the light-reflecting puddles adding a touch of glamour to the run-down estate, 'as things stand the last people to see Jennifer Baptiste were Bella Upton and her friends. Don't you think it's time we met the other two?'

By the time they arrived back at the office it was lunchtime and the two of them headed to the canteen together. Yannis plumped for his usual chips and beans followed by a muffin. Presumably all the fat he consumed was lining his arteries because it didn't seem to be settling anywhere else on his body.

Iona ordered chicken salad and a tough thread of the dry meat lodged itself in her teeth at the first bite. Just as she was trying to extract it with a fingernail, Maya came in. Too self-conscious to show her teeth she barely returned Maya's smile and the other woman walked straight past their table to sit with a couple of the uniforms. She said something and they all glanced over at where Iona and Yannis were sitting, and laughed. Her heart sank as she realised Maya probably fancied Yannis as much as everyone else did.

Electra Xanders agreed to speak to them when she got home from work at six. Yannis was pissed off. He had a date and wanted to go to the gym first to make sure he was suitably ripped when he got to the bar. He wouldn't say who the date was with.

Mrs Xanders lived in a basement flat on the edge of Pimlico, close enough that they decided to walk it from the station.

This was a mistake. It started to rain again before they'd got halfway, and by the time they arrived at the shabby Georgian terrace they were drenched and freezing cold.

Stepping carefully down the lethal concrete steps, Iona thought again how little she would like to live in central London. This dank, dark flat probably cost way more than her little house in Bexley.

The woman who answered the door looked exhausted and harassed, but possessed a sort of gaunt handsomeness that must once have been stunning. She was dressed all in black to match her tightly cropped hair, with high black boxing boots that squeaked along the laminate floor as she led them through to the kitchen. It was so dark in here, and even when the light came on the place felt oppressive.

She had children, they knew, but even so the flat was messier, grubbier and generally more shabby that Iona would have expected. The sink was piled with dirty dishes despite the fact that there was a dishwasher in the corner, liberally decorated with wax crayon. So far, so normal for a small flat filled with toddlers, but other things were less usual. Diminutive toe prints on the skirting board, as if a child had repeatedly kicked it in the same spot. An actual hole in the wall, recent enough for the smattering of powder plaster on the floor not to have been cleaned up. Several of the framed photographs had smashed glass, and there were no ornaments on any surface below chest height. Glancing into a darkened sitting room she saw, on the wall, the same photograph of the five women. In the gloom their eyes were black pits of shadow.

'Sit down,' Electra said. 'If you can find any space.' She moved a pile of laundry off a kitchen chair and sat heavily. 'Mind if I smoke?'

'Not at all,' Iona said, though after the reaction to the cat she was still wheezing.

She hadn't even offered them a drink, but Iona decided this was down to distraction, rather than rudeness. The woman was clearly on edge – or perhaps close to the edge.

'What can I help you with?' Electra inhaled deeply, retaining the smoke in her lungs for several seconds before exhaling.

'We wanted to talk about a friend of yours, Jennifer Baptiste.'

'Okay,' Electra said. 'What's she done?'

'Nothing, as far as we know. She's missing.'

Electra raised her eyebrows. 'Since when?'

'We're not entirely sure, but at the moment it would seem that the last time anyone saw her was at the gathering held at Chrissy Welch's house on the fourth of December.'

'The same day Ewan went missing?'

'Yes. You know about that?'

'Chrissy told me.'

Iona waited for her to say more, but she didn't.

'So, you saw her that night?'

'Yes.'

'How did she seem?'

Electra shrugged. 'Same as usual. In a rage with the world.'

'Anything in particular bothering her?'

'No more than usual. Jen could pick a fight in an empty room, though she would have struggled that night. Bella was comatose, Chrissy's far too polite and Skye's scared of her.'

'And what about you?'

Electra's eyes narrowed. 'What about me?'

'How did you get on with her?'

'We keep in touch because of the children, that's all.'

'But Jen doesn't have any.'

'Quite. I never understood why she comes along. I suspect it's to make us all feel bad.'

'In what way bad?'

'Well, she lost her baby, so when she's around none of us are allowed to talk about ours in case we upset her. It's tiring. I've got more important things to think about than nail bars and her boyfriend troubles. I'm sure she just comes to make us squirm. That's the sort of thing she would do. She's manipulative like that.'

'So the two of you don't get on?'

Electra blinked. 'I never said that. We're fine. We just don't have anything in common.'

'What about the others? Has she fallen out with any of them?'

Electra shrugged. 'I think Chrissy lent her some money that she never paid back. Oh, and she fell out with Skye. Skye said we shouldn't get scans during the pregnancy because the radiation was bad for the baby: that our bodies knew what to do and we should just let nature take its course. No one else paid any attention, but Skye's got a Ph.D., and I think Jen was sort of in awe of that. So after twelve weeks she stopped getting the scans. If she hadn't they would have picked up something was wrong. They might have been able to do something. I don't think Jen ever forgave her.'

The road outside grumbled with rush-hour traffic. Iona was looking forward to getting back to her warm little house. The heating and hot water would be on now. She could have a long hot bath, rinse away the misery of other people.

'How did she get on with Bella Upton?' Yannis said.

'Fine, I think. Bella's hard to fall out with.'

'She childminded for them, correct?'

'Yes.'

'Had there been any friction between the two women because of that?'

'What sort of friction?'

'I'll get straight to the point, if I may, Mrs Xanders. Could Jennifer have been having an affair with Ewan Upton?'

In the silence Iona noticed the hand that held Electra's cigarette was trembling, particles of ash drifting like dust in the stagnant air.

'Look, what people get up to in their marriages is nothing to do with me, okay?' She looked away, staring blankly at a wall with a large gouge running down it.

'For the purposes of the investigation, can you give us any information at all about Jennifer Baptiste's relationship with Ewan Upton?'

'No. And it's Miss.'

'Sorry.'

'Miss Xanders. The kids' dad and I were never married. He's looking after them now and I need to go and pick them up so he can get to work, so if there's nothing else?'

As Yannis climbed the treacherous steps to street level, Iona paused, hoping she might be able to extract some sisterly confidence. 'Was the Uptons' marriage happy?'

In the storm light, Electra's face was grey. 'I imagine he was bored out of his mind. When they met, Bella was in PR. I didn't know her then, but I'll bet she was a bit more fun than she is now. That's what happens to stay-at-home mums. Their brains turn to mush and then their husbands start looking elsewhere. Don't do it.'

Her tone was so bitter. Life here, in this messy, gloomy basement was clearly not easy.

'I won't,' said Iona, and followed Yannis up into the rain.

6

Mothers Club

18 Months Previously

The bathroom was in desperate need of a clean. There were brown stains around the plughole, pubic hair in the bath, dried toothpaste spatters all over the shelf. Was there time to clear up before the mums arrived? Not if she wanted to sort out her lip.

Peering into the smeared mirror, she inspected the injury. It was a neat split, from the bottom edge to the top edge of her lower lip, where it had struck her incisor, easily covered by lipstick, if she could just stop the bleeding. Tearing off a corner of toilet roll she pressed it to the wound, holding it until it stuck.

Then she moved on to her eye. This would be harder to cover up, and harder to explain away at work. He had caught her right on her brow and a dark bruise was spreading all the way around the socket. Dabbing it with concealer, she winced at the tenderness. But it wasn't pain but self-pity that brought tears to her eyes. And loneliness. Because there was nobody she could confide in. Who on earth would understand?

By the time she had finished off with powder she looked like one of the over-made-up waxworks that paraded up and down the Kings Road, but at least her lip had stopped bleeding. Smearing on a dark lipstick she went back to the kitchen and lit a cigarette.

She had said that sometimes she wanted to kill him. But it was becoming more frequent than just sometimes. Or if not kill him, have someone take him away. She was tempted, when he kicked off when they were out, to hit him with all her strength, then just stand there and wait for the police to arrive and take her away. The sense of relief, at the thought of being free from him, was enough to bring tears to her eyes.

And the other day it had come close to happening. When she thought back she wasn't really sure how she felt about it. Fear, yes, and shame, but also a yawning sense of possibility. A door opening that she could simply have walked through.

It had been a hot day. She'd had to come home from work because Pearl had been sick at nursery and Zack was stuck in a supplier meeting. As usual the problem had come at the worst possible time, as they were pitching for a new author: young, arrogant and thrilled by the bidding war for her straight-out-of-college literary masterpiece, the girl had preened and smirked throughout their meeting while Electra flattered her through gritted teeth. And then Suki had come in to say the nursery needed to speak to her urgently. The author's outraged expression as she left the room would have been downright funny if it hadn't spelled the end of their chances at signing her.

It had made sense to take both twins as she would be home anyway and Pearl was so miserable when she collected them that Electra promised to buy her some of her favourite sweets. Finally managing to get the double buggy onto the third bus that arrived – the owners of single pushchairs aboard the first two having refused to fold them to make room – she diverted to the supermarket nearest the flat.

Ozzy kicked off as soon as they crossed the threshold, climbing out of the pushchair and lying underneath it so that she couldn't move it. For some reason he hated this particular supermarket, probably because it was their nearest and he knew full well it would make things difficult. On the rare occasions they shopped here as a family Zack would take him off to the playground round the corner.

59

A woman tutted as she squeezed past the pushchair and Electra mumbled an apology.

The lights here were very bright and the place was always busy. They'd made the mistake of coming at lunchtime when the office workers were crowding the sandwich fridges near the till.

'Get up, Ozzy,' she said. 'We're in the way.'

Ozzy did not get up.

Another woman asked her to move the pushchair and she gave it a wiggle to show willing, but now Ozzy was gripping the wheel with his tiny, iron-strong fingers.

'If you don't get up right now,' Electra said sternly, 'there'll be no sweets for you.'

Ozzy did not even look at her. His face was entirely expressionless, the eyes shark-dead. Dislike for her child rose like vomit in her throat.

'Fuck's sake!' A young man had tripped over Ozzy's foot protruding between the wheels and dropped his sandwich box. It burst open, strewing mayonnaisey prawns across the floor.

'Sorry—' Electra began.

'Get out of the fucking way,' the man snarled, snatching up the remains of his lunch and thrusting past her.

'You know,' an old lady in the queue beside her piped up, 'if you can't control him you really shouldn't bring him here. Not at this time anyway.'

'I know,' Electra said. 'It's just that—'

But the woman had turned away.

'Ozzy. Get. Up. Now,' Electra said through gritted teeth, then muttered, 'or you will get a smack.' She was sweating now and the lights seemed even brighter. She felt her throat start to swell and had the urge to call Zack at work to come and rescue her. That was how pathetic she had become. A highly educated professional woman reduced to tears in a supermarket by an eighteen-month-old.

Now Ozzy was pushing his finger up between the pushchair seats and pinching Pearl's thighs. The sick toddler set up a frail wail.

Lights exploded in Electra's peripheral vision.

With a sharp nudge of her foot Ozzy slid far enough out from under the buggy that she could yank him to his feet. But he didn't stay on them for long. Hauling the snarling octopus into the air she threw him into the pushchair, forcing down his arcing body and snapping the buckle shut, before yanking the straps so tight that he squealed. That was when his little balled fist made contact with her eye.

Little fucker you little fucking fucker.

She stood there panting as he bucked and screamed, her whole face throbbing with the blow.

A middle-aged woman approached her, and she smiled wanly, hoping for a supportive pat, an *I've been there*.

'Ma'am.' The American woman did not attempt to hide her disgust. 'Don't kick your child.'

'I . . . I didn't kick him. I was just trying to move him because—'

'I *saw* what you did,' the woman spat.

Before the woman could say anything else, Electra yanked the unwieldy pushchair in a circle, almost taking out the old woman who was now at the front of the queue, and flew out of the shop.

When she got home she ran up to the bedroom where she crouched with her back to the door, emitting great gulping sobs until Pearl's quavering cry summoned her back downstairs. There she found that her daughter had been sick again, and her son had five fingertip-shaped bruises on the white flesh of his little arm.

Zack had told her to let her hair down tonight. By which he meant get catastrophically pissed without having to worry about getting up in the night to see to Ozzy – he would deal with it. But now Zack had gone to work and here she was, alone in the flat but for the sleeping twins.

She poured a glass of red and swilled it round, gazing down at her reflection in the dark liquid.

Dinner, for once, had gone fine. Ozzy had played with his spaghetti for hours, which gave her a chance to draw with Pearl. Electra drew her simple line pictures, a unicorn or a cat, and Pearl scribbled over them with her crayons. Then they watched TV together while Ozzy just sat in his high chair with his spaghetti, which was now in his hair, on the floor and all over the walls. He'd only kicked off when she tried to bath him. Usually he and Pearl shared a bath, but tonight he was so filthy she put him in on his own. He screamed as if the water was scalding, then, when she tried to lift him out, threw his head back, catching her lip.

She lit another cigarette. The line she was pursuing with Zack was that she only smoked when she drank, but it was bullshit. These days she had one on the way to the tube in the morning, another outside the office with the shivering young-sters who didn't know any better, another at lunchtime, and so on throughout the afternoon. Once she'd put the twins to bed she smoked in the dank stairwell, then changed her clothes and brushed her teeth so that Zack wouldn't be able to tell when he got back.

'Fuck.'

Seeing Bella's legs descending the last few steps she ran out to the hall, but didn't get there in time. The bell's urgent alarm echoed through the flat.

Forcing a smile she opened the door. 'Hi! Come in!'

Bella said something, but Electra wasn't listening. From behind the closed door of the twins' room she heard a coughing sob. It was followed by a moment of blissful silence, as if he had just gone straight back to sleep. But a split second later the full-blown wailing began.

'Somebody sounds cross,' Bella said, smiling. 'Lovely to see you. Gosh, you are so lovely and slim!'

'I've opened a red,' Electra said distractedly. 'Or would you prefer white?'

'Oh, I'll see to myself, you go and settle him.'

'I wasn't going to bother, actually,' Electra said.

'Will he get himself back off?'

No. He would scream until he was sick and sweating, hour after hour after hour, while Electra tried to block him out by listening to music on her headphones.

'Hopefully,' she said.

'Won't Pearl wake up?'

'Oh, she's used to it. She sleeps through anything.'

They attempted desultory conversation for a bit, but Bella's eyes kept flicking to the door, and Electra felt her chest tightening with the knowledge that her parenting was being judged, again.

'Honestly, go,' Bella said. 'I can look after myself.'

So then, as a good mother should, Electra took herself off to the twins' room and shut the door behind her. She leaned her head back against it as Ozzy howled. She could see him, in the cot nearest her, which was still raised to baby level because he had never tried to climb out and was always so difficult to lower in. His hands were stretching and twisting as he screamed, as if he was trying to fend off something attacking him. Was he dreaming of his mother?

And then suddenly she was hyperventilating.

A few minutes later there was a gentle knock at the door and Bella came in.

'Can I help? Oh, sweetheart . . .'

She couldn't speak, just nodded like a mad person as Bella stroked her arm.

'You go and have a drink, let me have a go with him for a while.'

Electra almost ran back to the kitchen, and lit another cigarette. The nicotine calmed her, as it always did, like an old friend, a gentle hand on her back. After a few moments she became aware that the screaming had stopped. Stubbing out the cigarette she went back into the bedroom. Ozzy was her problem to deal with, not her friend's; Bella had come here for a night off.

She stopped in the doorway.

Bella, whose fragility she had pitied, was walking up and down, rocking and singing to her son, and not gritting her teeth or crying, or squeezing him just that little bit too tight to try and shock him into silence, just walking and rocking and humming. The same song over and over again. Electra filled in the words in her head.

The night is black and the stars are bright and the sea is dark and deep.

It was Pearl's favourite TV programme. At the end, the little blue hero would sail off on his boat into the night. Electra had always thought it was an oddly lonely image to end a children's programme with, but right now she couldn't think of anything she wanted more than to be on that boat sailing away into oblivion.

Bella's lullaby was so soothing, Electra's diaphragm started to release and, with it, all the strength drained from her. She leaned against the door frame.

'Hey, hey, it's all right, Mummy,' Bella said in a soft voice, 'it's okay. I'm feeling sleepy now, aren't I? Yes, I am.'

Electra hadn't even realised there were tears running down her face. Bella walked across to her and, just for a second, her son's dark eyes were on hers, his little lips puckered with sadness.

'That's it, you cuddle Mummy, there's a good boy.' Bella passed him gently into Electra's arms and his head tucked into her neck. He was completely silent but for the snuffling of his breath, slowing and deepening now.

'I don't know what's wrong with me,' Electra murmured, sitting down on the toy box, 'I just can't handle him.'

'I don't think it's your fault.' Bella sat down beside her. 'He doesn't make eye contact much, does he?'

Electra shook her head gently. Ozzy had now fallen asleep in her arms. Bella would think it was so easy.

'And you said he's not making many sounds.'

'No, but he's not deaf. They've tested him.'

'Has anyone mentioned autism?'

Electra looked at her. 'No, why?'

'My cousin's son's autistic, and they're classic signs. He liked to be jiggled up and down and sung the same song over and over. There are questionnaires online, you know, checklists. You could have a read. Oh, listen, someone's coming down the steps. I'll intercept them before they can ring the bell.' She went out.

As she lay Ozzy in his cot Electra felt numb. Autism. The word conjured images of children banging their heads against walls, of rocking and moaning, of residential care homes. Surely not. Surely he was just a perfectly normal difficult baby. Plastering a smile to her lips she went back out into the kitchen.

Chrissy had arrived, and she and Bella were talking about the merits of freezing different types of vegetables.

'I'm lucky,' Chrissy said, 'when I get back from work, Haniah's got Chloe fed and bathed and ready for a story.'

'Oh, poor you, missing it all,' Bella said.

Electra looked away. Sometimes she made up an extra meeting at work so she could be sure Zack would have done all the drudgery.

'Don't you miss work?' Chrissy said.

Electra saw that instead of wine she seemed to have poured herself a glass of water.

'Not at all. I just love being a mum. Doesn't every woman? Sorry, I didn't mean to imply it's easy, because it's not, I—'

'Bella has just parented my child better in three minutes than I've done in eighteen months,' Electra said.

'Oh, no, not at all!' Bella cried, but Electra smiled.

Then she felt a sharp pain in her lip.

Chrissy said, 'You're bleeding.'

'Oh, it's nothing.' She touched the back of her hand to her lip.

It was the sight of the blood. It brought back memories of being a child. Of falling over and running home to be cuddled and petted. Suddenly she felt such a longing for her mum that she burst into tears.

She told them everything. The whole, shameful truth, her breath shuddering, snot streaming from her nose.

'But you know the worst thing?' she said finally. 'When I did it. When I . . . kicked him. It felt good. It released something inside me, like taking a breath when you're drowning. And if I'd been alone, I . . . I might have done worse. I might have picked him up and shaken him and shaken him and never stopped.'

There was a moment's silence, then Chrissy took her hand. 'Firstly, everybody feels like that sometimes.'

Bella nodded vigorously.

'Second, you didn't kick him, you tried to move him out of the way.'

'Thirdly,' Bella interjected, 'she's an interfering bitch who needs a good slap.'

Electra laughed through her tears and her lip stung again. 'Do you really think he might be autistic, Bella?' she said in a small voice.

Bella bit her lip guiltily. 'My cousin's boy is adorable, really. He gets *so* into his hobbies. You should see some of the things he's made with Lego. Like an adult made them and he's only four. And his IQ is so high. 130 or something.'

Electra nodded. What did it matter how clever Ozzy was if he couldn't hold down a job or a relationship? He'd be miserable forever.

'Say he is,' Chrissy said. 'It's so common these days, and there's so much more understanding. Once you learn what triggers a reaction you can learn to avoid it. And he's so young. If they start with him now he'll make really good progress.'

So Chrissy thought he was too. A lump lodged like a tumour in Electra's throat.

'Anyway, sorry.' She struck the tears from her eyes. 'Tonight was supposed to be fun. Why the hell aren't you drinking? Don't tell me you're fucking pregnant?'

'No, no. Dear God. I'm just off the booze for a bit.' She paused, and then added, 'I think it might be affecting our sex life.'

This was the most candid Chrissy had ever been, and Bella had been surprised into silence. To stop Chrissy regretting her honesty Electra jumped in, 'That's a good point. And it's not just that night it screws up. I'm always knackered for days afterwards. Just want to hit the sack at nine, so I'm fast asleep by the time Zack gets home. The poor boy,' she added ruefully, 'with his twenty-five-year-old's libido.'

'Don't rub it in!' Chrissy said.

'I wish I could,' Bella said in a pervy voice, and they all cackled with laughter. Zack was the hottie of the dads by some considerable stretch, but Electra was not the slightest bit bothered to think they all fancied him. None of them was a threat, apart from possibly Chrissy, and Russell was equally handsome.

'A toast,' she said, handing Chrissy a carton of pear and apple baby-juice from the fridge. 'To Chrissy's sex life.'

'Hear hear.' Bella knocked back her glass just as Skye came trotting down the steps.

'Sorry I'm late,' she said, bringing a blast of cool air into the smoky flat. 'My massage client was supposed to be there at four and he turned up at half five.'

'I hope he paid you for the wait?'

Skye rolled her eyes. 'Yeah right.'

Electra handed her a glass of wine. Committed ethical vegan as she was, Skye never complained about the choice of food or wine. Electra liked her for that. She left the door open to let some of the smoke out, in case the presence of it on Skye's clothes was enough to trigger an asthma attack in Juniper.

'The annoying thing was that Juniper was back from nursery and had to watch me pawing this half-naked man, all fat, hairy and sweaty. All for fifty quid.'

Bella giggled, but Electra could tell that Skye was serious. She was a bright woman, who had chosen an alternative lifestyle, but motherhood had sucked her back into the rat race.

Suddenly remembering the nibbles, Electra began emptying the packets of crisps into a bowl and unwrapping the cheeses.

The spread would not be to the standard the mums had become accustomed to, but she had a full-time job and no nanny so, like Zack said, they'd have to make do.

'Well, my basement plans have been approved,' Chrissy said. 'So we can get going on that soon.'

'Good luck finding a builder,' Bella grumbled. 'We got completely shafted by ours.'

'Already got one. Some Polish guy a woman at work used. Does everything, apparently. Plumbing, electrics, the works.'

'Ooh, you must give me his name. Our boiler's about a hundred years old and I keep waiting for it to go.'

Electra drifted off. She and Zack would love to improve the flat, but at the moment it came very low down the list of priorities. She'd been trying to squirrel away some money for his college fund, but it was so difficult to find anything spare at the end of each month. It was high time she got a pay rise. If they'd managed to hook the hot young author she could probably have demanded one, but apparently she'd signed with the other publisher. All of Electra's flattery and enthusiasm had been a complete waste of time. The other lot had offered her 100 k more.

'Door!' Bella cried, and ran for it as Jen's legs came down the basement steps.

Jen looked fantastic. Slim but healthy, her T-shirt stretched across breasts that were remarkably pert for someone who'd given birth. She sat down at the remaining place at the table and poured herself a glass of wine. When the conversation about woeful London contractors came to a natural end, she said, 'So, nobody's even noticed then. That was a waste of four grand.'

They stared at her and she looked pointedly down at her bosom.

'You haven't!' Bella cried.

'I have. They were dragging on the fucking floor. What do you think?'

'I'm horribly jealous,' Chrissy said. Her own were fashionably flat. 'What size are they?'

'Thirty-six double d.'

Electra whistled.

'Eliot loves them.'

'You're back together?' Bella squeaked.

'Oh, you know what I'm like. Can't stay angry with him for long. I haven't let him move back in, mind. It's been nice having the place to myself. Plus, I don't have to watch the football every bloody weekend.'

'Didn't it hurt?'

Jen went on to describe every lurid detail of the procedure, making them ooh and ahh and beg her to stop.

It was a good evening and ended just at the right time, none of them able to stay up past eleven these days. Bella was somehow persuaded not to open another bottle, and Chrissy helped her up the steps to drive her home.

When they'd gone and the flat fell silent once more, Electra felt somehow at peace, as if some poison had been drained from her body by the mere presence of her friends.

Pouring out the dregs of the last bottle, she opened her laptop and googled *autism in babies*.

Zack came back early. It was barely eleven fifteen when she heard the key in the lock. They could have an hour or so together before bed. She rose from the kitchen table to meet him, a smile on her lips. The more she'd read on the net, the more convinced she became that they should get Ozzy tested. Perhaps it wouldn't be so bad, perhaps he would only have it mildly, and now that she knew, she could be a better, more patient mother to him.

'Hey.' He came in and closed the front door softly.

'Hey.' She kissed him, inhaling the familiar scent of stale beer and Bar Keepers Friend.

'How was your night?' His tone was flat. He must be tired.

'Good. Great.'

'What happened to your lip?'

'Oh, I just . . . bumped it on the fridge door.'

'Right.'

It was such a poor lie, she expected him to pick her up on it, but he just took a glass from the cupboard and opened the bottle of wine they had managed to wrest from Bella.

'Shall we watch another one of that Swedish thing?'

For a moment he didn't reply, just leaned heavily on the sink.

'Zack?'

'Sit down, Lec.'

Her blood froze.

The new girl.

Thea.

She knew her name because Zack had mentioned her, what, three times yesterday? Thea's dad had gone to school with Zack's dad, a few years apart. Thea was working weekends at the bar to see her through med school. Thea was twenty-two.

Her legs went from under her and she sat, heavily. Zack came over and sat down opposite her.

'I didn't want to tell you before your drinks.'

Electra covered her mouth and stared at him. She should have known the day would come. It was always supposed to be a bit of fun. She'd been pushing thirty-five when they met, and couldn't afford to waste more than a couple of months on something that was clearly going nowhere. So she'd tried to keep a lid on her feelings. With zero success. Five months into the relationship she was considering abandoning her baby dreams just to spend a few years with this boy. Then she got pregnant.

And now he'd finally realised what she had got him into. What she had taken from him. His youth. His career dreams.

'This came this morning, when you'd gone to work.'

He took an envelope from his pocket and slid it across the table. She could not bring herself to touch it. Was it a letter from a solicitor?

'That American woman must have reported you. Listen.' He took her hands. 'We can deal with this, whatever happens,

70

okay? They'll realise soon enough that it's all bollocks. That we're great parents. It'll be over so quickly, and if it goes any further, you can get Chrissy involved.'

Sliding her hands out from under his she took the letter from its envelope.

Dear Miss Xanders,

We are writing to you because we have been contacted by a member of the public who witnessed an incident that led to them feeling concerned for the safety and well-being of your children.

Electra's heart stopped.

We would like to visit you and your children at home at your earliest convenience to assess the needs of the family. Please contact Kensington and Chelsea social services at the above email address in order to—

Her vision blurred. Blood pulsed behind her eyes. Her fingers had turned icy cold.

'Oh my god,' she whispered.

'It's okay.'

'Oh my god, they're going to take them away.'

'No. They're not. My parents have a councillor friend and she said if it's a thing from a member of the public they're obliged to check it out. Once they've assessed us and figured out that we're normal people, they'll close the file.'

But they weren't normal people. Electra was a monster who had admitted taking pleasure in hurting her own son. What if she was capable of more? What if she was capable of killing them? The council were right to think her children were at risk.

'I'll call them tomorrow.' She got up shakily and headed to the bedroom, climbing into bed fully clothed and pulling the duvet up to her trembling chin.

Zack followed and got in beside her and took her hand. His skin was rough from the chemicals they used to clean the tables. 'I love you,' he said. 'And whatever happens, we'll be fine.'

For once she didn't say it back. It was her love that had stripped him of a career, taken his carefree youth and now put him at risk of accusations of child abuse. She had ruined his life and if she really loved him she would let him go. Closing her eyes she let the tears roll silently into the pillow.

7

Iona

Present

More rain. The washing-up bowl she had just placed under the leak in the bathroom ceiling would be half full by the time she got back from work. She was sick of getting up in the dark, spending the whole day in a louring gloom, then going home in the dark to a darkened flat.

She thought she liked living alone, not having to excuse her habits or make desultory conversation when she'd rather just stare at the TV, but as Christmas approached she was starting to feel the first murmurings of a bleak future. When her parents died and her friends were busy with their families, perhaps she would not feel quite so pleased with her independence. She'd get a cat if she wasn't so allergic.

Walking quickly to the tube she was glad of the bright lights that greeted her, and paused to make conversation with a guard.

On the train she flicked through one of the free papers from an empty seat to see if the disappearances had received any publicity. But with yet more stabbings in London, one every night for the last four nights, all was quiet. At least until a body turned up.

The trains were delayed because of the rain, stopping for long minutes in tunnels, filled to bursting by the time they reached the margins of central London, and she was fifteen minutes late into the office. Maya was at her desk, on the phone. She glanced up as Iona passed and smiled, but then Iona realised that Yannis was approaching and she might have been smiling at him.

He looked tired.

'How was the date?' she said, leading him into her office. He was holding a sheaf of computer printouts filled with columns of numbers.

He grinned. 'Awesome.'

So they had slept together.

'Has the body turned up?'

'No. But the blood is Jennifer Baptiste's and we found Eliot Goulding's fingerprints all over the flat and his semen on the sheets.'

'We had his prints?'

'He was in trouble as a kid.'

'Any violence?'

'Nah. Just nicked some fags from a newsagent when he was seventeen.'

'But still no body. You checked the morgues and the hospitals?'

'Yup. And if she was in a park, someone would have come across her, so either he's dumped her further afield or –' he shrugged '– there's always the river.'

Iona's heart sank. Searches of the Thames never produced much. The river was tidal and very muddy. Bodies that did turn up had usually decomposed enough to float and be caught in the oars of some poor school rowing team. Plus, dive teams were expensive. But if there was any chance at all, she would just have to risk the wrath of the super, who was always on at them to keep costs down.

'Okay,' she sighed. 'I'll ask for a dive team to search the stretch between Chelsea Harbour and Albert Bridge.'

'It's not all bad, boss.' He sat down on the corner of her desk, making it creak alarmingly. 'We found some interesting stuff on Upton's computer.' He handed her the sheaf of papers. They were copies of bank statements.

Looking down the long columns of figures she whistled.

'I know, right? No sign of the actual money. I'm thinking it all happened online, and he was careful not to leave an e-trail. But at least we have a motive for the embezzlement.'

Iona scanned the pages. Column after column of debits to payees with names like PokerStars, Spin to Win, Game King.

The guy was a gambling addict.

'His credit cards are all up to the hilt, all his accounts are overdrawn, and recently he remortgaged the house. They're practically in negative equity now. I'm amazed the bank let them do it.'

'So, she *must* have known, then,' Iona said, laying down the papers and wondering, not for the first time, how people could be so stupid. 'The wife.'

'Not necessarily. The house is in his name, so the bank wouldn't have to tell her.'

Iona groaned. 'If it was that that made him run, the missing woman could be completely unconnected.'

'Doesn't feel unconnected, though, does it?' Yannis said, looking at her.

She looked up at him. 'Okay. Bring in the boyfriend.'

Eliot Goulding was not what she had been expecting. Tall and slim, he possessed the sort of clean-cut good looks that made his attire – trackie bottoms, a football T-shirt and a shaved head – seem like a posh boy's pretence at being a gangster. Even his London accent was gentle.

Yannis was doing the interrogation while Iona observed. That way she could concentrate on his reactions and body language.

'What's this about, then?' he said, all fake bravado. They'd made him wait half an hour alone in the interview room and he was already twitchy.

'What can you tell us about Jennifer Baptiste?'

'She's my girlfriend. Why? What's she done?'

'Nothing. Miss Baptiste is missing.'

Goulding sat up in his chair. 'Since when?'

'Currently we think she was last seen on the fourth of December, unless you can tell us differently.'

'But . . . but that's four days ago. And you're only telling me now?'

'We were under the impression the two of you had split up.'

'Y . . . yeah, but . . .'

'Did Jennifer end it?'

'We had a row. She kicked me out.'

'What was the row about?'

He eyed them for a second and Iona guessed he was trying to decide whether or not to front it out, tell them it was none of their business. But it took no more than a few seconds for him to crack. He was biddable, this one.

'She was taking me for granted. Not making any time to see me. Not returning my calls. I was getting sick of it.'

'So, you were angry with her?'

'No. Well, a bit, but . . .' His eyes widened. 'I wouldn't never of hurt her. I'm not like that. She's probably just gone off somewhere to wind me up.'

'There were signs of a disturbance in her flat.'

'What kind of disturbance?'

'Bloodstains, signs of a struggle.'

Eliot's mouth opened and closed.

'Her keys, purse and phone were still at the flat.'

The young man blinked rapidly. 'She left her phone?'

'When did you last see Jennifer?'

'Um . . . Wednesday. She called me to say she wanted her keys back. I left them with her neighbour because she don't trust the postboxes in the lobby.'

This tallied with what Mrs Kale had said.

'And then?'

'Then I went back to Mum's, watched the match, had a beer, went to bed.'

It didn't matter, Iona thought, Jennifer had been alive and well on the Thursday.

'And what were your movements on the fourth, fifth and sixth of December?'

'I . . .' He looked to Iona as if for help. 'I can't remember.'

'It was only last week, Mr Goulding.'

'Umm, well, I would have been working till about seven. Oh, I had a beer with the guys on the Friday. On Saturday I . . . watched the match and then went to the pub with some mates. Sunday . . . I went to the gym and then watched a film with Mum in the evening. *Dunkirk*. The war one.'

'Can anyone confirm your movements?'

Yannis noted down the contact details of the people Goulding gave him.

'I believe you're a driver for an executive cab company. Is that correct?'

He nodded.

'Do you drive all the cars in the company, or is one allocated specifically to you?'

'All of them. I s'pose, sometimes. But what's that got to do with anything?'

'We will want to look at any vehicle you've driven in the past week.'

He stared at the police officers and the colour drained from his cheeks. 'Wait, you don't think I . . . ?'

They all stood up as Eliot sprang from his seat, sending it clattering to the floor.

'I want a lawyer! Get me a fucking lawyer!'

The arrival of two other officers settled him down, and he stood panting in the middle of the room, arms tensed by his sides, fists clenched: fight or flight mechanism fully engaged. Not entirely the gentle giant Iona had taken him for at first, then.

They assured him that at the moment he was not under suspicion of any crime, and there was, as yet, no proof that Jen had been harmed.

By the time they led him back to reception Goulding was grey-faced and distracted and they watched him hurry to his car, fumbling the fob and stalling the engine twice before finally accelerating away.

'Seems like a no-brainer to me,' Yannis said, over lunch. 'His prints are everywhere, he had motive and opportunity, and there were no signs of forced entry. He murdered her, then somehow got rid of the body.'

Iona swirled her tea around the edges of the mug. 'His prints *would* be everywhere if they were in a relationship until very recently. A crime of passion I could accept – he clearly has strong feelings for her – but the removal of the body with no witnesses? It all seems too well planned for an impulse killing.'

Yannis looked unimpressed. 'They've just split up – most dangerous time for a woman. We've seen it all before.'

He was right.

'Okay,' Iona said. 'Get forensics to check all the cars at his firm.'

Maya walked into the canteen then, interrupting her train of thought. She and Yannis did not even glance at one another. Perhaps they were ignoring one another. People did play games like this, she knew, though she'd never understood why.

'Erm, haven't we still got one woman left?'

'Yeah. That one who told Jen not to get the scans,' Yannis said, gesticulating with his fork.

They raised their eyebrows at one another.

It was raining again. They'd had to park in a residential street off the embankment, and by the time they made it back to the river they were drenched. As the high tide lashed the green bricks, sending arcs of spray over the wall, Iona yanked her hood down, bunching it around her neck. She couldn't think of a worse day to be living on the river.

'So, what do we know about this one?' Iona said as they passed along the embankment towards the entrance to the pier.

'Sectioned in ninety-three after a breakdown,' Yannis said. 'Accused a teacher of rape the year before, but they were never convicted. Couple of warnings for cannabis possession and a dodgy tax return the first year of her massage business.'

They passed under a bridge and were, for a moment, engulfed in a urine-scented darkness. The darkened corners were littered with broken bottles and crumpled cans; evidence of rough sleepers. Rivulets of water ran like tears from cracks in the concrete bridge supports.

'Wonder why she does massage if she was raped,' he said. 'Why you'd want any contact at all with men's bodies.'

Iona shrugged. 'I guess this way she's in control.'

They emerged to see, up ahead, a straggling line of boats, of various size and impressiveness, arranged along a walkway connected to the metal pier. The boats jostled in the wind, making hollow booming sounds, and the surface of the water seethed. They were connected to each other, and to tall mooring posts, by lengths of rope draped with hanks of weed like green hair.

The river bent here, slowing the flow, and the flotsam and jetsam of the city had come to rest against the inner wall of the bend. Plastic bottles and cans, polystyrene fast-food cartons, takeaway cups, the odd bright blue Nerf gun bullet, all bobbed in a putty-coloured soup of scum.

'Which one is she?'

'That one, I think.' Yannis pointed at one of the smallest, perhaps no more than thirty feet from prow to stern. It sat low in the brown water, and the green and yellow paintwork needed restoring. Portholes studded the side, and anchor ropes fell away into the dark water at the prow and stern. The gangplank was scraping against the low wall as the boat rose and sank in the swell.

They went up to the metal access gate. On the railing was an intercom panel. Skye Demirel's boat was the fifth one down: the *Emmeline*.

Iona pressed the button and waited. A moment later there was a buzz and the gate sprang silently open. They went through and onto the gangway that led down to the pier itself. She had always imagined that living on the river would make you feel exposed, vulnerable, but the little walkway was bordered by a fretwork balustrade that gave a feeling of privacy from prying eyes onshore.

After passing several enormous and more luxurious vessels they eventually came to the little yellow craft. On either side of the gangway that led to a wooden door were terracotta pots that must once have held something blooming, but the twisted and bulbous roots that now coiled above the soil resembled nothing more than deformed foetuses. Iona crossed the gangplank and knocked.

'Ms Demirel?'

The woman that answered was heavily made-up with pale foundation and thickly kohled eyes that turned her face into a mask. She did not even glance at their badges, just turned and led them down steep wooden steps into the belly of the boat.

It took a moment for Iona's eyes to adjust to the gloom, and in that time she could smell a dense perfume. Essential oils for Skye Demirel's massage business, perhaps. Or maybe she was burning incense to mask the smell of cannabis.

'Sit down, if you can find space.'

They were in a narrow living room connected to a tiny galley kitchen. A green velvet sofa took up one side, a couple of book-cases and a dining table filling the rest of the space completely. Iona sat down on the sofa beneath a swinging ship's lantern that had been converted to take electric bulbs. Yannis remained by the steps. There simply wasn't room for him to squeeze in here while still retaining an air of professional formality.

It wasn't as bad as Iona had imagined. Snug-fitting portholes made the rain sound distant and, though they cast very little light, the lamps and lanterns dotted around gave the place a warm, reddish glow that made it feel almost womb-like.

The walls and cupboards were decorated with childish art. Pictures of Mummy and Daddy, of cats and birds and unicorns.

A Plasticine pig graced the windowsill above the sink and a blue inhaler sat on the kitchen worktop.

Framed on the wall above a rope of brass bells was the same picture of the five women that the others possessed. Having met them and seen glimpses of their personalities, Iona still could not get a sense of them from the shot. Each woman gazed inscrutably back at her, showing nothing of their true selves.

'Can I get you a tea or coffee?' Skye Demirel said.

She stood at the kitchen counter with her back to them. Through the thin fabric of her top Iona could see her ribcage expanding and contacting as she breathed rapidly. She glanced at Yannis to see if he'd noticed.

'I've only got decaf, I'm afraid.'

They gave the usual orders and watched her prepare them. Her body was slim and toned, but almost every inch of exposed skin was covered in tattoos, all the way up the back of her neck to where her bleached dreadlocks began.

'Has there been any news yet?' she said. 'About Jen or Ewan?'

'Not yet,' Iona said. 'We're currently working on the assumption that you ladies were the last to see Miss Baptiste, on the evening of the fourth of December.'

Skye brought the mugs over. As she laid them down on the table the tea sloshed over the sides. She didn't seem to notice. In fact, she looked distracted, glancing over her shoulder at Yannis as if to make sure he wasn't creeping up on her.

What must she have suffered twenty years ago after the rape claim? Iona wondered. In those unenlightened times she wouldn't be surprised if they had tried to imply that she was somehow responsible for the attack: that she had given out the wrong messages. *What were you wearing? Are you a virgin?*

'I don't see how I can be any help.' Skye spoke quickly and breathlessly. 'I came straight home after the drinks. It was Chrissy and Bella that saw her last.'

'How did she seem that night?'

Skye shrugged. 'Fine.'

81

'Did she discuss with you the issues in her relationship with Eliot Goulding?'

Skye rolled her eyes. 'I stopped paying attention to that little drama long ago.'

'Was she scared of him?'

'Like I said, I wasn't paying attention.'

Iona felt her irritation levels rising. The attempt at bravado rang false, somehow. At that moment the boat gave a queasy lurch and Skye grabbed the kitchen counter. Bit unsteady on her feet for a seafarer. Iona imagined you'd get your sea legs after a while, but Skye's posture was stiff and tense.

'Was she seeing anyone else, as far as you know?'

'I don't know.'

'Were there any tensions with any of the other mothers that evening?'

'There were always tensions. They're all jealous of each other, you know? Always comparing: looks and money and clothes. To be honest, I'm going to let the whole thing go when Juniper starts school.'

'Any specific issue between Jen and one of the others?'

Skye looked away, frowning in thought. 'Oh yeah, there was something with Electra. She thought Jen had reported her to the social services.'

Iona frowned. 'What for?'

'I think one of the twins had a bruise that looked dodgy, but you never know with Jen. She might have just done it out of malice.'

'Did the other women feel the same about her as you do?'

'What do you mean?'

'You don't seem to like her very much.'

Skye blinked and said nothing.

'What about the falling-out you and Jennifer had over the missed antenatal checks? Is it true she blamed you in part for the stillbirth?'

Skye hesitated before answering. 'I didn't know, okay? I didn't know there was something wrong with the baby.'

'Did you fall out about it again on the night of the fourth of December?'

'No,' she said. 'If we had, one of the others would have seen it, right?'

Not necessarily, Iona thought. Not if you went round to her flat after the drinks had finished and there was a confrontation.

'Okay. Can you tell me how well you know Ewan Upton?'

'Who?'

'Bella's husband.'

'Not very. Why? Could he be involved in Jen's disappearance?'

'We were hoping you could tell us that,' Yannis said.

Skye's fingertips drummed lightly on the counter, making the Indian patterns inked onto the tendons dance. Beneath the fitted T-shirt, her arms were sinewy, her stomach a grid of muscles, like a machine. Easily capable of overpowering a smaller woman.

'I mean, Jen flirted with him. She flirted with everyone. Even my daughter's dad and he's gay. Some women are like that.' She shrugged. '*Men's* women.'

Was there a touch of jealousy in Skye's tone? Was it possible this woman had feelings for Jen herself? Could this jealously have become something darker?

'She's an attractive girl,' Iona said. 'I suspect that flirtation was reciprocated by many men. Was Ewan Upton one of them?'

'I guess he might have been, but honestly, I very rarely saw—'

She broke off suddenly, with a gasp, as the boat lurched and a buoy clunked against the hull. Gripping the worktop she looked as if she thought the vessel was about to sink.

Catching Iona's eye she said quickly, 'I'm a bit jumpy today. My daughter was up all night with her breathing. I haven't slept.'

'In that case, we'll keep it short. Could you tell us what you were doing on the fourth, fifth and sixth of December?'

Skye stared at them. 'I . . . I . . .'

Iona smiled, patient.

'I came home, after the drinks—'

'Can anyone confirm this?' Yannis said.

'No. No one. My daughter was at her dad's. I just came back here and went to bed.'

'And what about the following days?'

Skye described her movements, which mostly revolved around her daughter. Many of them were solitary – a walk in the park, treasure hunting on the foreshore. The child was far too young to corroborate any of it, but it didn't matter. Like the others, Skye seemed to dislike Jen, or at least have complex feelings for her, but it would be a true psychopath who murdered for one of the petty reasons the women had outlined.

They thanked her and took their leave, Iona following Yannis up the gangplank carefully. The wood was slippery in the rain.

'Doesn't look as if the divers are out yet,' Yannis said, scanning the river. 'Mind you, in this weather the visibility down there would be even worse.'

'You have divers?' Skye said. 'Looking for Jen?'

Iona looked down to see her pale face staring from the shadows of the stairwell.

'Yes.'

She paused, expecting more, but Skye just closed the door.

Walking along the embankment back to the car, the rain began again, as if it had been waiting for them to come out of the shelter of the boat.

'I don't get jumpy when I'm tired,' Yannis said. 'Bad-tempered, yes, but not jumpy.'

'What, you think her behaviour was suspicious?'

Yannis shrugged. 'There was something going on. That comment about one of the others seeing if she and Jen had an argument sounded defensive, no?'

'Yeah, but it might have been just a reaction to us. Don't forget that her last contact with the police was when they failed to prosecute her rapist.'

'Alleged rapist.'

Iona looked at him sternly. In her opinion, most men accused of rape were guilty. She knew Yannis felt differently, that there were more than enough malicious women out there.

'She probably had something stashed away there,' he said. 'I could smell weed, couldn't you?'

They reached the car and got in. The air inside was damp and chill and Iona shivered. The rain had penetrated her bones. As Yannis pulled away she turned the heating up to max, then stared moodily out at the schoolchildren hurrying home, their eyes glued to screens.

Whatever the behaviour of Skye, or any of the other so-called friends, the only woman with any real motive to murder Jennifer Baptiste was, potentially, Bella Upton. Screwing your kid's babysitter wasn't exactly unusual, and there had been all those calls between Upton and Baptiste, plus the flirtation Demirel had mentioned. An affair would put Bella Upton's whole life in jeopardy. That was what made people kill.

Perhaps it was time to pay Mrs Upton another visit.

But when they got back to the station the chief was waiting for her. He didn't look happy.

'A word, Detective Inspector Chatwin.'

8

Mothers Club

1 Year Previously

The sun on the water was dazzling, the wave tips flashing as the clipper passed at speed on its way to Battersea Reach. Skye stood on the deck and let it mesmerise her, until she wasn't sure if it was the boat moving or her own body swaying like a charmed snake.

Summer was by far the best time to live on the river. She could see it in the envious eyes of those walking along the embankment, on their way home to gloomy flats with no gardens. To live on the river was to be blessed: there was something almost sacred about it. Sometimes she felt like offering a sacrifice: a coin or a bead, a sweet cake from the Lebanese bakery, to placate whatever spirit squirmed in the mud beneath the opaque surface of the water. To ask that it be kind to her over the coming winter.

Because a London summer was always so brief. Soon enough she and Juniper would be huddled in blankets by the wood burner, her pretending that it was all an adventure, making sure Juniper carried her inhaler at all times. They were overdue a hard winter. But when she asked Juniper if she wanted to move into a nice warm flat on dry land the little girl had cried and begged to stay on the *Emmeline*. Perhaps if it got really cold they could move in with Pedro for a bit.

A few minutes later she saw him jogging down the steps from the bridge. Her heart lifted at the sight of his black hair flashing in the sun. He moved easily, back straight, chin up, elbows pumping, pushing himself to speed up for the last few steps. He was on a fitness drive, having decided he was putting on weight: the mortifying phrase that could only be whispered: *middle-aged spread*. It made her smile. He was only a couple of years older than she was but made such a fuss about the lines around his eyes and the elegant streaks of white at his temples.

He'd come to collect Juniper's cuddly toy. The mums were over tonight and the boat was too small for a party *and* a sleeping child, so she was going to Daddy's. There were two of everything else: pyjamas, toothbrushes, underwear, one set at each of her parents' homes, but Meow could not be replicated.

'Hello, my darling!' he called, puffing to a halt and leaning over, hands on his thighs.

'How far today?'

'Five k.'

'Careful. You might start losing muscle mass.'

He straightened up, eyes wide with consternation. 'You are not serious?'

She smiled. 'Of course not. You've got plenty of fat to lose first.'

'And you are a bitch. Give me a drink. Something diet.'

He came down and slumped onto the sofa, red-faced and glistening with perspiration. Leaning over to give him his green Coke she inhaled the familiar scent of him appreciatively. Pedro didn't smell like other men: that sour milk fug that suggested a lax attitude to hygiene. Even his sweat was fresh and fragrant.

He chugged the drink back in one go, the muscles of his throat rippling, then deposited the bottle on the floor and leaned back, arms spread along the back of the sofa to reveal two neat sprigs of black hair.

'So.' He waggled his eyebrows. 'I have a date on Friday.'

'A date?' she laughed. 'Don't you mean a shag?'

Pedro waved his hand. 'Done that. No, this is actual *dinner*.'

'OMG.'

'I know, right?' The phrase always sounded funny with a Spanish accent. 'He asked me. I thought about it. I thought about the size of his cock. And I said yes.' He gave a flourish of his hand, like a prince bestowing favours.

Skye sat on the floor on the other side of the coffee table, cross-legged, a child ready to hear a good nursery tale. 'Come on then, spill.'

'Well, his cock is *massive*. I'm serious. It is like this.' Pedro opened his hands an impossible distance.

'Bullshit.'

'Not at all, I will show you.'

She sipped her detox tea as he tapped away on his phone, a smile playing on his lips. His cheeks were returning to their usual golden brown as he recovered from the run, but a muscle in his thigh still quivered slightly.

She thought, then, of the time those thighs had been between her own.

Closing her eyes she considered pushing the memory from her mind with the thought-stop technique she had learned after the breakdown. The problem was that the lovely bit could not be isolated. The part where his bare chest was touching hers, where his arms were around her head, his fingers in her hair. It was the last time she'd had a *cock* (thanks to Pedro she'd ceased being able to think of the portion of anatomy as anything else) inside her and the memory of it made her ache. But there was always the next part. The part where Pedro slowly stopped moving, where that sense of being filled diminished as he softened and then withdrew, and then, worst of all, burst into tears.

It's not you. You are a beautiful woman. It's me. I was stupid to think . . . I'm sorry. Oh, my darling, I'm so sorry.

The ache turned into a chill.

It had been the worst experience since her teenage years, conflicted as she was between wanting to comfort the man she loved as he sobbed, naked and hunched on the edge of the bed, and wanting to hurt him as he had hurt her. Because in her heart she had always believed his sexual orientation was as fluid as hers. She'd had relationships with women at uni – for a while she'd thought Tara was The One – the only requisite for her was love. She loved Pedro and Pedro loved her, so why couldn't he get over those simplistic urges? Didn't a woman lying on her stomach or on all fours look much the same as a man? Was her vagina so repellent to him?

In the end they'd gone to a clinic, and while their relationship remained close it was subtly changed by the experience. There was no more flirting or sleeping in the same bed, Pedro was more respectful of her body and her space. She missed it. The tacky warmth of his skin, the scent of his hair.

'Here,' he said.

She took the screen.

The penis was indeed huge. Large enough to have a slight bend in the middle, purple and rippled with knotty veins. Repellent.

'Looks painful,' she said.

Pedro waggled his eyebrows. 'Depends how much lube you use.'

She grimaced. 'What about the rest of him?'

Pedro scrolled through the pictures of a man who looked very similar to himself, only with a neat black beard and a more defined stomach and pecs. It always amused her that physically Pedro just fancied himself. It would be easier to wank in front of a mirror.

'Nice. What's his name?'

'Felippe.'

She shook her head. He was even Mediterranean.

'He's funny.'

She looked up.

'Very clever. Designs apps for this company in Shoreditch.'

'Wow.'

'He lives with his sister in London, but his parents are still in Portugal. He has a sister and a brother, but his brother is a drug addict. It is probably his father's fault. Very sad.'

They had talked a lot, then, in those brief periods before and after fucking.

'How many times have you seen him?'

'This will be the third. We're going to a place called The Bike Shed. Apparently it is *very* cool.'

'Right, sounds . . .' She tailed off.

'You will really like him.

'*Ohhhh.*' She put on a coy pretend-simpering face. 'I'm going to *meet* him, am I?'

'Yes,' Pedro said quietly. 'Yes, I think so.'

Pedro stayed until her client arrived, then, tucking Meow into his backpack, he set off for Juniper's nursery.

She was clumsy, leading the guy down the steps, and stumbled, knocking over a plant, spilling the soil all over the deck. Her head was filled with noise.

'I got your number from Amira Goel at Channel 4,' the client said. 'She said you'd sorted out a lower back issue she had.'

'Right.' Skye led him into the living room, where she'd set up the massage table while she and Pedro talked.

'I've had this problem with my shoulder for about three months. It's a bit embarrassing. I fell down a step when I'd had a couple and it just felt bruised for a while, but now I can only move my arm this far.'

She glanced at him as he demonstrated. 'Maybe you should go to a physio.'

'I've thought about it, but you came highly recommended, and I haven't had much luck with physios in the past. I had a bike crash and—'

'Lie down. Let's have a look.'

She knew she was being rude, but she didn't care. If they would just stop coming, these people, if the money would just dry up, then she could start claiming benefits, perhaps the council would find her a flat. Somewhere warm and dry, so that Juniper didn't have to go on antibiotics again this winter. But word of her massage technique seemed to be spreading around the media set of west London, and she found herself unable to refuse the income stream.

The man unbuttoned his shirt to reveal a typical, slightly pasty Englishman's body, a few fine fair hairs attempting to sprout between soft-looking pecs, a large mole or two, baby-pink nipples. She felt a moment's tenderness and tried to recall what he'd said his name was.

'Sorry, I'm a bit sweaty. I cycled here.'

'That's okay. Your muscles will be nice and warm. Now, which shoulder is it?'

The mums were coming at 7.30 and Chrissy was bound to be on time, so Skye jumped in the shower as soon as the client left, to rinse off the essential oils and the sweat from the effort she'd put into the massage.

His name was Mort and his shoulder was fucked. The fall he mentioned had shocked the muscles around the joint, making them contract, pulling the shoulder partly out of its socket. Her manipulation of the arm produced an alarming variety of crunches and clicks and the poor guy was chalk-white by the end. He'd actually felt so nauseous from the pain that she had to give him a cup of chamomile tea. To make conversation, as he slumped on the sofa looking rather pitiful, she had asked about his job – programme researcher – but he quickly shifted the conversation on to her and she found herself telling him about the Ph.D. she'd begun but never completed, on the effects of bacteria-rich food on brain neurology.

He was either genuinely interested in the research she quoted or just super polite. Either way, she found herself warming to him, despite his short back and sides haircut and Mr Average jeans and rugby shirt.

The shoulder would need a lot of work. She told him he'd be better off getting an NHS referral, but he insisted that the arm already felt more mobile and booked in for the following week. As she watched him cycle off down the embankment, indistinguishable from every other biking commuter, she thought about the nakedness of people under their clothes, the vulnerability they kept hidden. It was a privilege to have that vulnerability shared with you, and she vowed to be nicer to him next time.

Stepping out of the shower, she dried off and squeezed out her dreads. A glance in the mirror made her wonder again whether to give in and finally cover the self-harm scars on her upper arms with tattoos. At the moment her arms were a very obvious tattoo-free statement. *Look at my pain*. But she found she did not want to have to explain them to Juniper – not yet – and the little girl was already tracing the ridges with her fingertips. Perhaps a tree or leaf pattern would work.

Pulling on her vest and trousers she headed to the kitchen to blend up the garlic and mushrooms for the pâté.

When Chrissy arrived the two of them sat out on the deck and sipped vodka tonics. The sun was low over Chelsea Harbour, turning the windows of the Montevetro Building pink and gold. Chrissy looked tired and did not object when Skye took her hand and began massaging out the joints. Chrissy's fingers were gradually morphing from elegant to bony. They were all ageing, drying out, becoming stringy as old beans – except Jen of course, but her time would come. It was more obvious for Skye, who rarely wore make-up, but she was proud of the lines around her eyes and mouth, the sun damage that framed her face in freckles. It was a face that spoke of treks in Nepal, of summers working in Goan bars, tea picking in hill stations, conservation work in South Africa. A life well lived. But now contracting into a smaller sphere. A circle that contained herself, Pedro and Juniper. A circle of love whose limits sometimes made her afraid.

Bella was next to arrive, hurrying along the embankment.

'Thought I'd save some money and walk!' she called breathlessly when she came close enough. 'Boy, do I need a drink!'

'I'll make you one.' Skye got up and went down into the boat, which felt cavernous without Juniper. Dark too, even with the glinting river just outside the window. She suppressed a shiver of something: dread? Life was so short and fragile. She felt the urge to send the mums home and call Pedro, have him come back, and the three of them cuddle up on the sofa, skin to skin, limbs entangled. A family.

Opening the hatch, she tossed out the first thing that came to hand, a jade egg that had sat by the tea tin as long as she could remember.

Keep us safe. Keep us together.

The water received it silently.

'What was that?' Bella was standing behind her. 'Sorry. I didn't mean to make you jump, I just came to help with the drinks.'

'It's okay.' Skye smiled, trying to hide her discomfort at being watched. 'It was just a stone egg I picked up somewhere.'

'Why did you throw it into the water?'

'Sometimes I like to . . . you know, make a kind of . . . of offering to the river.'

Bella was looking at her with wide, encouraging eyes.

'I just reached for that instinctively, but I suppose it's quite appropriate because the egg is the symbol for the soul, and I'm offering my soul to the river.'

'Ah,' said Bella. 'That's . . . sweet.'

No one could ever really understand another person, Skye thought, as Bella bustled about the fridge. We were all ultimately alone.

Through the porthole that looked east, she could see the buses rumbling heedlessly across Battersea Bridge, their synthetic scarlet an affront to the natural colours of the sunset. Planes drew white scars across the sky. Humans self-harming the organism they were a part of. A lurch of depression made her lean heavily on the worktop.

These thoughts are grey but beyond them the sky is blue. Let them pass.

'Ooh, that's delicious,' Bella chirped. 'Shall we go back up and watch the sunset?'

She opened her eyes, followed Bella back up on deck.

Electra arrived next, her black trousers flapping in a cold breeze that had blown up. The sun had sunk below Chelsea Bridge and the river had turned to black ink, licking at the sides of the hull below them. Her arrival was the excuse they needed to withdraw downstairs. With the scented candles lit, their flames glinting off the hatches and drinking glasses, all was cosy and safe once more.

'Lovely brownies,' Chrissy said. 'Are they seriously sweet potato?'

'You can't tell the difference,' Bella said.

'Ha!' barked Electra, her open mouth revealing a wad of orangey brown sludge, and Skye smiled. Electra had on her black-rimmed glasses, which she only ever wore when she was seriously tired. Ozzy again, no doubt. The child needed some kind of therapy, or the impact of his pain would send hairline cracks throughout the whole family.

By the time Jen arrived darkness had fallen and the river lapped blackly at the hatches.

'Sorry I'm late!'

'You're always late,' they trilled.

'Eliot was being a twat. So what's happening with everyone?'

Skye said, 'Pedro's got a new man.'

'Ooh, titillate us, do!' Electra waggled her eyebrows.

'His name's Felippe and he's twenty-three.'

'Just your type, Lec.' Jen grinned and Electra flicked wine at her.

'Where did they meet?' Bella said, innocently.

'Oh, Bells.' Electra rolled her eyes.

94

The other three women chanted in unison, 'Grind-errrr!'

'What's Grindr?'

'A gay dating app,' Skye said.

'Oh,' Bella said. 'That's sweet.'

Electra snorted. 'You don't go on Grindr for *sweet*, just filthy sex.'

'Maybe I should try it,' Chrissy muttered, and Skye glanced at her. It was unlike her to be candid, even allusively, and she wasn't even drinking.

'It'll probably have run its course in a couple of weeks. Anyway, what about everyone else?'

'I've got a job!' Bella announced proudly.

They all woohed. Skye was surprised. Of all of them, Bella was the most natural stay-at-home mum. She seemed to love spending her time with Teddy.

'In PR?' Chrissy said.

'No. In Benjamin Brothers.'

'The department store?' Chrissy said, frowning.

'Yes. Menswear.'

There was a brief pause.

'That's great,' Skye said finally.

'Ewan says it'll help a lot,' Bella went on.

'Ewan made you take it?' Electra said.

'Not made, no. He thought it would be good for me to get back to work. To do something for myself.'

'Right.' Electra's tone was cold.

'Well, we'll have to come in and see you,' Chrissy said brightly. 'What are you going to do with Teddy?'

Bella's face fell. 'Nursery, I guess.'

'But if you're on a standard retail wage, won't that eat up the whole lot?'

'There'll be tax credits I suppose and . . .' She tailed off.

Even to Skye, who was useless at maths, it was obvious that Bella's take-home pay would be a pittance. How desperate were they for money that they would sacrifice Teddy for a few pounds a month?

'Let me look after him.'

All eyes turned to Jen.

'I'm cheaper than a nursery, and I might even consider mates' rates.'

For a moment there was silence. Jen had been a childminder before the stillbirth but had never gone back to work afterwards. As far as they knew she lived on benefits and whatever Eliot brought in.

'Are you sure?' Bella said doubtfully.

Jen smiled. 'Yeah. Of course. I wanted to get back to it eventually anyway, and if I can do it for a friend, and with a child I actually like, all the better.'

'Oh, thank you!' Bella lunged across the table and pulled Jen into her arms.

Skye and Electra left them talking and went upstairs for a smoke.

The night was opaque around them, the red eyes of the cars like creeping rats along the other bank. The river was a black gulf in between, absent of its gods. Somewhere out there, beyond the battalion of townhouses along Cheyne Walk, her daughter was sleeping in a Z-bed with a unicorn duvet. Her father beside her, soft-lashed and dreaming under grey linen, his love and protection a testament to the irrelevance of anatomical desire.

She thought of the man with the white chest and the ruined shoulder, hoped that she had not hurt him enough to banish sleep.

'God, it's peaceful,' Electra murmured. 'I can see why you love it.'

Skye smiled. 'It's not very peaceful when Juniper's stamping about like a herd of elephants.'

Electra looked at her. 'Try living in my house.'

'It's no better, then, with Ozzy?'

Electra shook her head. 'The social services come round once a month without fail. We tried to tell them that he might be autistic, that's why he's like that, not because he's disturbed by having a psychotic mother, but they won't believe it without a psychologist's report and that takes forever and costs a bomb.'

Skye touched her arm and tried to draw some of the negativity out of Electra's body and into her own. She knew the others thought that kind of thing was bullshit, but a moment later, Electra sighed. 'It'll be all right. That's what Zack always says.'

At eleven o'clock Chrissy announced that she was heading off and did anyone want a lift. They all did. Even inside it was possible to tell that the night had got noticeably colder. A thin chill seeped through the portholes. It was good that Juniper was at Pedro's tonight.

Skye followed them out onto the deck, pulling her cardigan across her shoulders as the river breeze bit. They kissed her goodbye, then trooped across the gangplank.

Watching them walk away, Skye thought how lucky she was to have them for friends. These women who she would never have given a thought to had she met them before, but who she had forged such strong bonds with, beginning with the bond of new motherhood but becoming deeper by the year.

She would do anything for them.

9

Iona

Present

The conversation with the chief had not gone well.

'Any progress on the embezzlement?'

'Not yet, but—'

'And the missing woman? Has she turned up?'

'No, sir. Not yet.'

'Do we have any leads?'

'We're working on it.'

'Could you explain to me why, when we have no body, and this is an adult woman who might very well have left of her own free will, and has currently been missing less than a week, you have decided to waste umpteen grand on a dive?'

She shrugged. 'It looks dodgy, sir.'

'*Dodgy?* You're a detective inspector not a beat muppet. I want to see evidence that this woman has suffered an untimely fate before I sign off that kind of expense.'

'There was blood. Signs of a struggle. She'd left her hair straighteners, sir.' She gave a weak smile.

The chief glared at her. 'Well you've had more than enough time to make an arrest. Here's a tip. It's the boyfriend. I want you off it because next week you'll be busy with the new mayor/Met forum.'

'What? Oh come on, sir. Don't punish me. This is a complicated one.'

'It's not a punishment, Iona. It's a diversity forum. And you're our most diverse member of staff.'

'What about Palvinder? He wears a turban, for Christ's sake.'

'Sikh.' He counted on one finger, then pointed it in her direction and flicked out a second finger. 'Woman. Gay. Double diversity.'

Iona's lip curled. 'Being a woman is not particularly diverse, sir. As you may know, we make up more than half the population.'

'Fine. We'll make a deal. Wrap this up, locate the missing woman and hand the embezzlement over to Fraud, and I'll make Palvinder do it.'

Iona sighed.

'Or you'll be discussing the difficulties of getting a wheelchair up Nelson's Column for the next three months.'

With characteristically perfect timing Yannis came in three minutes after her boss left, to inform her of a development. 'Upton turned his mobile on. He's in Germany. Polish border, heading east.'

'Did he try and make a call?'

'No. He was maybe checking to see if he'd received any.'

'From Jen or Bella?'

'We're tracking Bella's calls and there's nothing.'

'She hasn't tried to call him again? Doesn't that strike you as weird?'

Yannis shrugged. 'Either she's given up on him or she doesn't want us to think they're in touch.'

'I guess there could be a burner phone. But then why would he need to turn his on and risk us tracing him?'

'It's a mystery, boss.'

She sighed and leaned back in her chair. 'Tell me the truth, do you think we should just hand this over to Fraud? They can get Interpol on it.'

Yannis came in and sat down. 'The other bit of good news is that checks on Upton's car, and all the ones from Goulding's firm, came back clear. No blood. Nothing.'

'Great.' Diversity forum, here she came.

For a while they sat in silence. Maya's laugh drifted in from outside. Musical and soothing, it set up a tingling sensation at the back of Iona's head.

'I wonder if the wife knows more about Baptiste's disappearance than she's letting on,' Iona said. 'She was the last person to see Jen alive, as far as we know.'

'If you can describe it as *seeing* considering she was out cold.'

'Or was she?'

'What do you mean?'

'Maybe she wasn't as drunk as they all thought. Maybe when she got home she revived enough to have a row with Jen. Remember she said that she had to clear the dishwasher the next morning because the childminder hadn't turned up? If you were friends, or even just her employer, wouldn't you have called to check she was all right?'

'If they fought there, how come the DNA's all at Baptiste's place?'

Iona frowned. 'Didn't Marta say she'd seen her coming home twice that night?'

'Marta's a junkie. You can't trust anything she says. Besides, she claimed Bella was being *helped* home twice, by the other women.'

'Say Marta's confused about that part, but what if Bella *did* come back twice that night? Where did she go the second time?'

Yannis looked at her and she knew he was thinking what she was.

It was late afternoon by the time Chrissy Welch returned Iona's call, and she didn't sound happy to hear from the police again.

'I've told you everything I know. I don't see how I can be of any more help.'

'I'm sorry to bother you again, Mrs Welch.' Iona was careful not to sound too sorry. 'But as you can imagine, we are concerned for Miss Baptiste's welfare.'

'Yes, well . . .'

'On the night of the fourth of December, after you'd taken Bella home – around eleven o'clock, I think you said – did you see her again that night?'

'Of course not. I went to bed.'

'Was Bella asleep when you helped her inside?'

'Well, no, obviously not completely asleep or we'd have had to carry her. No, she could walk, just about.'

'So it's possible that Jennifer never actually tucked her into bed, because she was awake. Is it possible there was an altercation between herself and Bella?'

In the silence that followed Iona's heart quickened.

'There wasn't.'

'How do you know? You weren't there.'

'I know Bella went straight to sleep because a few minutes after I dropped them off we all got a text from Jen.'

'Can you send it to me?' Iona read out her number and a moment later a picture message pinged through.

It was a screengrab from a group chat that included all five women.

Jennifer Baptiste had sent the last message. It was captioned *Sleeping beauty!*

The image was of Bella Upton lying on her sofa wrapped in a blue throw. Her eyes were closed, her wine-stained mouth hung open and she looked as comatose as it was possible to be without being dead.

Iona thanked Chrissy and ended the call. Then she dropped her head into her hands.

10

Mothers Club

6 Months Previously

Jen sat on the sofa painting her toenails. Tonight she would wear the sparkly all-in-one playsuit with black sandals. She'd be overdressed compared to the others, but she always was. She could never quite understand why they didn't make more of an effort, for themselves as much as for their men. Bella, for one, had let herself go since Teddy was born and Jen could see, when they went round there, how Ewan's gaze skimmed over his wife, barely registering her physical presence. Chrissy ought to be his type – his age, his social level – but he would be intimidated by a woman like that. Whereas Jen herself always caught his eye. He probably considered himself more of a man for fancying a sexy younger woman, when actually it was just low self-esteem.

Balling up the toilet roll she'd used to separate her toes, she dropped it into the empty sushi box on the glass table. The flat was a pigsty, as usual, but it didn't matter. Nobody ever came here. No one but Eliot. She was still in touch with some friends from school, but she kept them at arm's length. So many of them had got pregnant in their teens and were now single mums, their babies with multiple dads. Jen's life wasn't going to be like that. It had gone awry, with what happened, but that was a blip. She refused to grieve for what she'd lost. She was young, she had plenty of time. The Mothers Club was her future. Professional, comfortably off, with a stable relationship and happy, healthy children at good schools.

That was the plan anyway. She just had to figure out how to execute it.

She went back to the bathroom and washed her hands. The water was ice-cold because the boiler was on the blink again. If the council moved at their usual sluggish pace it wouldn't be fixed before winter really bit. An elderly woman in the block had died of hypothermia last year waiting for them. Jen had liked her, but she'd never visited her in hospital before she died. She couldn't. Hospitals did her head in. After spending half her childhood in A&E with her mum, it was all she could do to step inside one when she was about to give birth. That was why she'd avoided the scans that might have picked up Zoe's problems.

After doing her make-up and fixing her hair into the fat curls Eliot liked, she pulled on the jumpsuit, shivering as her shoulders were exposed to the chill air. Then she sent him a selfie.

He responded immediately. **Shall I come round later?**

She smirked. **In your dreams.**

He didn't reply to that one. He was stroppy, she knew, because she hadn't let him move back in straightaway, probably egged on by his stupid mother who had always thought Jen was a manipulative bitch. Well, it took one to know one.

On the way out she knocked on Mrs Kale's door.

'Only me, Mrs K.'

The old woman opened the door wrapped in a dressing gown. 'You all right? Keeping warm?'

Mrs Kale rolled her eyes. 'They've given me an electric heater, but blow me if I can work it.'

'Let me see.'

The heater had two settings, one for timer and one for constant, and the dial to switch between the two was so stiff the old lady couldn't manage it with her arthritic hands. When

Jen got it working Mrs Kale insisted on giving her a glass of Baileys 'to get her evening going'.

It would mean she would be late to meet the mums, but that didn't matter, she was always late.

'Your father was always a whizz at technical things,' Mrs Kale said as they drank together on the foamy sofa.

Jen snorted. 'He could certainly work a corkscrew.'

'At least that was the only type of screw he fiddled around with,' Mrs Kale said, already slightly tipsy. 'My Del was always off at the first sign of skirt. There's nothing worse in a relationship than unfaithfulness.'

Jen raised her eyebrows. There was a lot worse as far as she was concerned. Like beating your wife senseless in front of your three-year-old, then storming out to the pub, leaving the little girl to phone the ambulance like her mother had taught her, because she knew it would be an invaluable skill for the little girl growing up. No, infidelity was nothing.

Once the room had finally warmed up and Mrs Kale was comfortably ensconced in front of *Love Island*, Jen let herself out.

As she was walking to the bar, Joe came past in his van and pulled in. She had been to school with Joe, they had got up to a lot of naughtiness in their teenage years.

'All right, gorgeous? Where you headed?'

She told him and he told her to jump in. The van smelled of Joe's overly strong aftershave. Hanging from his rear-view mirror was a picture of his seven-year-old daughter, her dark curls piled up in a tight ballet-bun.

'How's it going?' she said, helping herself to some chewing gum from the glove compartment.

'Me and Kelly have split up.'

'Shit, really?'

'It's okay. She's a fucking nutjob.'

'Well, yeah. But what about Aisha?'

Joe shrugged. 'I'll get her every other weekend, if Kelly feels like it, of course. How's you and Eliot?'

The atmosphere in the van became ionised. Joe had always had a thing for her. When she got together with Eliot at a party in an Islington nightclub, he had cried and punched a wall.

She looked across at him from the corner of her eyes. At his muscular body, clear skin and strong, handsome face. He didn't smoke. He worked out every day, he was pescatarian. She thought for a moment. And then she said, 'We're fine.'

Joe was black.

'Ah well,' he sighed, pulling into the kerb and hitting his hazards. 'You know where I am when you get fed up of the boring bastard. But don't be too long, I ain't gonna stay on the market for long.'

'Don't I know it.'

Grinning, she leaned over to kiss him, then got out of the van.

The bar was buzzing, Thursday always being the big night these days. She spotted them at a table in the corner, looking like the mums they were, at least ten years older than most of the other clientele.

'Oh my god,' Electra cried. 'I didn't know we were supposed to dress up!'

'What, this old thing?' Jen grinned. As she took her leather jacket off, she could feel eyes on her bare back, where the play-suit opened right down to the waistband.

They had already ordered. Some greasy bar snacks and a bottle of white wine.

'Ladies, what are you doing?' she said. 'It's happy hour for the next ten minutes. Two-for-one cocktails.'

She went to the bar and ordered a selection of long drinks and five shots of vanilla vodka. The barman was a local boy. She had seen him on the estate, and she returned his smile as he jiggled the silver cocktail shaker. If he was trying to impress, it wasn't working. Eliot could do the whole works, flipping and catching the shaker, pouring the liqueurs two at a time from high above the glasses. He'd learnt it when a group of them had worked the summer season in Malaga after they left school.

Back at the table she handed the drinks out according to personality. A classic mojito for Chrissy, a spiced el diablo for Electra, spring garden with actual herb leaves for Skye and an overly sweet and creamy piña colada for Bella. Jen herself had a raspberry spritzer, the least alcoholic on the menu. She never got drunk.

'So, so, so,' she said, sliding in next to Chrissy. 'What's happening?'

'You'll be delighted to hear that my basement extension is coming on a treat,' Chrissy said. 'And the Admiral hasn't complained once. Here, look.'

They never talked babies when Jen was around. It annoyed her that they clearly pitied her. She was looking forward to the time when everyone would be able to relax again. Hopefully not too far in the future.

'Who's the hottie in the vest?' Electra said.

'Atanis. My man of all work.' Chrissy grinned.

'He looks like a model. What the hell is he doing building your basement?'

Chrissy shrugged. 'He's Polish.'

'You should fix him up with your crazy divorcee client,' Skye said. 'Might take her mind off killing her husband.'

'I can't believe she wants six grand a month,' Electra said. 'What the fuck does she spend it on?'

'A lot of plastic surgery,' Chrissy said. 'And a very expensive gym.'

'I'd love to join a gym,' Electra said. 'But our local one wants two hundred quid joining fee.'

'Thought you were getting a raise,' Chrissy said.

'I did. Know how much the bastard gave me? Three per cent. Three fucking per cent, when my last five signings were bestsellers. But you know how it is. *Money's tight.* Unless you're a man. But I did get a bonus, which went immediately on Ozzy's autism report.'

'And?' Chrissy said.

'He is. But only level one, so the prognosis is good. Especially since we spotted it early. Thanks to you, Bells.' She leaned across the table and squeezed Bella's hand. She blushed. 'That's why me and him have been bumping heads so much. I just need to try and understand him a bit more. They've recommended some books. So, I guess things are looking up.' She clinked Bella's glass. 'I owe you.'

'I start my new job next week,' Bella announced brightly, clearly awkward at the attention. 'Teddy's so excited to be hanging out with Jen. Honestly, he's got even more energy than usual. I hope he doesn't wear you out!'

'He's literally never ill, is he?' Skye said. 'You two must have good genes.'

Jen's glass paused on the way to her lips.

Bella grimaced. 'I did breastfeed for ages.'

'So did I, but it doesn't seem to have made any difference. Juniper's allergic to wool now too. I don't know what I'll dress her in when it gets really cold.'

'How's the asthma?' Chrissy said.

'Okay at the moment, because it's been mild. But Felippe's moved into Pedro's flat, so we won't be able to go there if it gets worse.'

'Moved in?' Electra said. 'Don't tell me he's in *love*?'

Jen caught Skye's almost imperceptible wince. They all knew Skye was in love with Pedro, but Jen had little sympathy. Skye only went for gay men because she was scared of straight ones. She needed to move on from what had happened to her. Like Jen had. Find a man she could control.

'I hope not,' Skye said. 'Or he won't have as much time for Juniper.'

Or you, thought Jen.

'Stay with us,' Bella said suddenly.

Skye looked up at her.

'Really. We never use the top floor, only for storage. There's a bedroom and a bathroom. You guys could stay there.'

'Wouldn't Ewan mind?'

'I don't see why.'

'I couldn't . . .'

'Of course you could!' Bella was grinning and to Jen the glitter in her eyes seemed slightly manic. Perhaps it was just drink.

'I guess . . .' Skye said, 'if it gets really cold, in January, maybe just for a couple of weeks or so? Could you ask Ewan, just to make sure?'

Bella beamed. 'Sure.' She clinked Skye's glass. And then they all clinked glasses.

'To Mothers Club, and all who sail in her!'

She walked home slowly, ignoring the occasional car horn or shouted comment. She wasn't drunk, but the cold air had made her head even clearer. The night was beautiful, the stars bright enough to break through the light pollution and an ice-white moon gazed down from between two of the towers of the estate. Everyone she passed was looking at the pavement or their phones. She was the only one to see this huge expanse above their heads. This infinity of possibility.

She walked down the path that led onto the estate. It wasn't sensible to look at your phone round here anyway. You had to keep your wits about you if you wanted to be safe.

The ugly block looked almost cosy tonight, its million eyes lit up golden, the soothing sound of television and music drifting across from the lower floors. Her hands tightened on her keys as a hooded figure came towards her. But as she drew closer the moon illuminated his face.

'Evening, Tyler,' she said. She had babysat this boy, and now he was six foot four.

'All right, Jen.'

'Mum know you're out?'

He was fifteen and, as such, one of the most vulnerable people in the whole city, whatever he thought himself.

'Just getting some snacks. We're watching a film.'

'See you later.' She walked on to her own block, then swore under her breath. The door to the foyer was swinging open again. Anyone could get in. Stepping inside she closed it and made sure it was locked, then passed through the gloomy foyer.

What a dump. How had her mum stood it for forty years without going mad?

Jen was starting at Bella's next week. Bella had offered her cash in hand so she wouldn't have to stop claiming benefits. The money would go straight into her house fund. Before she got pregnant she'd been putting aside two hundred a month, and with Eliot's contribution they'd almost had enough for a little place out Bromley way. She would start looking on the property websites again. For a two-bed. With a room for a nursery.

Walking down the hall she could hear Mrs Kale talking on the phone, so didn't both to check in on the old lady, just let herself into the flat. Even though none of the kids would be hanging around outside on a cold night like this, she shut all the curtains and the blinds in the bathroom. She liked her privacy. Liked to be the one who did the watching.

Climbing into bed she lay gazing up at the light-strobed ceiling. She'd never needed much sleep. A childhood spent on permanent alert had trained her body not to need more than two or three hours a night. The sounds of the estate murmured around her like a beating heart, whispering its tales into her ear.

11

Bella

Before

She arrived at the shop early, and went straight to the staff entrance, down a flight of stairs off the pavement. The old man behind the security desk gave her a lanyard and a form and instructed her to wait on the sofa under a screen showing information on the previous week's sales figures. She filled in the form with her passport details and next of kin, and then sat with the board on her lap, watching the staff arriving, easily as terrified as she had been the morning of her first ever job as a fifteen-year-old waitress.

The uniform was black and white and somehow, since her last office job, styles of suit jacket had subtly changed. Hers was too short and wide, making her look fatter than she actually was, which was fat enough. Her size 12 trousers were straining at the bum-seam. She couldn't take the jacket off because nerves had made her sweat and she could feel that the dampness had spread out from under her armpits.

She was relieved to see, among the fresh-faced, fragrant girls, some of whom she recognised from visits to the beauty counter, a smattering of women her age. Nobody attempted to greet her or make conversation and the security guard had gone back to his tabloid.

Looking down at the comfortable shoes Ewan had told her to wear because she would be on her feet all day, she wished she had worn her patent ballet pumps instead.

She shrank into the sofa cushion as two young women came so close to look at the screen that their knees almost touched hers. As they began discussing the failings of the towels department Bella experienced a rush of terror so powerful she would have bolted from the seat and back up the steps to the street if the women hadn't been blocking her path. This was a mistake. She was going to make a fool of herself.

And poor Teddy was at home without her. Was he upset, wondering where Mummy had gone, why she preferred to go away and work in a shop than be with him? Her chin began to tremble.

'Bella?'

A tall, slim man was crossing the foyer.

'I'm so sorry you had to wait. There was a problem with the doors to the stockroom. We couldn't unlock the damn things.'

'Oh, that's okay.' She stood up.

From a distance he'd looked around her age, but as he came closer and reached to shake her hand she saw he was much older. Hairline wrinkles covered his fine-boned face, like crackleware pottery, and his hair was greying at the temples.

'I'm Rupert. Have you got your security badge? Great. So, go and put your stuff in a locker and I'll take you straight up.'

She did so, tucking the locker key into her trouser pocket, then returned to the foyer, where Rupert was waiting. He walked so quickly she had to scamper beside him.

'Do you mind if we take the stairs? I try to keep fit.'

'Not at all,' she puffed.

He smelled delicious, like spiced oranges, and the long fingers sliding along the banister rail were bare of a wedding ring.

'We're usually quiet on a Monday, so I should have plenty of time to show you the ropes.'

'Great.'

'Have you had much retail experience?'

'Not really. None, really.'

He waved an elegant hand. 'You'll be fine. It's not rocket science, selling cashmere cardis to a bunch of Chelsea queens.'

111

She laughed.

'Here we are. After you, darling.'

He held open the heavy swing door and she stepped through into Menswear. This was the one department in the shop she rarely visited. Ewan sneered when she told him which department she had been recruited to, that they had a cheek calling it *men's fashion* and that the only men it was *fashionable* for were American octogenarians. He got most of his clothes from Urban Outfitters.

The shop had been open for half an hour now, but the place was hushed, as if the piles of lambswool on the display tables absorbed all sound. Light shafts coming down from the skylight on the sixth floor illuminated dust motes swimming through the air.

'Right.' Rupert clapped his hands. 'Let me take you through the basics. This is underwear, obviously. This side's premium, and over there is the Basics range, which we don't sell much of, as you can imagine. No Chelsea-ite wants to be seen in polyester pants.'

After showing her all the menswear sections Rupert took her on a tour of the whole floor, which was bisected by the central escalators. On the other side was the beauty department, but it might as well have been a different world, populated by heavily made-up aliens. They cooed over Rupert as if he were a particularly divine Persian cat.

Then he took her to the stockroom. 'This is where they dump the stuff they don't know what to do with. I mainly use it to check my phone.'

She felt silly for following the rules in the email and leaving her own phone in the locker.

Back out on the floor he led her to the sales counter.

'They changed the till system recently, which was very stupid as it was much easier before, but now you have to do five steps before you're even on to the right screen. The customers get so stroppy waiting.'

He stepped up to one of the two computers and his fingers flew across the keys.

'Now, let's buy something. So, first you have to log in with the ID on your security pass.'

His fingers moved quickly enough that he did not give her time to process each step before moving on to the next. Eventually it all became a blur.

'Got it?'

'Could we run through it again?'

He did so and she still didn't take it in. When it was her turn she ended up on the wrong screen entirely and he had to take several back-steps to rectify her mistake. He gave no sign of impatience, but she could feel him judging her – a frumpy useless housewife, only fit for cleaning and childcare.

Suddenly tears sprang to her eyes. 'I'm sorry, I don't think I'm going to be able to do this.' Stepping back from the till she began taking off her badge. 'I won't waste your time any longer.' She was useless. A failure. *As usual,* Ewan would say. The smart feisty girl she had been before Teddy was dead.

Rupert laid his hands on her shoulders. 'Stop.'

She looked up at him, into his calm brown eyes.

'Deep breaths . . . That's it . . . You can do this. You are a strong capable woman. You are a warrior queen. You are a tigress. What are you?'

She smiled wanly. 'A tigress.'

'That's right. Now let's smack this bitch's arse.'

He moved aside and she took over. And, miraculously, this time she remembered the sequence.

'Woohoo,' she murmured when the sale went through correctly.

'See? You're a natural.' He grinned, and ridiculous though it was, her chest swelled with pride.

It really was very quiet. Though streams of people went up and down the central escalators, not many paused at the first floor, or at least not this end of it. Most were drawn to the lights and gloss of Beauty. Bella looked wistfully at the women her age getting makeovers. Arriving shabby and dishevelled, they returned twenty minutes later, with their backs straight, their chins high and the sparkle back in their eyes. It wasn't just the make-up, she was sure, it was the attention. It was someone telling you you had lovely skin or perfectly shaped lips or fine cheekbones. Once Bella had thought of herself as pretty, but not any more.

Rupert went on his break, so she stood behind the counter browsing the store's website – the only one they had access to. She looked at suits for toddlers, because they had a family wedding next year, and was scandalised by the cost. On her £8.50 an hour salary it would take three days to afford the cheapest one. Could this possibly be the excuse they needed not to go? It was one of the cousins that Ewan had declared a 'dick-swinging wanker' at the last wedding and proceeded to snub for the duration of the reception. But then again, there was no way he'd let her admit to her family that they were struggling financially. He said they were always waiting for him to fail.

Returning to the home page with a sigh she marvelled at how she used to spend her current hourly wage every single morning having coffee with the nursery mums.

'Ex*cuse* me.'

The woman spat the words like an insult. She was in her sixties, draped in floaty beige, with a rouged mask of a face, immaculate highlights and bloodshot eyes.

'I ordered a sweater three weeks ago and they said it would be available at customer collection, but those nincompoops downstairs couldn't find it and said I should see if there's one in stock up here. If there *was* one in stock I wouldn't have had to order it, would I?'

'I'm sorry, madam,' she said smoothly. 'If you give me the stock number, I can see if we have it on the floor or in our stockroom.' Rupert had taught her this just before he went.

'Oh, for heaven's sake, I don't *have* the stock number!'

'Umm . . . If you just describe it to me, then, I'll have a look on the floor.'

'Mustard. Cashmere. Medium.' It was as if she was uttering the scientific name of a venereal disease.

Bella went over to the cashmere display and riffled through the piles. Her heart was beating so fast, her vision had blurred.

'No mustards in medium, I'm afraid,' she said, going back to the woman. 'What was the name? We can see if it was delivered elsewhere in store.'

'Oh, for goodness' sake, you silly girl!'

Bella swallowed, on the verge of tears. There was one last possibility.

'I'll just check the stockroom.'

She almost ran through the door, then paused in the dusty silence, breathing deeply as she leaned on one of the metal shelves. She couldn't do this. Even this. Ewan was right. But if she quit on the first day he would be furious. As he said, she'd been nothing but a drain on his finances ever since Teddy was born. She *should* go back to work, like every other woman had to.

Something rustled.

The hand on the shelf was touching a package. She picked it up. It was soft and floppy enough to be a jumper. Surely. The name was Mrs E Gantry. Was it possible? Could the gods be that kind to her?

Fighting every instinct to cower in the safety of the little room for the rest of the day she walked back onto the floor.

Rupert was there. 'Ah, here we are, Mrs Gantry. Crisis over.'

Bella handed the package over with a beaming smile. 'Thank you so much for your patience.'

Mrs Gantry grunted and flounced off.

'One overpriced jumper for your pisshead husband to spill wine over,' Rupert murmured.

'Oh, she's a regular, is she?'

'She regularly tries to pretend the stuff came ready-stained, and last time I refused to refund her. She didn't like it. Mind you, most of our dear customers are total cunts.'

Bella's eyes widened and then she gave a yelp of laughter that was followed by a rush of happiness. She was going to like it here. She had a job, was using her initiative, earning money for the family. Perhaps she wasn't completely useless after all.

It was almost worth being away from him to see how Teddy's face lit up when she came home, scrambling up from his wooden train set and throwing himself into her arms, almost knocking her off balance. She lifted him up and buried her face in his hair until he squirmed free and went back to play with the trains.

'So, how was it?' Jen said.

'Not too bad.' She slung her bag down and sat on the sofa in front of Jen cross-legged on the floor. 'My back aches a bit, but my boss is really nice, and you know what, it felt great actually to be earning again.'

Jen smiled. 'And how were the customers?'

'Total cunts.' She slapped a hand over her mouth, laughing. That was a word she hadn't used in years and certainly shouldn't have done in front of Teddy.

Jen smiled. 'And how were the customers?'

Bella stopped laughing and stared at her. 'Sorry? Didn't you just say . . . ?'

Jen was looking at her expectantly. Had Bella misheard? Or had she imagined Jen had spoken?

The wine had lost its taste. 'Fine,' she said. 'They were all fine.'

Ewan didn't ask how her day had been. In fact, he was more morose than ever over the dinner table, and when she mentioned that she'd offered their spare room to Skye and Juniper for a couple of weeks if it got really cold, he threw down his knife and fork and looked at her like she'd just announced she'd shat in the bed.

116

'Why would you do that without asking me?'

'Sorry . . . Is it okay?'

'Sounds like it's too late for me to have an opinion.'

'Not at all, if you don't want her to, I'll say she can't.'

'Yes, you'd better do that.' He went back to his dinner.

She was in the kitchen filling up the water jug and wondering how on earth she was going to tell Skye that the invitation was rescinded, when she heard a sharp gasp, then Teddy started to choke.

She ran back to the table.

'He's totally overreacting,' Ewan said. 'I smacked his hand, that's all. He was picking up his peas with his fingers.'

Teddy's face was turning puce. He must have inhaled his food in surprise at the smack. Lifting him from the high chair she dashed to the sofa and laid his body across her lap. Then she thumped him hard on the back. A pea shot across the room. Teddy took a huge breath and began to sob. Holding him to her she rocked him back and forth.

'Why did you do that?' She tried to keep her tone even, but as she looked at her husband's face, dislike washed over her vision like ink.

'At his age he should be using a fork.'

'He's barely three!'

'Other children do. I've seen them. You just need to teach him.'

Teddy's sobs were subsiding and she wiped the sweat-damp hair from his forehead.

'*You* could try.' It was a classic passive-aggressive comment, she knew, but the poor baby could have actually died.

'I'm at *work*. The sort of work that actually pays some bills. Speaking of which, when do you actually get paid?'

'I'm not sure.'

At this new evidence of her shortcomings, Ewan curled his lip at her and shook his head. Getting up, he took his half-eaten meal over to the draining board and left the kitchen.

He was angry. But for once she didn't care. This was the first time she'd ever contradicted her husband's parenting and it made her feel strong. She'd had the balls and the confidence to stand up for her son when she knew it was the right thing to do. For so long she had doubted her ability to be any kind of parent. She had bowed to Ewan in every decision, from the controlled crying that left her a nervous wreck, to the exclusive breastfeeding for six months when the poor kid was clearly starving. She'd even agreed that it wasn't good for Teddy to be always in her arms and had instead let him lie for hours on his activity gym, with its arch of dangling dead-eyed animals that promised to aid his development, when all she wanted to do was cuddle him.

But as Teddy's sobs diminished and he wriggled out of her arms to pad off to the living room, her mood plummeted.

Ewan had put up with so much after Teddy was born, worked so hard to support the three of them while she was just a burden to everyone. What right did she have to criticise anyone's parenting?

Later, after she'd put Teddy to bed, she knocked on the door of the study, intending to apologise.

'I'm busy.'

He was upset. He would stay there all night now, as he had done other times when she'd said the wrong thing.

Sick with misery, she crept back to the kitchen and opened a bottle of wine.

As she sat there, alone, in front of the TV, it occurred to Bella that she hadn't experienced such an abrupt mood swing, from elation to despair over the course of a few minutes, since she was ill. She'd been a bit slack with the pills recently, not bothering to take one at all if she forgot in the morning. She would have to be more careful. She couldn't get ill again.

Her thoughts drifted upstairs to Teddy, sleeping in his cot, peaceful and trusting and so vulnerable.

12

Chrissy

Before

She stood by the window, gazing down at the pavement five storeys below. The street was bustling with office workers, flowing like tributaries of the river towards the entrance of the tube. Beyond, where the street became Blackfriars Bridge, the river was a flashing strip of bronze. It looked hot. The air would be choked with dust and traffic fumes: the intoxicating smell of summer in the city.

But not here. Here the air con was pumping out cold, flavourless air, and the room smelled of the lilies in a huge vase in the corner. Funeral flowers for unhappy people.

It had been a difficult afternoon. The client she'd tried to persuade to go to mediation had changed her mind, provoking a perfectly reasonable reaction (in Chrissy's opinion) in her long-suffering husband. He had now retracted his offer and was digging his heels in, pushing for joint custody with half the maintenance Joanna was demanding.

After two decades frittered away at Pilates classes and coffee bars, with the occasional dabbling in flower arrangement and life drawing, Joanna seemed surprised when her husband finally threw in the towel and began an affair with his boss.

Chrissy couldn't help but like him for that. A man so secure in his own masculinity that a woman more powerful than him did not threaten it. His name was Harry and she quite fancied him. The uneasy truth was that, these days, she quite fancied most men.

As the afternoon ticked into evening she became twitchy and unfocused, barely paying attention as Joanna droned on about how difficult it was for a woman left at home to look after the children with *no help whatsoever* apart from the cleaner and the au pair.

Get a job then! Chrissy felt like shouting in her taut face. *Get a job, get a life and some self-esteem and maybe your husband will change his mind.*

Because Joanna still loved Harry. A love that had been so poisoned and twisted that she said things like, 'I hope he gets bone cancer.'

Chrissy glanced surreptitiously at her watch. It was approaching seven. Yet again she had missed teatime, bathtime and storytime. Russell would have taken over from Haniah and be putting Chloe to bed.

She turned to Joanna, now literally spitting with rage, showering Chrissy's desk with a fine spray of poison.

'I'm sorry.'

Joanna stopped mid-flow.

'I must get on.'

She gestured towards the door, and a gaping Joanna picked up her bag and swept out.

Chrissy followed, passing her client on the pavement and stealing the cab she was attempting to hail. Glancing back as the vehicle accelerated away she saw the bedraggled woman standing bereft on the kerb. She felt a mild sting of guilt, but Joanna had brought it on herself.

As the cab eased through the rush-hour traffic she gazed out at the river. A nice evening to be out on a boat. Perhaps they should reschedule tomorrow's drinks to Skye's place. Maybe they could raise anchor and chug upriver, to where the Thames moved through the leafy countryside of Runnymede or Windsor. And then maybe just keep going.

The cab paused at the traffic lights and more people streamed across to Embankment tube. They strode with heads bent, brows furrowed, no one speaking or smiling.

Was it so hard to be happy?

She and Russell were blessed. They had a healthy, happy child, enough money, careers they loved. And yet they had let something slide. They had become the sort of couple who administered their lives together, rather than living them. She did not want to end up like Joanna and her husband.

Taking out her phone she texted him.

Nearly home. Looking forward to seeing you.

It just took a bit of effort, that was all. Check in now and again with each other's feelings. Try to listen, to understand, to love.

The reply came back.

Took Chlo to Mum's. Grandad wore her out playing horsey. And she wore him out!

She smiled at the picture of her daughter on her father-in-law's lap, both fast asleep.

Let her sleep over. We can have an eve on our own. Maybe go to the pub . . . She added a grinning emoji.

Okay. Came the reply. She had to force herself not to bristle at the dismissive tone. But then again, he wouldn't have brought any of Chloe's things, so it might be a real pain.

We can go wild and order a Deliveroo!

A thumbs up emoji from Russell.

She sighed and put her phone away. Maybe she expected too much. Like Jen. Always hungry for more more more. There was a time when you had to be satisfied with what you had, when you had to accept that life wasn't going to just keep giving.

The setting sun had turned the river to blood. A sudden flash came to her, of the minutes after her daughter was born, when she began to haemorrhage. Watching the blood gushing out of her, spattering the floor and walls like some nightmare. She had been certain she was going to die. She had clung to Russell to save her. And Russell had gaped and stuttered, unable to take

121

charge when his capable wife needed him most. Pushing the thought away she closed her eyes. She was tired, that was all.

The house was dark and silent when she got home. Turning on the lights she saw that his running shoes were gone.

She stepped straight into the shower in the en suite, determined to rinse away any of the negativity she had brought home from work. Marriages were not all doomed to end in hatred and despair.

Drying off, she tied up her hair and put on her moisturiser, then regarded herself critically in the mirror. The windswept natural look that used to suit her so much was now looking more like raddled and harassed. Perhaps she should try some fillers and peels, like the client wives. Then she remembered – they had all been abandoned. She smiled grimly at her reflection. She didn't want the faff of putting all her make-up back on, so she would just have to distract his attention from her face.

Slipping on a silk oyster-coloured slip, a light cashmere cardigan and a pair of jewelled flip-flops, she went back downstairs, opened a bottle of wine, put some music on and began scrolling through the Deliveroo app.

At every breath the cool silk grazed her nipples, setting up an electric circuit through her nerve endings.

'Hi! I'm back!'

She heard the thud of his trainers hitting the hall floor, and the rustle of his jacket.

'I'll get showered and I'll be down.'

'Do you fancy Thai?'

'Yeah, great.'

She ordered, and then she went upstairs.

The shower was already running and she followed the line of sweaty, discarded clothes into the en suite. He stood beneath the flow, head bent, fair hair forming a point from which the water streamed. His body was lean, his back smooth and unblemished, without the carpet of hair that seemed to afflict most men his age, judging by those at her gym. Physically he was still as fanciable as he ever was.

Stripping off she opened the door and got into the shower with him.

The way he jumped made her laugh, but as she tried to put her arms around his neck, he pulled back.

'Chris, please. Let me just get showered.'

She hesitated a moment, wondering whether to persevere, wondering if he wanted her to, but one glance at his flaccid penis decided her.

The humiliation was as sharp and real as a paper cut as she sat back at the kitchen table, her cardigan pulled tight around the silk shift. She sipped her drink slowly, trying to calm her breathing, hoping it might slow her heart back to normal. She should cry. Show him how much he was hurting her with his rejection. But she couldn't. The only emotion she could feel was rage. So that when he entered the room, in jeans and a sweatshirt, whistling as if nothing had happened, she could not hold back.

'What is wrong with you?'

He paused in the act of pouring a glass of wine. 'What?'

'Well, something is, because I've forgotten what sex feels like.'

He finished pouring and glugged from the glass, all without looking at her.

'Isn't it supposed to be the woman who goes off sex after the kid's born?'

'Yeah, it is,' Russell said. Now he looked at her, pointedly.

'What's that supposed to mean?'

'Well, you're not exactly *like* most women, are you, Chris?'

She folded her arms across her chest. 'What does that mean?'

'Well, you're not particularly feminine, are you?'

It took a second to recover from the slur. 'Oh, so you want me to wear more pink?'

His lip curled. 'Is that all you think being a woman is?'

'No, no, no, I get it. If I was the sort of woman who couldn't get a spider out of the bath, or read a map or, most importantly, never ever earned more than you—'

'It's nothing to do with that.'

'Oh, I think it is.' She laughed grimly. 'What you need is Bella, Russell. Then maybe you'd actually be able to get a hard-on. Why don't you just admit it? Say the fucking word. Impotent. That's what you are. Imp—'

Russell slapped her across the face.

There was a moment of absolute silence. Then Russell seemed to remember how to breathe again.

'Was that what you wanted, huh?' he panted. 'Does that make you feel like more of a woman?'

'Stop.'

The man's voice surprised them both into silence.

For a moment she couldn't place his face, then she realised. It was the Polish builder. Atanis. He must have come in through the tarpaulin.

'That's enough, Mr Welch.'

As Russell stared at him, breathing heavily, Chrissy looked from face to face, wondering what was about to happen. The idea that Russell might get back what he had just inflicted upon her made her heart beat faster.

For a moment her husband's face registered naked fear. The builder was six foot of solid muscle. But Atanis made no move towards him, and eventually, with a sneering laugh that was more of a sob, Russell left the room.

They heard him stomp up the stairs and slam the front door. Silence descended on the kitchen.

Eventually Atanis said, 'I stay late to cover the brickwork because we are having rain tonight. I am sorry to come in like that, but I want to make sure you are okay.'

Chrissy nodded blindly. She felt like crying. And then, for the first time in years, she *was* crying.

'Oh. Oh hey. It is not so bad. My father used to throw my mother across the room. This? This is nothing.'

She gave a weak laugh and then suddenly his arm was around her shoulder. The shock of this physical invasion by someone she barely knew made her freeze. Underneath the silk slip she was naked.

'It's okay, Mrs Welch. He will calm down. He will be sorry.'

She found herself melting into him, snuffling into his shoulder, inhaling the scent of him through his T-shirt. Immediately, the ache between her legs began again, like a restless animal waking.

Really?

She had accused Russell of wanting someone to make him feel like a man. Now here she was turned on by an action hero, bursting in to rescue the damsel in distress. All that education and ambition, for this?

She shuffled out of his embrace. 'I'm fine. Thank you.'

'I will stay, until he returns,' he said but even now was backing away to put a more appropriate distance between them.

'There's no need.'

'If you don't mind, I will stay.'

'Okay, sure. Sit down.' She poured them both a glass of wine and clinked him shakily. 'Thanks. For *rescuing* me.' She had wanted it to sound ironic, but it didn't.

Atanis looked at her. His eyes were so pale and clear. 'He seemed very upset.'

'Yes. We're, er, having some relationship problems.' She raised her hand to her stinging cheek and felt a rush of fury. She had never in her life been hit before.

Atanis smiled. One of his incisors was grey, the only flaw in his otherwise perfect looks. 'Relationships are always a problem.'

'You're right there. Not married?'

'I have a wife and daughter, your own daughter's age, in Kalisz, near Warsaw.'

'Oh.' She looked away. 'I'm sorry you have to leave them to come over here.'

'It's okay, we are not really *together* together. That's what you say here, isn't it?'

Chrissy laughed. 'What about your daughter? How often do you get to see her?'

Atanis took his phone from the pocket of his jeans, tapped the screen and then held it out for Chrissy to see. It was a picture of a light-eyed little girl in a blue dress. 'Not often enough. We fathers are not as good as you mothers, I'm afraid.'

'Nonsense. You're doing your bit. You're providing for them.'

'I am building us a house near the coast at Gdansk. So we can have holidays by the *seaside*.' He laughed and started describing his plans for the house.

But she had stopped listening to his words, distracted by the ache, by the way his lips moved as he spoke, the subtle rise and fall of his pectorals under his T-shirt. Would it be so bad to fuck him? The self-righteous part of her screamed *NO*, Russell deserved whatever he got. The calculating part muttered that Russell would never even find out. The sexual part of her, the part she had repressed for six months, pretending her sexuality was nothing, put her glass down, walked the length of the table, took Atanis's face in her hands and kissed him.

He kissed her back, for the briefest, softest, most yielding of moments, then he moved her hands from his cheeks.

'You are a beautiful woman,' he murmured. 'But you have just argued with your husband. Your head is hot. You will regret it.'

She sighed, smiled and brushed a blond strand from his forehead. 'You're right. Thank you.'

She rinsed out the glasses as he pulled on his jacket, not meeting her gaze, then she walked him up to the front door. Normally he let himself out of the side gate. This was the first time he had been inside her house. He seemed to fill the space more than Russell. The building itself seemed to have woken up, become rawly aware of his presence. Not exactly disapproving: interested.

He opened the door and a chill autumn wind ruffled his hair.

She reached past him and closed it.

'My head isn't hot any more.'

13

Bella

Before

Jen arrived early and they all had breakfast together, even Ewan. It was fun. Ewan actually smiled, actually laughed when Jen told Teddy that Daddy was eating snot on his toast. They had stopped buying avocados because of the expense, but now that she was bringing in a wage, Ewan had started getting them again, from the pricey Whole Foods shop near his work. It was nice to see that she had done something constructive, even if the avocados were only for Ewan. Yesterday morning she had transferred her first wage payment to his account to help pay off their overdraft.

'How come I only got jam?' Jen pouted.

'Yeah,' Bella said, joining in the joke. 'You used to say you needed a special energy breakfast because you were cycling into work, but you don't any more!'

'That's because my bike was stolen,' Ewan snapped. 'I need it more than ever now that I don't have time to exercise.'

The atmosphere fell flat. Kicking herself, Bella excused herself and went upstairs to take her pill. Picking up the bottle and shaking out the little white tablet onto her hand, she heard them laughing again. It was a long time since Ewan had laughed at anything *she* said.

By the time she went back downstairs Ewan had gone to work and Jen was already making a pasta picture with Teddy.

His sturdy little fingers were too clumsy to make anything but the most basic shapes and Jen had to help push them into place. After kissing him goodbye, Bella left them to it and went to work.

The first thing Rupert said to her was that she looked like she hadn't slept all night.

She grimaced. 'I didn't. My brain was racing.'

'Tell me about it,' Rupert drawled. 'Try audiobooks, darling. I have to listen to them all night if I want a wink of sleep.'

In the dead time after lunch he said he had an important job for her. She swallowed, suspecting that she might very well have reached her limit of absorbing new information.

Taking her by the shoulders he walked her across the floor, past the escalators to Beauty and up to the MAC counter.

'Sabine,' he said to the young dark girl standing by a mouth-watering display of lipsticks. 'Make her so delicious even a queen like me will find her irresistible.'

Sabine grinned. 'Piece of cake.'

Rupert had clearly arranged this in advance because Sabine had a range of colours ready, all of which Bella knew from her life pre-Teddy would suit her perfectly. She closed her eyes and let the beautician work. The feeling of the cool brushes and paints on her skin was so soothing, the way it was when Teddy would walk his fingers up and down her arm. Her breathing deepened as the pleasure washed over her in waves. Everybody needed physical attention. Not just sex. It didn't matter so much that she and Ewan weren't really sleeping together any more, but what she did miss was physical touch.

When Sabine announced that she had finished, Bella sighed regretfully and opened her eyes.

Her breath caught. It was as if the mirror was a kind of time machine. Her twenty-five-year-old self gazed back at her, eyes bright, lips plump, skin aglow.

'Wow,' she said. 'Thank you. You've done an amazing job.'

'I had amazing materials to work with.'

She felt like hugging Sabine as she got up off the stool. As she walked past the escalators back to Menswear, she could feel eyes upon her. It straightened her spine and neck and put a spring in her step and that afternoon she found that laughter and wit came more easily to her.

The elation ebbed as she walked home. It would be to an empty house because Jen had taken Teddy to the park and had texted to say she was running late. Bella might only have an hour or so with him before Ewan got home.

Nearing the house, she saw Ewan's bike chain dangling from the railing and felt a surge of sympathy. There he was, crushed onto a sweaty tube to get to work to earn money to support his family, while his carefree wife enjoyed free makeovers.

She would make him his favourite lemon drizzle cake. Perhaps she could somehow pour her love and commitment into the mixture, and then, when she ate it, she would feel something for him again.

God, that sounded weird.

Turning on the kitchen TV to try and refocus, she set about making the cake. Measuring out the ingredients and being forced to focus on the weights and measures calmed her.

The only eggs left were Ewan's special organic Whole Foods ones. Ewan's mother had hammered it into her that you should never add eggs straight to a mixture in case they were off – not that she'd ever in her life encountered an off egg – and she'd got into the habit now, so she took a bowl from the cupboard and began breaking the eggs into it.

The eggs certainly looked good quality. The shells were thick and brittle as porcelain, the yolks a rich orange, holding their dome shape until the blades of the mixer bit into them.

She broke the second, and then the third.

She dropped the mixer. It fell with a clatter to the tiled floor, split in two and its mechanics spewed out, the motor grinding and squealing before finally falling silent. But Bella's gaze was focused on the white bowl, now spattered scarlet.

The third egg had been filled with blood.

Sweeping the bowl into the sink she ran the tap until every vestige of egg had glooped down the plughole and every speck of blood was washed away, then she picked up the scattered mixer parts, wrapped them in newspaper from the recycling box and dropped them into the bin.

It took long minutes for her heartbeat to slow, and she had to force herself to count her breaths, focusing every jumping neuron on the number sequence. Finally she sank down at the kitchen table, head in hand, and wondered if she really was going mad.

The egg had seemed to be filled with blood, literally filled, as if someone had bored a hole in the bottom, then somehow injected it in. The only logical explanation was that the egg had been partially fertilised. The chick foetus had developed and then died and the blood was . . . was part of its decayed body.

She felt queasy.

But there had been so much of it.

Or had there?

Had she imagined it? Was it just a delusion?

If so, it was a small one. A bit of blood in an egg and her mind had just made it seem there was more of it. An exaggeration. Like a child describing a spider as *this big*. Not so bad.

Shakily, she got to her feet and put the kettle on.

She would just carry on as if nothing had happened. Nothing *had* happened. She was blowing a minor incident into a grand symbol of her own mental unbalance. Which was just silly. And dangerous if she indulged it.

She tottered to the corner shop and came back with some barn eggs and cautiously broke them into a fresh bowl. The shells of these were frail, held together by a membrane like white cling film. The whites were watery, the yolks colourless and runny. But she didn't care, because they were just eggs. White and yellow: no blood, no bones, no feathers. With a balloon whisk she mixed them into the other ingredients, then poured the batter into a tin and put it in the oven.

By the time the oven pinged she felt herself again. The cake had worked perfectly, and after drizzling over the lemon syrup, she left it to cool on the rack and started preparing a shepherd's pie.

Jen and Teddy came home.

Her son was pink-cheeked and wild-haired and when she hugged him he smelled of cut grass. She held him a long time, until he wriggled and grunted to escape, but she wanted his pheromones, to inhale them into her brain, let them absorb into her synapses and bring her back to reality, to her solid place in the world.

'Can you stay for a coffee and a bit of cake?' she said to Jen.

Jen looked at her watch. 'Actually that's a good idea. Eliot needs to come back to the flat for his football boots, so if I stay here a bit I can avoid him.'

'Have you broken up again?'

'He's being a twat, so I kicked him out. It's his mum, really, going on at him all the time that I don't treat him right. I told him he'd better choose, me or her.'

'Is that fair?' Ewan's mother had died and she couldn't understand Jen's wanting to deprive Eliot of his.

'I don't care. I'm not having it.'

Bella smiled and shook her head. 'I wish I had your balls.'

'Fake it till you make it.' Jen grinned. 'Loving the make-up by the way.'

'Thanks. The MAC people did it.'

The egg incident had rather put Bella off the cake, so she brought a piece over for Jen and sat down beside her.

'Did Teddy nap at all?' The relative number and duration of these naps would bode either good or ill for the night ahead.

'Just once. I kept him awake until we came home at lunchtime, then I gave him beans on toast and he slept for an hour and a half. God, he's got an appetite, hasn't he? And it all seems to go straight to his muscles! He's so strong.'

Bella beamed. She may not be able to do much, but she could produce a robust child.

'How was work today?'

'Good,' she said, and her face froze under Jen's cool gaze. She wondered if there would be some other odd turn to the conversation. She would have to be careful, concentrate on Jen's words, answer them sensibly.

Jen said, 'Are you okay?'

'Yes. Fine, why?'

'I don't know. You seem a bit distracted.'

Bella swallowed. 'Do I? Sorry, just a bit tired.'

In the pause that followed, Bella felt the stirrings of panic in her chest. Whatever was going on in your mind, it was only when someone else noticed that you started to worry.

'You are . . . taking your pills, aren't you?'

Bella bit her lip, ashamed. 'Yes.'

'Maybe you need to go up a dose?'

'Maybe.'

'Ach, it's probably just tiredness. With work and everything.' Jen leaned across and took Bella's hand. 'Forget I said anything.'

Ewan didn't even notice her make-up, disappearing straight into the study when he got home and only emerging for his dinner, which Teddy objected to because she hadn't chopped the onion finely enough.

In the end she didn't even offer him the stupid cake, letting him go back to his precious work, while she finished the bottle of wine and she and Teddy munched through the cake in front of a documentary about orangutans. He made her laugh with his impressions, dragging his little arms on the stairs as they went up for his bath.

By the time she put him to bed she was drunk enough that she had to squint at the smaller sections of type in the picture book. But Teddy didn't notice. Exhausted by his long single-nap day, he curled in a ball against her, his arm across her tummy, his thumb in his mouth, and was soon breathing deeply. She lay with him, inhaling the delicious musk of his hair until her glass ran dry, then she extricated herself and went downstairs.

On the way she paused by the study door. She could hear the erratic tapping of the computer keys. Ewan didn't normally type like this, so what was he doing? Apparently not the report he claimed he had to finish.

From the other side of the door came a groan.

She froze, eyes wide in the gloom. Was he looking at porn?

Was he seriously in there looking at porn every evening, rather than being with his family? Was he *addicted*? Should she knock on the door and have it out with him?

Don't be silly, she told herself. Maybe he was just groaning because he'd made a mistake on the report. Maybe he hadn't groaned at all and it was just the chair creaking.

Weariness settled on her back, as heavy as piggybacking Teddy. Last night's lack of sleep was catching up with her. Going back to the kitchen, she refilled her glass and drank solidly until she passed out in front of the TV.

It was past one by the time she woke, heavy-headed, with a foul taste in her mouth and eyes scratchy with mascara. Dragging herself up the stairs, the banister creaked under her full body weight, but no one came to see if she was okay.

In the bedroom her husband's shape under the duvet threw a groping shadow over her side of the mattress. Why hadn't he woken her? He must have come in to turn the TV off, and yet he had chosen to leave her there in the cold darkness, not even laying the throw from the back of the sofa across her.

But as she undressed her irritation diminished and she began thinking about the eggs.

Ewan had bought them from the Whole Foods near his work. Skye said that the egg was the symbol of the soul and Ewan's had been filled with blood.

As she removed the mascara, which had smeared across her face, she tried to talk herself down. She was just drunk. She wasn't going mad, and her husband wasn't evil. And yet,

133

her thoughts weren't quite right. Could he be drugging her? The face in the mirror stared back at her, wild-eyed, make-up streaked into a crazed tribal mask.

No, no, no. That was crazy thinking.

But as she slid in beside her husband's inert body she felt only blank dread.

14

Electra

Before

Hearing the door close, she quickly got out of bed to stop him coming and telling her not to bother.

She walked quietly out into the hall. The twins were snuffling in their cots, Pearl gathered into a ball topped with a shock of Zack's sandy-blond hair, and Ozzy stretched out, his toes poking through the bars. The psychologist who had diagnosed the autism suggested moving on to a toddler bed with side supports as he would enjoy the feeling of security.

Glancing at the sleep-trainer clock on the chest of drawers, she saw it was past two a.m.

Zack knocked off at half eleven, was usually out by midnight, home by quarter past as the roads were pretty clear by then. Had he stayed for a drink afterwards? He used to, when Alex worked there, but Alex had left when he got the trading internship. But Thea was still there.

Padding down the hall she could hear him in the kitchen. Sometimes he made himself a snack before coming to bed and his mouth would taste of Marmite when she kissed him.

Stumbling on a Duplo brick, she felt her belly judder under her T-shirt and wished she'd pulled on a hoodie. All the other mums, except Bella, had managed to lose their baby weight, and it didn't even matter for them. Their husbands were old.

At the kitchen door, her heart began to thud with fear, that she would find him texting.

She pushed it open.

He wasn't texting. He was leaning over the worktop, head bowed in an aspect of exhaustion or despair. Somehow this was worse. Was there more bad news that he'd been keeping from her?

'Hey.'

'Hey.' His voice was flat. He didn't turn.

'You okay?' She noticed with a plunge of her heart that he had poured himself a whisky. Were things *that* bad?

'Shitty night.'

It was always a shitty night. He shouldn't even be there – wouldn't be if it weren't for the twins. It was supposed to be a blip, the bar job, something non-stressful while he got over his dad's death.

'What happened?' She walked across to him and touched his shoulder. Under the shirt he was damp with sweat and he smelled different, a musky salty scent. She swallowed. God, surely not . . .

He raised the glass to his lips and it clinked against his teeth. His hand was shaking.

'Babe, please. Has something happened?'

When he finally looked at her, she gasped.

His left eye was almost completely closed, the lid swollen and purple. A cut on the socket had bled down onto his pink shirt and blood had dried at the corners of his mouth. There was so much blood, on the shirt and on the back of the hand that held the whisky glass, where he'd tried to wipe his face. That was the smell – not another woman's sex.

'Oh my god. Zack.'

She grasped his shoulder and he winced, as if there were more injuries to his body.

Sitting him down at the kitchen table with the pathetic little first-aid kit they'd only ever needed for plasters and bite cream, she set about cleaning and dressing his wounds.

'Do you remember that guy I told you about? The squaddie?' His voice was thick where he'd bitten through his tongue. 'He was paralytic. We refused to serve him and he went mental. Started smashing up the place. Throwing chairs. We had to get everybody out. Thea called the police and he went for her, literally jumped over the bar, pulled one of the bottles out of the optics and was going to smash it over her head. I managed to get between them.'

A stab of jealousy. He had been protecting Thea.

'I got the bottle off him but—'

He broke off with a sharp intake of breath as she dabbed antiseptic onto the cut beneath his eye.

'Sorry.'

'But he punched me, then kicked me in the stomach when I was on the floor.'

'Fuck, Zack . . .' she breathed. 'We should go to A&E.'

'I thought I might have broken a rib, but I reckon it's only bruised. The police came really quickly, but then we all had to give statements. Took fucking ages.'

He tore off a strip of the kitchen roll and spat pink froth into it. The state of his tongue would make eating agony for the next few days.

With clumsy fingers she managed to Steri-Strip the wound, pressing the tape to his cheek as gently as possible while he told her how the police hadn't even offered to take him to hospital, just let him drive home with a head injury.

She opened her mouth to let out a stream of expletive-ridden outrage, then closed it again. Did she really want to remind him that he shouldn't even be there? That he was wasted managing a fucking bar? That he was so clever and capable he could do anything?

Because she was the reason he *was* there. The reason he was bleeding onto his best shirt. The one his father had given him that last Christmas before he died, that he was supposed to wear to his first day at work, never imagining that would be a sports bar in Chelsea. What would his mum say?

Oh god.

As she smoothed arnica cream onto his eyelid she saw that the hair on the crown of his head was becoming downy. A prelude to the male pattern baldness that had affected his father. She wouldn't tell him. He'd always hoped he would take after his mum's dad.

She bent to kiss his head. His skin smelled the same as the twins' and she closed her eyes to breathe him in, the downy hair tickling her nose as she inhaled. There had been a time when she would have been delighted at any sign of his ageing. She'd avidly watched for any suggestion of a wrinkle, taken the piss out of the hair that had started to spread down from his chest to his stomach. The tiniest paunch from all those late-night bar meals, finishing off the chips when the kitchen closed.

But now. Now this sign of his declining youth was a knife in her stomach. She had taken his best years and used them for her own gratification. His friends had barely finished uni, some of the medics were still there. Others had got graduate places in their dream careers. But Zack, the best of them all – the funniest, hardest working, kindest, most loyal – was nothing. He would become the James Stewart character in *It's a Wonderful Life*, having to swallow the line that fatherhood is the most rewarding thing in the world. Like women were supposed to believe was true of motherhood.

Well, it was a lie. If she could go back now, she would have done things differently. She would have gone on the pill instead of trusting that stupid coil.

'Can we go to bed?' he said shakily.

Leading him by the hand to the bedroom, she tucked him in and he was soon asleep. But Electra lay awake, staring at the ceiling, until dawn lightened the curtain edges.

Next morning she let him lie in and got the twins ready and breakfasted herself. Afterwards, she sat them in front of the TV while she made muffins, cleaning the kitchen while they were cooking. She'd taken the morning off and the twins were going to nursery after lunch, because today was Sue day.

Forty minutes after Sue was supposed to be there, when Electra's false smile and even more forced patience with the twins had turned to barely suppressed fury, Sue arrived, plump and pink-faced and unapologetic. The social services department never had to apologise, and woe betide you if you complained.

'Good morning, Electra!' she breezed, wiping her feet on an imaginary mat before bustling past Electra's fixed grin. 'What a lovely morning! Shame to be inside, isn't it? Are the twins in the garden?'

'No,' Electra said through gritted teeth. Firstly, she had been trying to keep them clean and presentable, and secondly, the 'garden' was a postage-stamp-sized yard of uneven stones and weeds that got the sun for about thirty seconds when it was directly overhead at the summer solstice, and mostly just smelled of pizza grease from the takeaway next door. 'They're drawing all the animals we saw at the park yesterday.'

'Ah well,' Sue sighed. 'It's hard in London unless you're prepared to make a huge effort.'

Fuckofffuckofffuckoff, Electra thought, but knew better than to reveal her irritation.

Sue walked into the living room uninvited and greeted the children with alarming jollity.

'Hello,' Pearl replied wanly. Ozzy just looked darkly at her.

'Would you like a cup of tea?' Electra said, her voice shrill.

'So,' Sue said as they leaned against the kitchen counter, their bodies directed into the living room that adjoined the kitchen, where the twins were now fighting over a yellow crayon. 'How are things?'

'Fine,' Electra said. 'Good. You got the letter?'

'Yes. We did. I must say I wasn't surprised.'

Electra resisted the urge to slap her. If she'd known, why the fuck hadn't she said something before?

'Of course there are a great deal of challenges with an autistic child, even a level one. How do you think you'll cope?'

Electra was about to bluster that she would be absolutely fine, that there were books, that she had learned an awful lot already. But she didn't. Exhausted, her nerves frayed by last night's shock, she had lost the ability to dissemble any more. Sighing, she sat down at the kitchen table.

'I think it's going to be tough,' she said quietly. 'I suppose I've always been a bit of a control freak. I expected the kids just to fall in, do as they're told. But I guess Ozzy's going to be more of a control freak than me.' She smiled up at Sue. 'I hated it at first, you coming. But now, I think –' she took a deep breath '– I probably need you.'

Sue was about to say something when the door opened and Zack came in.

Electra winced. If possible he looked worse this morning. The redness had darkened to indigo and even the uninjured side of his face had a greenish tinge.

'Hey, Sue,' Zack said. 'How are you?'

'Good. Thank you. The children seem well.'

'Yeah, they're great. Ozzy's made a friend at nursery, so things have been a bit more peaceful on that front.'

He went on to tell Sue about Pearl's prize for her minibeast garden and Electra flushed with shame. She'd been so concerned about putting the social worker at her ease that she'd failed to behave in a way that would do so – namely by showing a loving interest in her children.

Sue nodded and smiled, but when Zack paused to take a sip of his own coffee, the social worker said, 'Can I speak to Zack alone?'

Electra's heart lurched.

'Of course. I've got laundry to put away.'

Sitting on the bed she stared listlessly at the dust motes filtering through the bars of light. Warmed by the sun the bedding had started to smell of Zack's body. She wanted to press her face into it, to gather it in her fists and hold it to her body. Sue was asking him if she'd hit him. Not content with beating her child, she clearly thought Electra was also a domestic abuser.

The babies' wide eyes stared back at her from the professional studio shot Zack's mother had paid for. It had always made her cringe, the way they reclined on that artfully strewn blob of sheepskin, Pearl with a ridiculous pink bow somehow attached to her bald head, Ozzy scowling, his shock of black hair like a fancy dress wig.

Five minutes later the door opened and Zack came in. 'Come on out,' he said. 'Sue wants a word.'

She followed him out into the kitchen, her heart pounding. What had he said to her? That he came home the other day to find her crying because Ozzy had smashed her mobile screen again? That she had smacked Ozzy's leg when he bit Pearl? That she was back up to the twenty a day she had smoked when she was a teenager?

As Sue raised her head and their eyes met, Electra experienced a rush of something other than her habitual dislike for the woman. She'd been trying to help them, that was all. And Electra had treated her like the enemy. Well, it was time to give up, surrender herself to the help she so desperately needed. There was nothing shameful in finally admitting it.

She smiled at Sue, then, a warm natural smile, the first she had ever treated the social worker to. Sue would be there for them as Ozzy grew up, as he became more challenging Sue would help them find support and advice. Not an enemy at all, a partner in Ozzy's journey. A friend.

'So, I've just had a chat with Zack and that conversation has confirmed what my observations over the past few months have led me to believe.'

Electra's eyes widened in dread. This was not Sue's normal tone. What was going on? Was she going to take the children away?

'It's clear to me that you're capable, loving parents who have faced this difficulty with Ozzy with as much patience as any of us could have managed.'

141

Electra looked at Zack, but he wouldn't catch her eye.

'In light of the medical assessment confirming Ozzy's autism diagnosis, it was decided by me and the other case officers that his challenging behaviour is in line with common symptoms of the condition, and not evidence of any shortcomings in your parenting.'

Electra stared, trying to keep up with the formal language.

'You'll receive a letter from Child Protection Services to tell you that the Section 47 enquiry is concluded and no further action is required.'

Sue picked up her bag and slung it over her shoulder. Now she was smiling. 'It's been a pleasure knowing you both and I wish you and Pearl and Ozzy all the very best of luck for the future.'

She hugged Zack, and then came over to Electra. 'You don't need me,' she said softly. 'You've got each other. And you're a great mum.'

Electra accepted her embrace numbly, numbly returned her goodbyes and stood in the kitchen as Zack led Sue to the front door. They were laughing, saying something about the weather, Zack was calling a hello to someone passing on the street.

The door closed and he came back.

She looked at him, eyes wide as a child waiting for a parent to explain that the monster is just a dressing gown hanging on the back of the door. He came over and held both her hands in his. They were warm and strong, one nail black from where a barrel had overturned.

'It's over. It's fucking over.'

Pulling her into his arms he cradled her head against his shoulder and held her as she sobbed.

She thought they'd never make love that way again: with the carefree abandon of a desire uncomplicated by children or responsibilities. They laughed, they overbalanced, their clothes snagging on toes and heels. Even the twins co-operated, sitting quietly in front of the TV without coming to find their parents who lay entangled in a sweaty fug of happiness.

Afterwards they went for lunch in the café opposite the cinema: pasta followed by ice cream sundaes loaded with marsh-mallows and chocolate sauce. Groaning, they drank tea as their bodies processed the sugar, phones sacrificed to the twins' sticky grasps, Electra not even caring what other parents thought.

It was a revelation, that. Not caring. Not seeing other adults as spies in the pay of the social services, waiting for her to slip up and shout or slap a chubby leg. Without the pressure to sing-song good-parenting bollocks – 'Now, darling, how do we hold our fork?' 'Can I have a drink, *please*' – she ignored them and concentrated on her beautiful lover.

The bruise had come out properly now, drawing a purple panda-ring around his eye. He looked like a teenager who'd been in a punch-up over some girl. She smiled at the thought, but the smile faded when she noticed that the young woman behind the counter was looking at them.

'That's too loud,' she said to Zack, meaning the iPad Ozzy was playing with. It was lazy, but Zack had the patience to persevere with Ozzy without losing his temper.

'Quieter, Ozzy.' Leaning over the table Zack touched his son's head to make sure he was paying attention. But Ozzy did not turn the volume down. Zack sighed. Electra shifted in her seat, sipped her glass of water.

'Oz, mate. Turn it down. People don't want to hear it.' A fine line had appeared between his eyebrows.

Electra glanced over at the woman behind the counter who was now muttering to a colleague. The older woman looked across at them. Electra lowered her head, but not her eyes, so she saw the raised eyebrows and shake of the head.

'Ozzy, don't make me take it away from you.'

Their son did not raise his eyes from the screen. He seemed entirely unaware that Zack was speaking to him. He hadn't let them brush his hair this morning and it stuck out from his head like he was holding a Van de Graaff generator. He had at least let Zack clean his teeth, but not wipe the excess paste from around his mouth. It made him look like he was foaming at the mouth.

Pearl's face was pinched with anxiety and Zack's phone hung limp in her little hands. She knew what was coming.

Zack tried to take the iPad from Ozzy.

'NO!'

Nought to sixty in a microsecond, Ozzy's eyes were wild, a white-knuckled grip on the device. Electra glanced around, the familiar sense of shameful apprehension crawling over her skin.

The hooded stares of the women behind the counter expressed their disapproval. Other customers were turning in their seats.

'Let Daddy turn it down, Ozzy,' Electra said desperately. 'Only a little bit.'

'Ozzy. Give it to me.'

Zack's face had turned hangover grey. His Adam's apple bobbed as he contemplated what was about to happen. He was so much braver than she was. He would see this through calmly, doggedly trying to teach Ozzy what was and was not acceptable.

'I'm going to count to five, and then I want you to turn the sound down or give the phone to Daddy. One.'

Ozzy started to growl.

Electra should do something. Step up, be a parent, but the whole experience in the supermarket had made her scared of what she was capable of.

'Two.'

Zack's chest rose and fell, making the baggy T-shirt ripple. He was scared. The poor man was scared of what was going to happen, but he was doing it anyway because he was a responsible parent – and she was letting him.

'Three.'

He was still in his twenties. A boy himself. He should be drinking in bars with his mates, having on-off relationships with unsuitable girls, taking drugs, lying in bed to midday, finishing a degree. What had she done to him?

'Four.'

Tears coursed down Pearl's cheeks.

'Five.'

Ozzy started screaming.

She took Pearl home while Zack wheeled Ozzy round the park until the tantrum ended. Free from her brother, Pearl trotted happily inside and went to play with her dolls. Electra followed, dumping her purse and keys on the coffee table and sinking down onto the sofa. Faces beamed from the walls and shelves. Neon toys cast hard-edged shadows. Her keys gleamed. The cheap plastic of the photo-frame key ring was scratched and yellowed as if she was gazing at a memento from years ago, when they were still young.

She was old. She'd had her fun, there was no going back. The rest of her life would be a loop of what she did now, until she became too old to do it any more.

But it wasn't too late for him.

In the morning Zack tried to make love again, but she told him she hadn't slept, and he said to have a lie-in while he did the kids' breakfast. Afterwards he took them to nursery.

She got up and dressed like a frail geriatric, barely able to do up the last button of her shirt. It was as if someone had drained half her blood and replaced it with water. In the bathroom she washed her face and cleaned her teeth. She needed to be presentable, professional, to look like she meant this.

She waited for him in the kitchen, nursing a cup of tea and her fourth cigarette of the day. 'I called in sick,' she said when he came back.

'That bad, huh? Shall I make you a Lemsip?'

'No. I wanted to talk to you without the kids here.'

He stopped in the act of hanging up his jacket. Turned round. 'What about?'

He came over, pulled out a chair and sat, legs splayed, one arm across the table, forefinger tapping: like an insolent boy in the head's office. 'So, what, you lied to me about being tired?'

She nodded.

His eyes were hard. It wasn't often she'd seen him angry, but he was now. This was good. Anger she could deal with.

'You got something to tell me?'

She laid the palms of her hands carefully on the table.

'Is it someone at work?'

'What? Of course not.'

'Well, spit it out then.'

She saw then, as he inhaled, that he was trembling. He knew she was about to hurt him. She must do it quickly.

'I don't think it's working.'

'What?'

'Us.'

He blinked, his fair lashes catching the morning sunlight.

'I'm not happy, you're not happy, and it's going to affect the kids in the end.'

'I'm happy.'

'No, you're not. You never wanted this life. You're twenty-six. You don't want to be living like this. All the stress, no money. Ozzy. You should be finishing your degree, getting a—'

'Don't tell me how I feel.'

Somehow, from somewhere, she dredged up some anger of her own. 'And I'm sick of feeling guilty about ruining your life.'

'You haven't ruin—'

'That's what your mum thinks, and she's right.'

'Fuck my mum—'

'I've got some self-esteem, you know. I don't want to feel like the fucking child-catcher all the time.'

'Jesus, Electra.'

'You go back to your life and I'll go back to mine. We can share custody of the kids. You can move back in with your mum.'

He stared at her.

'It's over, okay? Us. I'm not living like this any more.'

'No.'

She looked away. 'I've made up my mind. You can stay here as long as you need to get your stuff together and then—'

'No.'

'Zack.'

'No, no, no. I love you.'

A gasping pause, like the page of her script had torn. Then she found her place. 'It's not enough. We—'

'It *is* enough! I love you, and I love the kids, and I don't give a shit about a fucking degree. I can get my own bar, start making some proper money. We'll get a bigger place.'

'It's not the money.'

'This is bullshit!'

The anger again, weaker now. 'My feelings aren't bullshit. I've made up my mind.'

He put his palm over his mouth, squeezing his face until his features distorted, became ugly.

'Zack, please. Please don't cry.'

'You're taking my family away from me!' he roared. 'What do you expect me to do?' He hurled his mug at the wall and it shattered. A shard of porcelain rebounded and struck her cheek. The pain was clean and refreshing, but Zack fell to his knees in front of her. 'I'm sorry, Lec. I'm sorry. Did it get your eye?'

'It's okay.'

He took her hands and squeezed them so tight the bones crunched. 'Now they've signed us off, everything will be fine. I love you, you love me, that's all we need.'

'No,' she said. 'It isn't.'

15

Bella

Before

From upstairs in the en suite Bella heard Jen arrive and the murmur of conversation between her and Ewan. It wasn't as effervescent as usual. Were they talking about her? Was Jen telling him her worries about Bella's mental state?

Of course not. They'd both agreed she was just tired.

Forcing down the negative thought she took her pill, taking a moment as she swallowed to close her eyes and think about how her body was feeling and her expectations for the day, using the mindfulness technique Skye had told her about. She was looking forward to seeing Rupert, and to the lovely warm feeling of coming home to Teddy when she hadn't seen him all day. She was hoping that by the time she got downstairs Ewan would have gone to work.

He hadn't. He and Jen were in the kitchen and they stopped talking when she walked in.

'Morning,' she said brightly. 'What are you two up to today?'

'What do you think, Ted?' Jen called across to the living room. 'Shall we go and see the dinosaurs?'

'YEEEEEEEESSSSSSSSSSSS!' Teddy came roaring into the kitchen and threw himself into Jen's arms, making the chair squeal alarmingly. Then, snatching the corner of toast from her plate, he marched back to the TV.

Bella shook her head, smiling. 'That boy.'

'You should watch what he eats,' Ewan said. 'He's getting fat.'

'He's not fat, he's just sturdy,' Bella said.

Ewan looked her up and down. 'That's one way of putting it.' He smiled like it had been a joke.

'You get going, Bells,' Jen said. 'I'll make sure he does his teeth.' She was pale today, Bella thought. Whatever she said, she was probably missing Eliot.

'I think I can manage on my own,' Ewan grinned.

As Bella set off down the street, she wondered if Jen had just been being considerate, or whether her friend had noticed the way Ewan was speaking to her and sent her away to stop her getting upset. People always treated her with kid gloves. Sometimes she resented it. She wasn't that pathetic, was she?

Rupert was beaming when she got in. The way he stood, in a shaft of sunlight, made him look like an angel. He came over and slipped an elegant arm across her shoulders.

'I've arranged for Chloe in Lighting to cover my break.'

'How come?' He wasn't going somewhere, was he?

'So that we can take our breaks together. Today, my darling, we are going clothes shopping.'

She clapped her hands like a little girl.

'How was your day?' she asked brightly as Ewan sat down on the sofa with his plate of chilli.

'Fine.'

She waited for him to return the question, wanting to tell him how much fun she was having, and how she should have done it years ago. She wouldn't tell him about the purple lace underwear set Rupert had made her buy with her staff discount. She'd let him discover that for himself.

But the smile slowly subsided as he began forking food into his mouth.

After dinner, unable to concentrate on the documentary he was watching, she got up and started looking for something constructive to do.

Teddy was already asleep, lying on his tummy with his bottom poking up, the duvet bunched up in the corner of the cot. She tucked it back over him and pulled up the sash window. Glancing down she saw their tiny backyard was littered with leaves and twigs. He and Jen must have been to the park today. She hadn't thought to ask. It was good for him, being with Jen. She had more energy, took him to exciting places, like pond dipping and art sessions at the local galleries. It should have made Bella feel bad, but surprisingly enough, despite the fact that she was now a working mother and so, by definition, neglecting her child, she didn't feel half as guilty as she used to. Before, everything she did seemed substandard or damaging in some way, and yet still she had striven to do everything right. But amazingly, now that she'd handed all of it – the healthy eating, the fresh-air outings, the creative play – to Jen, she didn't feel an ounce of guilt.

Not even about the ready meal she had just served up for her husband. He hadn't even noticed. Perhaps that was another thing she could let go a bit – the constant pressure to provide wholesome home-cooked meals. What was the point if no one noticed the difference?

Unloading the laundry basket she sorted the colours. She would do a dark wash. Hang it out first thing before she went to work. But as she rooted through the pockets of Ewan's work trousers for discarded tissues or coins she felt something.

Drawing out her hand, she frowned at the object nestled in her palm.

How strange. Ewan worked in a high-rise in the city, and yet here, in his pocket, was the wing of a butterfly. It was pure white with a single black spot like an eye, and attached to the inner corner was a shred of black carapace where it had torn away from the body.

Something stirred in her chest, like a sleeping worm coming back to wakefulness.

She brought her hand closer to her face, until a shaft of street lamp fell on it, turning the wing a dull orange. Tentatively, she touched the wing. It rustled. It felt solid and real. She wasn't imagining it.

The poor creature must have blundered into his pocket as he cycled home. But the bike had gone weeks ago, and these trousers weren't in the basket when she did the last wash. She felt in the pocket for the other half, not liking the idea of the fragile body disintegrating in the machine.

But it was empty.

Why would Ewan have half a butterfly wing in his pocket?

She stood in the darkened room and forced her breathing to stay slow and regular. There was nothing to be afraid of. Odd things happened all the time, and this wasn't even that odd. Perhaps Teddy had found it in the park and put it there.

She balled up the washing and took it down to the utility room, binning the wing fragment on the way. She was about to push the load into the washing machine when she saw another pair of Ewan's trousers were already inside. Why hadn't he put them in the laundry basket with everything else? She pulled them out to check the pockets, then stopped. The inside of the groin was spattered with something white and stiff, like egg white or . . . dried semen.

So it *was* porn he was looking at in the study.

Leaning against the thrumming machine she tipped her head back and gazed up at the damp-speckled ceiling.

Porn wasn't great, but most men probably did it in their private time when their wives weren't around.

The problem was, Bella *was* around. Ewan was choosing to look at porn over spending time with his wife. And it wasn't as if he was bringing his freshly awoken sexuality to the bedroom. She couldn't remember the last time they'd had sex.

But maybe that was her fault. The makeover had reminded her what she looked like when they first met. Back then he couldn't get enough of her. He used to love seeing her in the underwear he'd bought her. It wasn't fair on him that she had let herself go so badly. Well, she would start to make more of an effort. Become the woman he had married.

151

She returned to find he had switched off the documentary and gone to bed. Resisting the urge for just one more glass of wine she went up after him. After she'd cleaned her teeth she washed and put on a little of the perfume she hadn't used for years. It smelled slightly off.

Climbing into bed beside him, she thought he might be asleep. But the vague sense of relief this produced made her determined to see her plan through. He was facing away from her, so she slid an arm under his and moved her hand to the crotch of his pyjama bottoms. His breath caught.

It took a long time to get him hard and then she had to pull him over onto his back. He didn't open his eyes as she pulled off her vest and lowered herself onto him. She had taken off the bra but still had the purple lace knickers on. If he opened his eyes he would see.

His hands stayed by his side as she began moving up and down. He was clearly too tired to help her, so she bent forward and let her nipples brush his chest until she was fully aroused.

Minutes passed and she wondered whether this had been a good idea after all. Ewan's eyes remained closed and his mouth was twisted into what looked like an expression of pain.

Then, out of nowhere, Rupert's face flashed into her thoughts. The way he smiled when he saw her after the makeover, his face when she was modelling the underwear for him. And suddenly his body was so clear in her mind. If she was lying on him now, his chest would be hard beneath her breasts, his hips sharp against hers. He would smile and sigh and—

Suddenly she climaxed, with a gasp like a drowning woman resurfacing.

Ewan's eyes snapped open. 'Did you just come?'

'Yes, sorry.'

'For fuck's sake, I'm nowhere near.'

'Don't worry, I can . . .' She crawled down the bed, but he caught her shoulder roughly.

'I'm not in the mood now.'

'Oh. Look, I'm sorry. I just got carried away, I guess.' She laughed.

'It's not funny.' Pushing her off, he treated her to one final, baleful glare, before turning his back on her.

16

Skye

Before

Skye dressed carefully, in her Thai fisherman's trousers with the midriff vest top and loops of beads, then put on make-up. Almost as much as she used to in the old days: heavy eyeshadow and liner that curled into Egyptian loops at the corners of her eyes. Proof that women were beautiful – and a mask to hide her feelings.

Felippe was coming again today. This would be the tenth time she had met him in just over a year. Pedro invited his lover to everything: family brunches, Juniper's plays, impromptu drinks on the boat on his way home from work. Family time should be for the three of them. Affable as Felippe was, he was not family.

Her mobile rang. Perhaps they were calling to cancel.

It wasn't Pedro, it was Mort.

'Wow, long time no see. How are you doing? How's your shoulder?'

'Fucked again.'

'Oh no. What happened?'

'Gym injury. I was trying to lift weights that were too heavy. What a knob, eh? Are you around this afternoon?'

'Got some people coming for lunch. What sort of time?'

'Any. Whenever you like.'

'Two?'

'Sure. See you then.'

She ended the call feeling slightly better and went out on deck to wait for Pedro. Disappointing that the injury had returned. She thought she'd done a good job on it. She'd certainly tried, working on it more diligently than she usually did, pulling a muscle in her own shoulder in the process, because she'd liked him. Despite his dull appearance, Mort was funny and nice. And she imagined, if she could read auras, that his would be a good one. Pale green or blue. Calming. He was a good person to have around, and if he wasn't a client she'd like to have him as a friend.

There they were, Pedro and Felippe, walking up the embankment. For once they weren't holding hands and their expressions were rather sombre. Perhaps they were coming to tell her they were finished. She smiled and waved.

Felippe kissed her on both cheeks and Pedro gave her the loveliest hug, holding the side of her head and kissing her hair, like he did with Juniper. He smelled as delicious as usual. To her, Felippe smelt faintly like uric acid, but perhaps they just had incompatible pheromones.

'We brought salami and cheese and tomatoes from Don Juan, and bread from Poilâne!' Pedro waggled his paper bag proudly.

'Lovely. I'll get the plates. It's nice enough to eat outside, isn't it?'

'I'll get them,' Pedro said. 'You sit down and relax.'

They sat on the rickety metal chairs of the garden set. Felippe, usually so voluble, didn't seem able to catch her eye.

'Juniper looks gorgeous in that new dress you bought her,' Skye said. 'It's lovely.'

'She looks good in everything,' Felippe said. 'Takes after her mama.'

He looked peaky, that was the only word to describe it. As if he hadn't slept. She would give him a cranial massage later, to reduce tension. She regretted the pleasure she'd felt imagining them having relationship problems.

'She didn't want to go to nursery this morning. Apparently some little bitch has been teasing her about her lisp.'

Skye's heart lurched.

'I told her that had happened to me when I was her age, about my teeth. I was so goofy! We talked about how there will always be nasty people in the world, and they're usually that way because they're unhappy. We just have to ignore them and feel sorry for them.'

'Oh, okay,' said Skye. She'd probably have handled it the same way.

'We had a little cuddle at the gate and off she went, happy as usual.'

Skye's heart clenched. Felippe had cuddled her daughter back to happiness. Was he becoming part of the family? Should she try and embrace that fact?

They ate in uncharacteristic silence, punctuated by the occasional observation about the weather or passing river traffic. Pedro's cheeks were flushed and he looked distracted, almost unhappy. He stared out across the water, as pensive and subdued as the morning after their failed lovemaking. Had something really bad happened? Was there a reason for his weight gain? Oh god, he wasn't ill?

Leaning over she took his hand. It was ice-cold.

He turned and looked at her, and the expression in his brown eyes made her breath catch.

'What is it?' she murmured.

He looked over her shoulder, at Felippe, who stopped talking.

The salami turned to a flavourless pulp in her mouth.

'We wanted to . . . ask you something,' he said.

There was a sudden hush: not a single boat engine, chatting jogger or plane grumble. The traffic on the bridge died away to a distant hum.

'What?' she said. But it wasn't Pedro that spoke.

'You know how much we love Juniper?' Felippe said. 'That will never change. Whatever. I will always think of her as mine as much as she is Pedro's.'

156

'It's true,' Pedro went on, backing him up. 'Nothing could ever change our feelings for Juniper.'

'But?' she breathed, eyes wide.

'No but. Nothing. I love her. She is my daughter.'

'It's because we love her so much, because she has made us so happy, made us feel like a family . . .'

'That we want to make that happiness bigger.'

Skye stared.

'We want another baby.' Her ears were ringing so much she wasn't even sure who'd said it.

'But we want you in our life too.' This was Pedro.

'We can't imagine that anyone could make a lovelier child than Juniper.'

'And we want her to have a *real* brother or sister. With the same wonderful genes.'

There was a pause.

'I don't understand,' she said, shaking her head.

'We would love it if you would agree to be our surrogate.'

She couldn't breathe. Getting to her feet she walked to the rail and leaned over, gazing down into the dazzling water, gasping the dank cool air that rose from the surface.

They loved Juniper. They wanted a *proper* brother or sister for her. But not a mummy.

She pushed harder against the railing, until it hurt her inside.

'Skye?' Pedro said. 'Darling? Are you okay?'

Somehow, God knows how, she managed not to throw up. Gripping the rail she breathed, thinking about her toes, her ankles, her knees, her thighs, her pelvis, her chest: loosening them, relaxing her whole body until her lungs could expand enough to take a breath.

'Skye?' Felippe said. 'I'm sorry, we should have . . . it was too sudden.'

And finally she found the *now* her: the balanced, stable, in-control, yoga-practising her who could take this without breaking.

157

'It's okay.' She straightened and turned.

Pedro's hand had closed over Felippe's.

'Really. It was a bit of a surprise, that's all.'

Felippe pressed his lips together and started to cry.

'Hey,' she said. 'Hey, don't be silly!'

Pedro pulled Felippe's head into his shoulder and patted his dark hair, rolling his eyes at Skye.

'I told you it wasn't fair,' Felippe was saying to Pedro, his voice thick and more heavily accented than usual.

Pedro dipped his head. 'We should not have asked you. It is my fault. I wanted us to stay . . .' He inhaled. 'A family.'

But what they were asking would not make them a family. She would be a donor, nothing more. Some genes and a vessel. She wouldn't be allowed to feed this baby or cuddle her to sleep, she wouldn't choose her clothes or take her out in her buggy, teach her to read, clean up her grazes. At best she might be a glorified godmother, excluded from every moment of her child's life bar Christmas and birthdays.

'We have . . .' Felippe began haltingly. 'Money. For expenses.' Pedro groaned softly, but he carried on. 'We are allowed to give you up to twenty thousand pounds. If you would accept it, we would be happy to.'

Skye swallowed down the surge of nausea. Twenty thousand was more than enough to move out of the boat into somewhere warm and dry. Somewhere Juniper wouldn't wheeze and cough from October to March.

With an effort of will she didn't think herself capable of, she went and sat beside them, closing her own hand over their clasped ones.

'Let me think about it.'

Mort arrived twenty minutes early, on foot. She saw him circling the broader patch of pavement, glancing at his watch, waiting until the right time. It gave her a rush of gratitude. She'd entirely forgotten he was coming, and now had time to clean up her face and dab at her eyes with an ice cube wrapped in a flannel. She set up the massage table and finally, after some deep breaths to unjangle her vocal cords, called down to him.

Trying to stay in the present she concentrated on watching him take off his T-shirt, taking in the details of his body. A light tan had taken the edge off his bluish skin tone and turned him a rather pretty shade of peach. The hair on his arms had faded to gold, and he had a slight sunglasses mark. As he bent to deposit the T-shirt on a chair, she counted the freckles on his back. Three large, five small, a few fine hairs just above the waistband of his faded blue twill shorts. A glimmer of sweat in the small of his back.

Sure enough, she was calming down.

He lay down on his stomach on the bed, punched out a hole in the couch paper and settled himself into position.

Placing both her hands on his shoulders she closed her eyes and breathed, trying to absorb the calmness he exuded through the warmth of his skin, swaying gently with the motion of the boat. Then she set to work on his shoulder.

'Does that hurt?'

'No.'

'How about that?'

'Not really.'

There was a moment's silence as she concentrated on pushing a little harder, waiting for the resistance so that she could stop before she hurt him. The muscles seemed loose and springy.

'How have you been?' he said.

'Not bad. Not as busy as I'd like. Everyone loosens up when the weather gets warm.'

'Ah, sorry. I'll try and fall off my bike again.'

She smiled. Still unable to find the sweet spot of his pain she rolled his arm until the inner elbow pointed upwards.

'How's that?'

'Okay.'

159

For a moment she thought he was holding something small and dark in the palm of his hand, but then she saw it was a tattoo, of a death's-head moth.

'Wow, you have a tat.'

'You sound surprised.'

She paused at the delicate spot on his wrist, his pulse tapping at her fingertips. 'Oh, I don't know. Just that you're an accountant. You dress really smartly all the time. I just thought you were a bit too . . .'

'Conventional?' He laughed. 'It's a long story.'

'I'm not in a hurry.' The sound of his voice was pleasant enough at the best of times – soft and lyrical, almost girlish – but today it was a tonic flowing through her veins.

'Okay, then.' He twisted his torso to look up at her. 'What were your parents like?'

She shrugged. 'Pretty crap.' She paused, then made a decision. 'When I got raped they just pretended it had never happened.'

'You got raped? Shit. I'm sorry.'

'They didn't want to think or talk about it, so of course I ended up having a breakdown.' She didn't want to talk about it any more herself. It was past. Today she was a different person. Pushing him back down she circled her thumbs around his shoulder joint, still unable to find the injury. 'Why do you ask?'

'Mine were goths.'

She snorted. 'You are kidding.'

'They changed their names by deed poll from Simon and Helen to Belial and Lucrezia. That's why I'm called Mort. It means death.'

She had to pause while she laughed. 'I thought it was short for Mortimer.'

'For a while at primary school I made everyone call me Ben, but when I was about seventeen I decided to embrace the whole thing. That's when I got the tat, dyed my hair black, pierced my eyebrow.'

She bent down and saw the tiny white dimples above his right brow.

'But it wasn't me. I just felt stupid. Turns out I actually *want* to be conventional.'

There was a pause.

'Me too.'

'Seriously?'

She took a deep breath, letting her hands rest on his shoulder blades. 'I didn't want to be like my parents, hiding everything, pretending complicated feelings didn't exist. I guess that's why I ended up like this.' She held out her inked arms.

Mort raised his head from the bed. 'They're beautiful,' he said. She wasn't sure if he meant the tattoos or the grid of pale scars.

'But I just want what everyone wants. A family. To be loved and protected. I want to give that to someone else.'

She drew away from him, holding her arms across her body, covering the womb they wanted to rent out to make a child that would not be hers. The love she thought would be hers forever did not exist.

'Hey,' Mort sat up. 'Hey, it's okay.'

'Don't say that. You sound like my parents. You don't know me.'

'I'm sorry,' he said, and stood up. 'I'll go.'

She turned away from him and bent double. It was as if some band of elastic connecting her chest to her pelvis had suddenly contracted, pulling her from the inside, trying to close her up.

The rustling of his movements had stopped and she was aware of him standing behind her.

'Or . . . I, er, did bring a couple of beers, in case you fancied one. Because it's so nice outside. And everything.'

The elastic slackened. She straightened and turned back. Mort stood in the middle of her living room, his T-shirt held loosely at his side, his white skin gilded by the dusty sunlight lancing through the porthole. She had never seen anything so solid, so real and immutable. It was as if the whole world revolved around his still, pale body.

'If a man called Death offers me a beer, who am I to argue?'

Mort grinned. 'You know,' he said as they walked up the steps into the sunlight. 'There's nothing wrong with my shoulder.'

17

Bella

Before

When she arrived at work Rupert took her aside.

'Are you all right?'

'Of course, why?'

'Oh god, I don't care if you get someone's change wrong, I just wanted to make sure you were okay.'

'Did I get someone's change wrong?'

'Don't worry about it. They never even noticed.'

She frowned. She had dropped a couple of things this morning too, smashing a particularly expensive lamp Merchandise had brought down to show off the silk tie display.

'Maybe I need a sit-down. I haven't been sleeping well.'

She went to the stockroom and poured herself a glass of water. As she sat staring at the shadows and wondering whether she was, in fact, becoming unwell again, her phone vibrated.

Snatching it from her pocket she hoped it might be Ewan wanting to make up.

It was a message from Jen.

I found this. I guess Teddy must have done it when I wasn't looking. So sorry.

The picture came through slowly, pixel by pixel.

Out of nowhere, she started hyperventilating.

Rupert found her a few minutes later and made her sit with her head between her knees until her breathing returned to normal. But for the rest of the day her hands trembled and she kept messing things up, putting the wrong product through the till, miscounting change, dropping things.

She left five minutes early and walked the long way home. It was nearly rush hour and the traffic was almost stationary along the Kings Road. When she came in sight of the house she stopped and leaned against the wall of the health centre, breathing heavily.

The picture that had eventually come through from Jen was one from their wedding. It featured her and Ewan cutting the cake. She looked as good as she had ever looked, smiling and beautiful. Ewan had been smiling too, as she recalled, and gazing at her face.

But the image of Ewan had been defaced. Someone had scratched his eyes out, leaving just sightless white pits. Jen said it must have been Teddy, but a three-year-old wasn't capable of that sort of precision.

But she was. Bella looked down at her hands with a creeping dread she thought was long gone. What had she done?

Jen and Teddy had been to the Science Museum and played with the water fountain in the basement, pushing coloured plastic boats around and doing 'experiments'.

Bella tried to focus on the happy pictures on Jen's phone, but her lower lip trembled.

'You okay?' Jen said, when Teddy had wandered off to watch TV. 'Were you bothered about the picture?'

'A bit.'

'Maybe the photographer kept the files? I binned it, in case it upset you seeing it. Was that okay?'

'Thanks. Yes.' She attempted a smile.

'Don't worry about it. Kids do that sort of creepy stuff all the time. He might just have been having an anti-Daddy moment.'

'Did he seem okay with Ewan this morning after I'd gone?'

'Yes, fine. I shouldn't have told you. It's the last thing you need.'

'What do you mean?'

'Well, you know. You just seem a bit distracted at the moment.'

Distracted was where it all began, being dissociated from the real world. And then came the delusions . . .

'Hey.' Jen laid a perfectly manicured hand on her sleeve. 'I didn't mean anything.'

'I'm not upset. I'm fine. Really. Now, take extra today because you probably had to pay for lunch, didn't you?' The ten-pound note she held out trembled like a leaf in the breeze.

That night she drank too much again. A glass of wine at dinner with a predictably taciturn Ewan, another two in front of Teddy's TV programmes and one that she sipped at while reading to him. This finished the bottle and she opened another, ploughing solidly through it while clearing the kitchen and watching the start of a Netflix series Rupert had recommended.

Ewan was in his study.

Working? Or wanking. She laughed hazily. It was too loud in the silence.

When she heard him go up she followed, intending to attempt some kind of light conversation to try and defuse any fallout from the sex debacle.

But by the time she had cleaned her teeth he'd turned off the bedside light and rolled over to face the wardrobe.

As she lay in bed, sleepless as ever, her thoughts churned unpleasantly. Was Ewan addicted to porn? Did she have an unhealthy crush on Rupert? Was it Teddy who had defaced the picture? Or something worse?

To give her a chance at sleep, Bella decided to take Rupert's advice and listen to an audiobook. A light novel about shopaholics that she had given up on a few months ago would be the perfect distraction from her troublesome brain.

As usual it took a few moments for her to rustle and fidget her way to comfort. Finally she was ready, and closed her eyes to concentrate on the story. The narrator sounded slightly different than she remembered, throatier, more intense, as if he was whispering urgent secrets into her ear.

'It is impossible to say how the idea first entered my head. There was no reason for what I did. I did not hate the old man; I even loved him. He had never hurt me. I did not want his money. I think it was his eye. His eye was like the eye of a vulture . . .'

Her eyelids snapped open.

'The eye of one of those terrible birds that watch and wait while an animal dies and then fall upon the dead body and pull it to pieces to eat it.'

She punched the off button and the device fell silent. Then she stared into the darkness. What the hell had she been listening to? It certainly wasn't the shopaholics book. Had she downloaded something else by mistake? Gingerly, she powered up the device again and hit the audiobooks app.

Afterwards, she got out of bed, went downstairs and opened a third bottle of wine. Sitting drinking it at the table she tried to rationalise what had happened.

'The Tell-Tale Heart' by Edgar Allan Poe. There was no way she would have ordered such a heavy book by mistake, but it appeared she had, because her account told her she'd bought it for 99p.

Anyone could access her account though, once they'd tapped the pin into the device. Could Teddy have done this too, playing around with the game apps she'd downloaded for him?

Or was it Ewan, trying to freak her out?

No, no, no, no. Of course not. No.

She gulped a third glass, felt her thoughts turn syrupy.

Was she losing her mind? Please God, not again.

*

166

Next morning, she got up early, dressed without showering and went straight downstairs. She didn't think she would be able to look him in the eye today (*his vulture eye*) without blurting out an accusation.

She polished off the dregs of last night's final glass but managed not to refill it. Her veins were buzzing.

Jen was uncharacteristically late and Ewan left before she arrived, skipping breakfast and leaving the house with a curt goodbye, without even kissing Teddy. As soon as he was gone Bella felt the strength drain from her legs and sank down onto the kitchen chair where she remained, listlessly watching Teddy watching TV, still unbreakfasted.

The knock at the door pushed air back into her lungs and she hobbled over to answer it. Jen came in, complaining about the wind that had blown dust under her contacts.

'Can I talk to you?'

Jen paused in the act of hanging up her coat. 'Course.'

They went through to the kitchen.

'Everything all right?'

'You know how I said I wasn't really sleeping. Well, I'm a bit worried that I might be . . .' She inhaled. 'Getting ill again.'

Jen touched her arm. 'Why? What's happened?'

Bella tipped her head back, blinking away tears as she gazed at the dusty cornicing around the light fitting. The shame of having to admit this again.

'I've been having delusions. Hallucinations.'

She told Jen about the egg and the butterfly wing, the audiobook.

'Are you sure you didn't download it by mistake?'

'I thought I might have done, but for it to start at that passage? Where the mad person decides to murder the old man? I did all that without knowing about it. My god.'

She covered her mouth with her hand.

'There could be a reasonable explanation, though, right?' Jen said. 'For all of it. I mean, like, if the egg was fertilised then you might find some blood.'

'But this was literally filled to the brim with blood and nothing else. But of course it wasn't really. I know that. I know it's a delusion. Which is a good thing because last time I didn't. I didn't know. And then there's the picture. Teddy couldn't have done that, scratched the eyes out. What if it was me?' She clamped her mouth shut.

Jen was staring at her.

'Don't be scared,' Bella pleaded.

'I . . . I'm not. I'm just worried.'

'I should go back to the doctor, shouldn't I?'

Jen winced. 'I don't know, Bells. Honestly, though, we all get confused, do stuff and then forget about it, right?'

Bella nodded bleakly. 'The doctor might make me go back into hospital and . . .' She didn't need to finish her sentence. Jen knew what she meant. Jen remembered.

It had come upon her so suddenly. Yes, the birth had been difficult, but most births were. Teddy had had a brush with death, but everything had been fine in the end. The bleeding afterwards had been horrible, but again, not so rare, and until that moment she'd never had a day's mental illness in her life. It didn't run in the family, nobody could have predicted it.

Ewan never let her forget the day he found her standing over the cot holding the pillow, or how lucky she had been that he'd come home when he did. During subsequent arguments – which became fewer as she realised that he was right, he *was* the sane one – he'd thrown it back at her a few times. 'Shall I mention to the social services that you tried to murder our baby?' This always struck such fear into her heart that she could barely breathe. She couldn't lose Teddy. She would rather die a million times over than be without him.

But she had got better within two weeks. The medication had been effective so quickly, and with such a mild dose, that the doctor thought it was more likely to be a single psychotic episode brought on by stress, rather than full-on postpartum psychosis. The risperidone dose had been low enough that she could still

168

breastfeed, and the doctor said she wouldn't have side effects coming off it if they did it gradually. But she'd never quite had the courage. Ewan told her that after you'd had one psychotic episode there was a ninety per cent chance of a recurrence. She couldn't risk it. Couldn't risk them taking Teddy away.

She stopped the thought mid-flow. She wouldn't even go there.

Looking up she smiled wanly at her friend.

Jen's forehead was creased in thought. 'Last time, after Teddy was born, you were different. You totally believed what you were seeing, but now you seem sort of *aware* of it, that they're just delusions, not real. Maybe if you keep telling yourself that – they're not real – and try to push them away, you can keep it under control. And if they get worse, then you go to the doctor.'

'You're right. I'll wait,' Bella said. 'You won't tell Ewan, will you?'

Jen shook her head.

'Because whereas last time it was all centred on Teddy, this time it seems to be about him.'

'Is everything all right with you two?'

'I guess we're having a bit of a rough patch. But I don't want my crazy brain to latch on to that and make it something else. Like he's evil or something.' She laughed grimly, but the word quivered in the air. *Evil.*

Jen reached out and took her hand. 'Okay, listen. You need to stop worrying and try and keep calm. What about that meditation app Skye uses? Try that, give yourself some headspace, keep out of Ewan's way for a bit and just try and focus on yourself.'

Bella nodded, her head hanging. She felt like a little girl again: lost and scared.

Jen reached forward and pulled her into her arms and Bella sank onto her friend's shoulder. Burying her face in Jen's fragrant hair she wished she could stay there, in the warmth and darkness of another person's bodily protection, forever.

18

Jen

Before

She'd chosen a table at the back of the café, in a booth shielded from passers-by, but even so she couldn't help glancing at the door every few seconds. *Hurry up.* She wanted to get this over with as quickly as possible. It was Saturday morning. Anyone could be wandering past.

Her phone vibrated. She glanced down. He was trying to call her. She waited for it to ring off and then exhaled. At least she wouldn't have to listen to a message.

Then her breath caught. Out on the pavement, hand in hand, stood Bella and Teddy. Wincing, her phone at the ready to cancel, she waited for them to spot her and come in. If their gazes had been focused on the interior of the café they would have done, but they were looking at the menu card.

Shrinking back against the wall Jen held her breath.

Bella glanced at her watch and shook her head. Teddy's bottom lip popped out and, snatching his hand from hers, he stomped away. Bella went scurrying after him.

Jen exhaled. She sipped at the mineral water that was the only thing she could face this early.

The door jangled.

Thank God. Jen stood up and beckoned. 'Did you see Bella?'

'No.' Chrissy looked round in alarm. 'Is she here?'

170

'It's okay, she was looking in, but now she's gone. Probably to the park to give Teddy a run around, so we've got a bit of time.'

Chrissy called her order over to the waitress behind the counter. 'Is this about what I think it is?' she said, her expression dour.

But before Jen could answer Electra slid in beside her. 'Hello, ladies.' Her tone was flat and she looked exhausted. Around her was the miasma of unwashed hair and her nails were bitten to the quick. Something was wrong, but now was not the time to discuss it. They were here for Bella.

The coffees came and they waited impatiently for Skye, who eventually arrived, brimming with apologies. In contrast to Electra, Skye looked well, her cheeks flushed from the chill autumn morning.

'Right,' Chrissy said. 'We'd better make this quick. Jen says Bella's in the area. So, what's up?'

All eyes turned to her.

'I think . . .' Jen began, suddenly self-conscious under the weight of the attention. 'I think Bella's getting ill again.'

After she had told them everything there was a long silence. The women stared into their mugs or gazed sightlessly at the bustle of the café.

It was Chrissy who broke the silence. 'Well, it's not great. I think we can all agree.'

The others nodded, their faces grave.

'To me,' Jen said cautiously, 'it seems as if some of it could be just paranoia, blowing slightly odd things out of proportion.'

'Oh god,' Skye said suddenly. 'It was me that told her eggs were the symbol of the soul.'

'It's not your fault,' Electra said. 'She could have picked up on anything.'

'The amnesia thing is worrying though,' Chrissy said. 'It sounds like she went into a dissociative state for a while. Although I don't think that's totally abnormal in periods of stress.'

'Doesn't sound normal to me,' Electra muttered.

'As far as I can see,' Chrissy continued, 'there's not much we can do at the moment. It wouldn't be fair to contact her doctor or anything while the symptoms are this minor.'

'Would they try and take Teddy away?' Jen said.

'Probably not with Ewan around, and not if there hadn't been any specific incident, but it's not worth the risk.'

'She'd never forgive me,' Jen said quietly.

'Have you told Ewan?'

'No.'

'Well, at least you're there,' Skye said. 'You can keep an eye on things until he gets home in the evenings.'

'I've been getting there before he leaves, to make sure she's not alone with Teddy.'

They all winced.

'Is it that bad?' Electra said. 'Is she dangerous?'

The question hung in the air like the smell of food gone bad.

Around them crockery clinked, children babbled, bacon hissed on a griddle, but they were enclosed in a bubble, its walls quivering with tension.

Eventually Chrissy spoke. 'Look, if she starts behaving irrationally or threateningly towards Teddy again then I guess we'll have to do something about it, but for now let's just watch and wait. Agreed?'

They agreed. And then, one by one, they left the café, quickly and without fuss, dissolving into the morning crowds just as it started to rain.

Next morning Jen tried calling Eliot. He didn't pick up. She was tempted to leave a message. Tell him he had to come and get the rest of his stuff. Make him think she meant it this time. That would give him a fright.

Because, of course, *he* didn't mean it. He'd pulled this stunt several times in the past when he thought he wasn't getting enough attention. Flounced off to his mum's to wait for her to come crawling. Except that she never did. It was always him who came running back when he realised how much he missed her.

And she missed him. She was sorry about what was happening, but there was no other option. She was doing it for them. And it wouldn't be for much longer.

She got dressed and set off for Bella's place. It was only a couple of minutes' walk, but the blast of cold air was enough to shake off the nausea that had clung to her since she woke.

Late again this morning, she was surprised to see Ewan still there.

The tension in the house immediately set off a headache, and the sight of the eggs, bleeding yolks across his greasy plate, brought the nausea crashing back. Teddy ran towards her brandishing a plastic superhero, but she batted him away blindly. 'In a minute, darling,' and ran to the downstairs toilet.

There wasn't much to come up. Last night she'd only fancied mango, and had eaten two straight, gnawing and sucking them in the kitchen until she was a sticky mess. The vomit had a disgustingly sweet tang and she flushed it away quickly.

'Oh dear.' Bella had come to the bathroom door.

'Think I must have picked up a bug from one of the kids in the museum. Has Teddy been okay?'

'Oh, you know him. Iron stomach.'

Jen got to her feet and rinsed her mouth under the tap. In the mirror she saw with a jolt that Ewan was watching them from the hall.

'I suppose you'd better take the day off,' Bella said. Jen could hear the regret in her voice. She was desperate to get back to work, and who could blame her with the atmosphere in this place.

'I'm so sorry. Will they still pay you?'

'I'll just pretend it was me off sick,' Bella said, passing her a towel. 'Don't worry about it. You go home and have a lie-down, and we'll see you tomorrow if you're up to it.'

'Thanks,' she said wanly. 'These bugs never last long, so hopefully it'll be fine.'

She went out into the hall. Standing in the shadow of the bathroom door, Ewan's face was unreadable.

'Alternatively *you* could take the day off,' she said to him. 'I'm sure they could manage without you for one day.'

'Oh, no,' Bella said behind her. 'His job's far more important than mine.'

Jen rolled her eyes. From the shadows Ewan's black pupils gleamed.

'Get well soon,' he said.

19

Bella

Before

A full day with Teddy was lovely. Having so much time away from him meant she appreciated him far more. For two whole hours they sat and made a jigsaw, her finding the pieces and him slotting them in, murmuring to himself. It was as soothing as a lullaby. Afterwards, because she could now that she was working, they went out for a pizza. She left a quarter of hers, aware that she was full. This wouldn't have happened before: hanging around at home, she used to think about food all the time.

When it was time to go she actually tipped the waitress, who gave Teddy a toffee from a huge glass jar.

It was the end of Bella's first full month of work, and it had been such a pleasure to see her bank balance suddenly jump up to four figures, even if half of it went to Jen and most of the rest to Ewan. They had agreed she should have an allowance of four hundred per month for groceries.

They skipped home and made cookies, which they ate in front of *Toy Story*, and then, for the first time in a month, Bella had time to make a full meal from scratch.

The evening went as it always did, with Ewan heading to his study after supper, but at least he'd complimented the lasagne, and kissed Teddy goodnight.

At nine thirty, bored of the TV, she went up to bed.

Was it a coincidence that nothing strange had happened today, or a consequence of not being stressed? Perhaps she should cut her hours. Although Ewan would probably have something to say about that. She tried to stay awake for him, to make the suggestion when he was relaxed, his work done, but she dozed off before he came up.

Next morning Jen was well enough to come back. Seeing her pallor Bella debated telling her to go straight home to bed, but she was itching to get back to work. Rupert had the next fortnight off, so she only had today and Friday to enjoy his company.

'Are you going to make it to Chrissy's tonight?' Bella said, handing her a strong coffee.

'I reckon I'll be all right by lunchtime,' Jen said. 'My stomach's been much more settled.'

'Well, don't go out. Teddy will be fine just knocking about the house.'

Ewan came in. 'Morning all.'

Bella swallowed. Suddenly she had forgotten how to speak naturally to her husband and, for once, Jen seemed disinclined to make conversation.

'Hi. You worked late last night. Got a lot on?' It sounded clunky. As if she was making small talk with an unfamiliar work colleague.

'Nightmare,' he said, without turning round from the breadboard.

'Oh poor you. I can leave later tonight, if you need to get stuff done.'

She heard Jen sigh but ignored it, suppressing a flash of irritation. How could Jen understand what it was like to have a high-pressure job like Ewan's? Eliot was a chauffeur.

'As long as you put him to bed before you go, I won't need to do anything.'

'Unless you want to check he's okay later on,' Jen said.

Bella's chest tightened. Why was her friend being so provocative?

Ewan turned around, smiling, then held his plate of wet scrambled eggs under Jen's nose. 'Want some?'

'Ewan!'

'It's okay. I'm used to that sort of mature behaviour from Teddy.' Jen's laugh was forced.

When Ewan went upstairs Jen murmured a request for Bella to hang on until after he'd gone. This wasn't a problem, Bella only ever got in early to go and enjoy a coffee with Rupert in the staff canteen, but Jen's tone worried her. She wasn't thinking of handing her notice in, was she? The prospect of returning to lonely housewifery made Bella's heart plunge.

But after Ewan left, Jen just asked how she was feeling.

'Fine,' Bella said. 'Good. Nothing happened at all yesterday. No delusions or paranoia. I didn't sleep very well, but that's par for the course these days.'

'Good,' Jen said with genuine warmth. 'Now go and enjoy your day. Me and Teddy will be fine.'

Rupert was on top form and by four o'clock her cheeks were aching from laughing. After admitting the purple underwear hadn't had the desired effect, he promised to bring her back some special Turkish herb, which supposedly had strong aphrodisiac qualities. Bella wondered idly if it would have the power to make a gay man fancy her. She felt almost tearful when they hugged goodbye.

Jen looked much better when she got home and they had a cuppa standing at the counter. Her friend laughed when Bella told her about Rupert's outrageous comments to the rude woman from Merchandise, but she looked a bit wistful afterwards, Bella thought. Perhaps Jen was lonely, looking after a monosyllabic three-year-old all day, and envied Bella's work life.

They didn't linger because both wanted to get ready for the evening at Chrissy's. After paying Jen and seeing her out,

Bella fed Teddy and got him ready for his bath, then had the quickest of showers.

Sitting down at the dressing table she tried to apply her make-up as Sabine had done it. Why not make an effort for once, even if it was only the mums that would be there? She'd learned from the makeover that knowing she looked good made her much more confident. Perhaps that was a bit tragic, but what the hell.

She blow-dried her hair, clipping it in sections and dropping the clips into her dressing gown pocket when she wasn't using them. She was almost done. Her hair tumbled in loose, Kate-Middleton-style curls. The colour, now it was washed and shiny-smooth, wasn't dishwater brown after all, but golden chestnut with flashes of auburn. She couldn't imagine why she never liked it.

There was just one more section to dry. But when she went to retrieve a clip something rustled under her fingers. An old tissue perhaps. And yet it felt, somehow, bristly.

Holding the pocket open she peered inside. Then she screamed, tore at the knot of the cord and wrenched the thing off. She stood, naked, in the corner of the room, shivering.

The pocket was full of spiders.

Downstairs, she could hear Teddy's TV programme. Was it acceptable to summon your three-year-old to save you from a *minibeast*? This was what he thought of all bugs as, something to be studied under his mini microscope, with fascination not babyish terror, but Bella's flesh was still crawling.

The pocket gaped, but nothing scuttled out.

Eventually her heart rate slowed and she could think straight. Maybe Teddy had put them there after rescuing them from the bath. The door frame above where the dressing gowns hung was a bit dusty, and there were a few cobwebs in the corners. Perhaps the spiders had dropped down into the pockets and then been unable to get out.

For what reason she could not imagine. Old age? Her laugh was sharp in the empty room.

Venturing back across the carpet, she lifted the dressing gown and turned the pocket inside out. There were three of them. Three dead husks, black and gristly. Perhaps discarded skins rather than the creatures themselves, but that was no better. Going into the bathroom she tore off a couple of metres of toilet roll then, grimacing, picked up the spider husks and flushed them down the toilet. She flung the dressing gown into the laundry basket.

Afterwards, she sat down on the bed, staring into space.

Blood, dismembered butterflies and now dead spiders. Even the audiobook had been about death and violence.

Was this a message? Was somebody trying to tell her something? To *warn* her of something?

Ewan's dressing gown hung on the back of the door. Alone. Like he always wanted to be. Without his troublesome, whining, frumpy, boring, insane wife.

Was she in danger?

Then she started to wonder if she'd seen the spiders at all.

Ewan came home at 7.15, just after she'd put Teddy to bed. He was never this late normally. Had he done it to try and screw up her evening?

She was waiting in the kitchen, a glass of wine already on the go so she wouldn't have to play catch-up. As soon as she heard the door she put his pasta in the microwave.

He came into the kitchen.

'I'm just heating up your dinner,' she said. 'And then I'll be off.'

Something inside her shrank at the lack of response. She hated pissing him off. If she'd thought it would have brought him round she would have cancelled tonight.

'Did you have lunch at Pizza Express?' He was holding the receipt that had fallen out of her purse onto the table when she paid Jen.

'Yes. Teddy ate an entire pizza. An adult one. That child, I swear—'

'Twenty seven pounds.' He looked at her.

She bit her lip.

'What's wrong with buying some bread and cheese and making a sandwich at home?'

'I just thought, because I'm working now, I'd treat us.'

'You're working because we need the money, Bella. For important things like the mortgage and bills, not to fritter away on fucking pizzas. Half your salary goes on Jen anyway.'

'I'm sorry, I—'

'And tonight you're going out, again. And I suppose you'll have to bring wine and food.'

'I won't. Chrissy won't mind. She—'

'Forget it.'

He walked out of the kitchen.

Anger bubbled up in her throat like stomach acid. She was not angry with him but with herself. For apologising about taking their son for a pizza. The sort of thing everyone did once in a while – no, more than once in a while: regularly. But she wasn't allowed. Oh no. Ewan said she shouldn't have. So, like a good little girl, she had apologised.

Jesus, just how much of a doormat was she?

Her blood pressure must have shot up because she was seeing stars. *Calm down.* Nothing constructive would come of picking a fight.

But she couldn't quite dampen the fire kindling in her belly. Had he gone off to the study to look at porn again?

Taking off her shoes she tiptoed down the hall, her adrenaline pumping.

When challenged Ewan tended to flip immediately, like a switch, shouting the cruellest things he could think of before flipping off again just as fast once he'd reduced her to tears. It was deliberate, she was sure. To cow her into submission early on so that he didn't have to give any ground, make any compromises.

And yet, for the first time, she wasn't scared of confronting him. Determined, yes, and angry. Because he had ignored and dismissed her for months. Because they hadn't had sex since the spring. Because the woman she used to be before him, before Teddy, before the illness, was finally waking up and *she* wouldn't take any more of his shit.

She would tell him and he would listen. That she was not just a mother or a wife but a *woman*. She needed love and attention. Her emotional and physical needs had to be catered for or . . . Or what? She would leave?

Maybe. Maybe she would. And Ewan could spend the rest of his life in a sad little flat wanking in front of his laptop.

Pausing, eyes closed, palm to the wall, to wait for the adrenaline to subside, she heard a noise, like the padding of feet, but accompanied by small clicks, as if Teddy's toenails had grown too long. It sounded heavy, too heavy for Teddy.

Her eyes opened.

The hall was deserted.

She stood there, breathing deeply, trying to suppress the emotions that coursed through her like a virulent infection, turning her blood to acid, sensitising her skin, making the air smell of burned matches. It wouldn't do any good shouting. She had to stay calm if she wanted anything constructive to come of—

A tiger walked out of the kitchen.

She froze.

It was huge, its sloping back at least up to her chest, each paw as big as Teddy's head and crowned with curving white talons. It regarded her with bright eyes that shone with intelligence, gold fur rippling in the ceiling lights.

She managed to snatch a breath.

Had it escaped from a zoo? Or a Chelsea millionaire's mansion? Would screaming shock it enough to give her time to barricade herself in the living room?

No: it was coming towards her, its eyes still fixed on her face. It stopped in front of her and she could feel its huge breaths on her forearms. She gazed into the eyes that were amber and emerald and every shade in between. She felt the tiger looking back, peering into her soul, seeing every shameful emotion that cowered there, all the fear and self-doubt and shame. It did not look away. It held her. It *saw* her. Herself, bare and exposed and vulnerable, and it did not turn away.

Her fear left her.

The tiger lifted a huge paw and took a step forward. Now Bella could feel the living heat coming off it in waves. It bumped its massive head into her hand and suddenly she understood. This was her spirit animal, come to protect her. From danger. From evil.

The tiger turned and they walked up the hall together, to the door of the study. Then the animal sat down, curling its silken tail around Bella's bare heels, panting quietly. From the corner of her eye Bella could see a pink tongue moving in and out between yellow incisors like scimitars. Its breath was coppery with fresh meat.

Bella knocked.

There was no response.

She knocked again.

'What?' His tone was petulant. She and the tiger exchanged glances and the tiger's eyebrow twitched. Bella looked away to stop herself laughing.

'I want to talk to you.' She was amazed at how strong and even her voice was. Beside her the tiger's purrs were like the low rumble of a vast underground machine.

'I'm *working*.'

'This is important.'

'Is Teddy okay?'

'Yes, he's fine, I just—'

'Then it's not important.'

The tiger growled softly.

'We need to talk about things,' Bella persevered. 'Sort things out.'

'Not now.'

'Yes, now.'

'Oh, fuck off, Bella.'

It's funny, isn't it, Bella thought-spoke to the tiger, *how men treat women when they don't know there's a tiger sitting beside them.*

The tiger grinned: yellow teeth and blood-red gums.

What should I do now?

The tiger butted the door with her pink nose. The quiet thud was ignored by Ewan.

Bella went to the knife block in the kitchen and slid out the little fruit knife with the snapped-off end. She had used it once when Teddy accidentally locked himself in the toilet. All the locks in the house were made up of little domes of brushed steel with notches into which, in an emergency, you could insert a blade or screwdriver and turn manually.

When the tiger saw the blade in her hand it nodded its massive head.

Bella inserted the tip into the lock and turned it until it clicked.

Then she opened the door. The scene before her imprinted itself onto her retinas.

The room was hot and foetid. Her husband had swivelled towards the door, his face twisted. Behind him, on the computer screen, there were no spreadsheets, or even naked women. There was just fruit. Brilliant-coloured waterfalls of cherries and oranges and bananas and stars.

She blinked.

It was a gambling site. He was gambling. All the time he said he was working he had been doing this? Frittering away their money and then castigating her for coffees and pizzas.

Ewan stood up, the coloured fruits tumbling down the screen behind him. His eyes were fixed on her face, taking her breath away, scrambling her thoughts. Their expression was almost triumphant.

'Wh . . . what are you doing?'

'What does it look like?'

'Gambling.'

'Spot on, Sherlock. And now you've made me miss a spin.'

'Turn it off, we need to talk.'

'No.' He stood protectively before the screen.

'Turn it off.'

He laughed grimly. 'Don't you want me to win back the house, then?'

'What do you mean?'

'What do you think I mean? The mortgage is in arrears and they're threatening to repossess. I've been working my arse off to try and make the money back.'

'*Working* . . . ? Money that you lost, because of this?'

He folded his arms, his chin tilted arrogantly.

'We could lose the house? What are we going to do?'

Ewan laughed. 'I don't know what *you're* going to do, darling, but I've got a bit stashed away that the bank can't get hold of. Maybe I'll just head off somewhere. Let you deal with it for once.'

'A bit . . . Money?'

Ewan gave a seedy grin. 'Let's just say it's a gift from my employers.'

'You stole it? Oh my god, Ewan, we're going to go to prison!'

'Again, that *we*.'

'But . . . Teddy.'

'You'd better get on the emergency housing list I guess. I hear single mums are priority.'

'But Teddy's your son. You have a responsibility—'

He shook his head. 'I don't owe either of you anything. You're only living in this house because of me.'

'But I gave you money for the . . . the—' Her thoughts were scattering like spilled sugar.

'High time you got off your arse and did something constructive. You've always been a lazy cow, and that boy is just like you.'

'He's . . . he's beautiful.'

'Well, good luck keeping him. With me gone you'll probably have another breakdown, try to kill him again, and he'll be given to some nice normal family. Then you can sit around talking to the fairies to your heart's content.'

She spun round, stumbling blindly down the hall to the down-stairs toilet, where she threw up her pasta and red wine. When there was no more left to come up, she hauled herself to her feet. The mirror above the sink showed her that all the pretty peaches and golds of her make-up had smeared to shit-brown. Her curls had flopped. She looked like what she was, an overweight house-wife who had deluded herself that she was worth something.

She had to get out of the house, away from him.

Forgetting her coat and only just remembering to pick up her keys she burst out into the cold night air and stumbled down the front steps. Without looking left or right, she pelted across the road, making the drivers swerve and honk and shout that she was *fucking mental*.

And she was. Spiders were one thing, defacing a picture was another, but imagining a fully grown Bengal tiger stalking through her house was something else entirely. She was ill. Properly ill. The pills weren't working. She needed to get back to the doctor and ask for a higher dose before she could even think about how to deal with what she had just discovered.

She would book an appointment first thing tomorrow morning, but right now she needed to calm down. Leaning against a wheelie bin she closed her eyes and breathed deeply, counting slowly in and out, murmuring one of Teddy's favourite nursery rhymes through teeth that chattered with shock and cold.

The wind was gnawing through her silk top. To think she had dressed up for tonight, imagining it would be fun.

But she would go. She would go and cry on her friends' shoulders. Apart from Chrissy, they had all been through worse – a rape, a stillbirth, the threat of your children being taken away – and had all survived. Now it was her turn.

Chrissy would know what to do. She was a divorce lawyer. Ewan would have to leave, and then she would be able to claim benefits. Maybe the council would pay her mortgage.

The first drops of rain fell on her bare head.

She opened her eyes and found she was crying. People hurried past her, oblivious, unwilling to linger in the rain. There was little enough to linger for on this street anyway. It had been a bad decision to buy here. Like her decision to marry Ewan. She had made excuses for him for so long, justifying his dislike for her family, his refusal to socialise with her work friends until they stopped being invited to things. He had reduced the circle of her life until it included just himself, Teddy and the mums. No doubt he would soon enough find a reason for her not to see them.

And the craziest thing of all – forget the blood and the book and the tiger – she had let him.

Feeling eyes upon her, she glanced back at the house. Perhaps Ewan wanted to come after her, to apologise.

The tiger stood in the living room, resting its huge paws on the windowsill, its breath misting the pane as it watched Bella hurry away down the street.

She blinked into the darkness, blind and disoriented. The last thing she could remember was crying while clinging to someone's arm.

As her senses returned she realised she was lying on the sofa, wrapped in the turquoise mohair throw. A cushion had been tucked under her head, a glass of water laid on the coffee table beside her.

She tried to sit up but immediately flopped back down, sucked into a maelstrom of vertigo.

When it subsided she tried again and this time made it to a sitting position. Hunched and shivering she reached for the water. In the gloom her hand looked dirty.

What kind of state must she have been in when she came home? Had she fallen over? Crawled home along the dirty pavement? Tears of shame sprang to her eyes.

As she stood up something thunked to the floor.

It was the fruit knife she had used to get into the study.

Had she confronted Ewan again when she came home? If so, perhaps they'd come to some kind of reconciliation, because he had tucked her in down here. This most negligible show of tenderness was enough to bring tears to her eyes.

The room spun as she navigated it gingerly, every step making her head pound. Passing the downstairs toilet, she wondered if she would be sick again, but the tide of nausea was retreating, leaving just pain.

Everything hurt. Her head, her feet, her back. All she wanted was her own soft bed.

Teddy's door was open and she tiptoed over to his cot. Looking at him, so beautiful and peaceful, cuddling the soft monkey whose tail hung by a chewed thread, sorrow swelled in her chest. She and Ewan could not let their own failings ruin his fragile happiness. Whatever happened to their finances, they still had each other, they could still make a home for themselves. Ewan said that he'd stolen some money. He claimed it was his escape plan – leaving them in the mess that he created – but presumably that was just to hurt her, and his real intention was to gamble it away in some desperate attempt to recoup his losses. Well he would have to pay it back. Perhaps if he did so before the company audit no one need ever find out, he might keep his job. Then he could get some help for his addiction. By the sound of things the house would have to go. She would have to go back to proper work. Nine till seven and the occasional weekend. Teddy would go to nursery, with all the other abandoned babies, where he would learn *independence*, which really meant learning not to trust anyone again.

Dislike for her husband twisted in her stomach like an intestinal worm.

How had he brought them to this?

She leaned down and kissed her son's soft forehead. He smelled of the lavender bubble bath that Ewan had complained was too expensive but that she had carried on buying anyway because it was organic and paraben-free. Such tender care was a luxury they would no longer be able to afford.

Tiptoeing out of the room, she closed his door so that he wouldn't be woken by the noise of the pump when she ran the tap.

As she walked down the landing she suddenly remembered the tiger. Earlier she had not been sure, but she knew now, for definite, that it had been a hallucination, and that was reassuring. They had a difficult few months ahead of them, though, so perhaps she would ask the doctor if she should up her dose of risperidone. She wouldn't mention the tiger, or they might try and hospitalise her again, she would just mention the dissociative episode with the audiobook. Hopefully that would be enough.

She went into the bedroom.

Ewan was asleep. She could just make out the broad shape of his body spread across the mattress. The bed was all white and beige: the effect as close as she could manage to The White Company, only for Ikea prices. And yet there was a darker patch right at the centre of the bed. Discarded clothing or a spilled drink. Perhaps Ewan had got off his face tonight too.

There was also an odd smell. Greasy and metallic, like the saucepan drawer, or the motor of the food mixer.

She went into the bathroom to take off her make-up. Her eyes felt puffy and irritated and she wanted to clean her teeth.

The sudden blare of the light blinded her and she had to feel for the cotton wool pads and lotion. The cool liquid felt so good against her hot eyelids. She cleansed her whole face, then dropped the cotton wool into the bin under the sink, then she straightened up and opened her eyes.

Gasping, she gripped the edge of the sink.

Her face wasn't clean. It was smeared with blood. There was so much blood on her hands that she had transferred it to her face and the side of the sink, and the cotton wool bag and lotion bottle. It was spattered like freckles on her silk top.

Was she injured? Had she hurt herself falling over?

Washing her hands, she looked for the gash that had produced so much blood. The water ran clear. Her hands were white and smooth, the nails unchipped. Stripping off the silk blouse and cocktail trousers, she saw that the rest of her body was unblemished. The pain she felt was caused by a hangover, and from lying for too long in one position on the sofa, and wearing too-high heels.

Should she wake Ewan and ask him if he knew what had happened?

Instinctively, she glanced into the bedroom where her husband lay. The bathroom light fell in a shaft across the bed, illuminating the tasteful shades of white and stone and oatmeal, and the dark patch on the duvet.

Except now she saw that it was red.

20

Iona

Present

She and Yannis were drunk. Good, intense drunk, instead of singing and shouting drunk, which the rest of them were. Even Maya was jiggling on her bar stool, eyes closed, arms raised like a teenager at Glastonbury.

It was somebody's birthday. She couldn't remember whose, but this close to Christmas, everyone was ready to celebrate.

The two of them sat on stools at a high table by the window looking out on a small cobbled mews. Iona thought it would be a relief to let down her hair for a night and not think about the case, but she found she couldn't get it out of her head. Ever since the knife attack her habit of rubbing her jaw while she thought just irritated her scar, and now it ached. It was probably bright red. At least it was on the window side so that Maya wouldn't see.

'You know I was saying Bella Upton knows more than she's letting on,' she said, raising her voice above the jukebox.

'About the missing money?' Yannis said.

'More the missing friend. I mean, something's obviously happened to Jennifer Baptiste. Whoever was in there knew what they were doing, they didn't leave a hair or a thread or a footprint.'

Forensics had told them nothing they didn't already know.

'So, what are you thinking?'

Iona's scar throbbed. 'What if the scene was staged?'

'By who?'

Iona looked out of the window. The cobbles glittered in the rain and the windows were decked with fairy lights, the tasteful, clear kind, not the coloured sort favoured by the housing estates in Bexley.

'Say Chrissy takes them both to Bella's place, Jen promising to tuck her in.'

'Which she does. We've seen the photo.'

'But what if, afterwards, when she thinks Bella's out cold, Jen goes upstairs to see her lover?'

'Ewan?'

'Yeah. And what if Bella wakes up, goes upstairs, finds them together in her bed, and murders her. Then she goes round to Jen's place and makes it look like she was attacked there, and . . .'

Yannis smiled, shaking his head. 'Oh my god, you really don't want to do that diversity forum.'

'You tell me then, because it's not adding up at the moment.'

'So how come Upton flees rather than coming to us?'

'Maybe he thinks we'll pin it on him. Maybe he's just scared.'

'Okay, so, where does she put the body?'

'She couldn't have done it alone,' Iona said after a pause.

Yannis freed one finger from his pint glass and pointed it at her. '*That* I agree with.'

'So, maybe she had help from one of her friends. By the sound of it, none of them liked Jen much. What about Chrissy Welch? She's been having a basement dug, right? So who's going to notice a bit more disturbed ground?'

Yannis laughed. 'What, you'd do that for your friend, would you? Bury a body in your garden?'

Iona shrugged. 'Depends how much I liked them.'

'Not at all, in their case, right? You know what, though. We've never actually searched the Uptons' house.'

There was another pause, then Iona said, 'Remember what Marta said?'

'The junkie? I'm not sure her word can be relied on completely.'

'No, but she saw Bella being helped home *twice*. What if, the second time, it wasn't Bella that Marta saw?'

Yannis's pint glass paused on the way to his lips.

'What if it was Jen? Marta probably wouldn't notice any difference.'

'But she said the woman was out of it. Totally pissed. Had to be carried in.'

'Okay, how about this for a scenario: what if she wasn't pissed? What if she was injured? What if she was attacked at her flat, knocked out on the table, then brought back to Bella's?'

'You've lost me,' Yannis said.

'Ah God, I don't know.' Iona shook her head, raised her eyes to the ceiling. 'There's something going on that we just don't understand. Some escalation of the grudges they admitted to, or something they never told us.'

'If it was Jen they were bringing home that night,' Yannis said softly, 'then maybe she's still there.'

They both jumped as a drumbeat as loud as a gunshot heralded the start of one of the more popular jukebox selections, and soon all other sounds were drowned out by the roaring and yowling of a drunken choir.

Iona thought about Jen. The spectre at the feast. The dark fairy who came to the party only to sew bitterness, whose gift was guilt, who made the other mums feel ashamed of their happiness, of their healthy babies. Wouldn't you eventually come to hate her?

First thing tomorrow morning, Iona vowed, whatever the chief said, she would get a warrant to search Bella Upton's home.

21

Chrissy

4 December

She lay above the duvet, her skin flushed with heat. As the perspiration dried she would cool down, have to crawl back inside the bedding that smelled of sex and sweat, but for now she relished the cool night air on her body, like a touch.

Gradually her heartbeat settled and the pounding of the blood in her ears subsided, allowing the more familiar sounds of the city night to filter in: a distant siren, a suitcase trundling down the pavement even at this hour.

Everything seemed slower than usual: the minutes dripping like treacle into slowly spreading pools of time. It reminded her of the long nights of her childhood when she would lie watching the shadows move on the ceiling: when thoughts had time to grow and develop, when her dreams were forged. The other mums thought she had been born posh, but they were wrong. She had just been born hungry.

His arm felt so comfortable lying across her bare stomach, as if they were two halves of the same entity. She loved the smell of him. To her palate his sweat and his come tasted sweet.

Turning over, she found him looking at her. The street lamp pouring through the open curtains turned his irises almost translucent. She felt a rush of something in her chest. For a moment she pictured what it would be like to be with him properly. To walk in the park, drink in bars, hold hands and kiss on street corners.

'This is nice,' he said.

'Yes.' She stroked his face and smiled. It was just sex. Nothing more. Sordid, if you wanted to look at it that way. Russell had gone to a production meeting in Salford, where he would be staying the night. She couldn't cancel Mothers Club, but she had always planned to stay sober. She didn't want to miss a thing about tonight. In fact, she sent the mums home far earlier than she would normally have done, on the pretext that Bella had had enough. Which she had, of course. She was in a terrible state. Crying all night, drinking herself incoherent. Chrissy had promised to help her with the perilous legal and financial situation her shitty husband had left her in, and she would. Just not tonight.

Because tonight they had the whole night together. She'd expected to want to spend every moment not asleep fucking but found she was quite happy just looking at him.

'*Nice* nice.' He grinned. His teeth were perfect but for that single grey incisor whose root, he told her, had been snapped by his father when they had fought about him leaving home. She and Atanis had learned a lot about one another in the snatched hours they had spent together. He learned that she only wanted him for no-strings sex, and she learned that he was an intelligent, educated, sensitive man who deserved to be treated with more respect.

Recalling their first conversation on the subject still made her wince.

'I'm not leaving my family,' she had said. 'Don't try and make me.'

'I won't.'

'You won't tell Russell?'

It had only occurred to her after it all began that she was now in someone else's control. That Atanis could ruin her life if he chose to.

Atanis had frowned. 'I would never do anything to hurt you. That is what love is. It does not need to be returned to mean something.'

Love. He had said the word. It should have frightened her off and she told herself when she had satiated her appetite she would end it, but her appetite had changed. It seemed now to require more than just a willing body and a pretty face.

No. She turned her head away from him. She loved her husband. She loved her daughter. She did not love this Polish builder who smoked strong cigarettes and got drunk on strong lager and wore the wrong colour jeans and the wrong-shaped leather jackets.

'Hey,' he said. 'What's wrong?'

'Nothing.'

He sighed and slipped his arm from her waist. 'It's okay. I know.'

'What do you know?'

'That the build is almost finished. That it is almost time to say goodbye.'

It was true. She had watched Atanis and his assistant fit the French doors with something akin to despair.

A sob swelled in her throat, but she held it in, spoke evenly. 'I'm sorry it has to be this way.'

Now he turned over and she could feel the warmth radiating from his chest.

'I am going back to Poland.'

'Why?'

'I should see more of my daughter. Your husband is a good father to Chloe. I am a bad father.'

'At least you're looking after them financially.'

'There is more to love than money.'

'Yes.' He was right. She had spent all this time blaming Russell for not being more of a breadwinner, ignoring the fact that he got home from work in time to feed his daughter, to put her to bed, to read her a story.

'Besides, I would miss you too much if I stay in London.'

She pressed her eyes shut and swallowed. 'I'll miss you too.'

'I know we cannot stay in touch, but if you ever need me, for anything . . .'

She turned and kissed him, and then they were making love again. Love. Not fucking, which was all she thought she needed. When what she really needed was love.

When the phone rang she almost didn't pick up, but Atanis went still and then moved off her. It occurred to her then that people didn't ring in the middle of the night with good news.

Chloe.

Reaching across Atanis's chest she snatched up the phone.

But it wasn't Chloe. It was Bella.

22

Electra

4 December

When she got back from Chrissy's she carried on drinking. After all, it didn't matter how pissed she got because the kids were staying at Zack's mum's place. She'd made him take them straight from nursery, ignoring his protests that they would want to come back and say goodnight to Mummy. It was mainly to avoid seeing him, but also to ensure he didn't see the state of the house. Every day she returned from work too exhausted to do anything but stare at the TV.

She'd imagined there would be some respite after the first few weeks, but seeing him every day when he dropped them off just kept the wound open.

He was young, still young enough to recover from heartbreak, as she had done in her twenties, but she would never get over this. The cut would never heal even to a scar. It would bleed and weep forever.

She glanced at her phone for the fiftieth time since she'd got in. The drunken late-night texts had stopped. He was moving on. Well, why shouldn't he? She'd made her position perfectly clear. It was over.

The next kick in the guts would be when he met someone else. He'd lost weight, looked peaky around the eyes, but he was still beautiful. He would meet a beautiful girl his own age and she would be a wonderful stepmother to the twins, full of youthful brightness and energy. Perhaps when he realised the joyless life they were leading with their mother he would apply for custody. Maybe that would be better for them. It might even be better for her, not to have to put on a brave face every single fucking day. She could sink as low as she wanted. Like Bella. They could wallow in their misery together. But at least Bella's hadn't been self-inflicted. She'd made a bad choice, that was all, and may have lost everything by it. But Electra had made an excellent choice and then thrown it all away.

She picked up her phone and opened Instagram. He was top of the list in the search bar and she clicked through to his page.

Luckily she made it to the sink before she threw up, splattering the dirty dishes with red wine, which was all that had passed her lips all night. Then she managed to carry the phone over to the windowsill, as carefully as if it were an IED, to avoid the temptation of texting him to ask where he was, *who* he was with.

Because she didn't need to, did she? The woman he was with, apparently in a nightclub, his arms around her pretty young shoulders, could only be one person.

Thea.

When the phone rang she spilled the entire glass of red wine across the table, soaking the drawing Pearl had done at breakfast. Without bothering to clear it up she leapt up and flew across the room. It had all been a lie to try and force her hand. He wasn't really on a date with Thea, he was just trying to frighten her into capitulating. He knew full well she was struggling and was just waiting for the perfect moment to come in with the killer blow.

Well, he'd won. She couldn't do this any more.

Snatching up the phone she gasped, 'Zack?'

But it wasn't Zack, it was Chrissy.

23

Skye

4 December

The drink hadn't helped. She was hoping that it would numb her brain, but the bracing wind on the walk back from Chrissy's had blown the cotton wool from her mind and left her thoughts painfully clear. When she got back to the boat she re-downloaded the meditation app: something she long ago stopped bothering with. Focusing on the narrator's soothing voice, she tried to *watch the thoughts pass by, like traffic, and not go chasing after them*. She really tried, but her head broiled and she blundered into the road and the cars struck her and spun her and crushed her with their wheels.

She had made her decision, and would make the call tomorrow. She'd wanted to discuss it with the mums tonight, but Bella's problems required more immediate attention. Besides, how could they tell Skye how she would feel, and that's what it came down to. Could her heart survive this?

She thought it would be easier, once she made the decision, but things had got worse, not better. She'd gone running and swimming, did teacher-led yoga at vast expense in a Chelsea gym, but the fact was she had too much time on her hands. Without anything to distract her, her thoughts raced round her head like a lunatic dog.

She was going to say yes.

They would go to a clinic and Pedro or Felippe's sperm would be inserted into her womb. Then, if her body worked as it should, she would get pregnant, with a baby that was hers and not hers. She would spend nine months not thinking about the little hands developing, the little brain becoming aware, the little heart starting to beat in time with its mother's. Because it wouldn't have a mother, it would have two fathers. Which was fine. Perfectly fine.

And they would pay Skye twenty thousand pounds for the privilege.

With which she would put down a deposit on a nice warm flat and she and Juniper would move out of their little boat and onto solid ground. Fixed forever. Juniper would finally be able to breathe. And Skye would suffocate.

She tried to refocus on the app. It told her to concentrate on her breathing, counting in and out, focusing on the sensations of her body. But the boat's gentle rocking, instead of being soothing, was unsettling, as if someone was trying to dislodge her from her life, to drown her.

Yanking the earphones out, she stumbled out on deck and gulped down the cold night air, like water.

Pedro and Felippe could never be described as the patriarchy. They were not sexists or chauvinists or misogynists. They loved women. They loved Skye.

And yet they were treating her in the way men always had: as a body to be used. That was what her teacher had told her. That she was nothing, just a collection of holes he could stick his dick into. She would never be worth anything.

Maybe not to men, but she was worth something to her daughter. That was what she had to focus on now, she and Juniper, alone in the world. Because once their baby was born Pedro and Felippe would not have time for Juniper. Skye would have to be her everything: mother, father, sister, friend, confidante, protector. She would give Juniper the life she never had. One free of the malign influence of men. How could she even have considered embarking on a relationship, when her daughter should be her absolute number-one priority?

She texted Mort.

I don't want to see you any more.

Though it was now past midnight, he called her straightaway. She let it ring out, then trill as the voicemail came through.

'That text was weird. Can you call me?'

A few minutes later it rang again. She was standing by the sink heating up miso soup, craving the comfort the hot umami always brought, so she almost didn't look at the screen.

But this time it was not Mort, it was Electra.

24

Jen

4 December

The car was freezing. Presumably worried that Bella was going to vomit all over the cream leather, Chrissy had all the windows open and Jen shivered in her thin jacket. She pulled Bella closer and brushed the hair out of her eyes.

'How is she?' Chrissy said, glancing in the rear-view mirror.

'Asleep.'

'Not unconscious?'

'Doesn't seem to be. Bells?'

Bella moaned and shifted.

'How much did she have anyway?'

Chrissy sighed. 'I don't know. We drank quite a lot of vodka on top of the wine. Do you think it'll be okay to leave her? I guess we could wake Ewan. But considering what she told us tonight, I think if I saw him I'd knock him out.'

Jen snorted. 'What a shit. And I thought Eliot was bad.'

Chrissy smiled at her in the rear-view mirror. 'You know full well Eliot's an angel.'

Jen grunted. 'I know you lot think he's Mr Perfect, but he can be a right twat sometimes.'

'I'm sure you can handle it.'

Jen raised her eyebrows. 'Course.'

'Right. Here we are.' Chrissy pulled up to the pavement outside the Uptons' house and killed the engine. Red lights from passing cars strobed her face as she turned round in her seat. 'So, what do we do?'

'Bella?' Jen shook her gently.

'Shall we wake him up?' Chrissy said, glancing up at the darkened house.

'How about I see her in? I know the alarm code. I can put her to bed, make sure she's okay.'

'I guess you could tell Ewan to keep an eye on her . . .' Chrissy shrugged, grimacing.

'Okay. Help me get her up the steps.'

Bella could just about put one foot in front of the other, mumbling incoherently as they lugged her up to the front door.

When a woman emerged from the adjoining property they hesitated. It looked bad somehow, Bella lolling on their shoulders, like the victim of a date rape.

'What are you looking at?' the woman snarled, and now they saw she had the shrunken features of a drug addict. The tight jeans and cropped top looked out of place on her wizened frame. Apparently she didn't feel the cold.

'We're just helping our friend inside,' Chrissy said. 'She's had too much to drink, that's all.'

'Silly bitch.' The woman's lip curled and she tottered off down the steps in four-inch heels from which most of the faux snakeskin had rubbed off.

Finally they made it to the top of the steps, where they paused for breath, propping Bella against the door frame.

'Do you want me to come in and help?' There was something in Chrissy's eyes, a sort of pleading. She clearly had somewhere else to be.

'It's okay,' Jen said. 'I can manage.'

Leaning across Bella, Chrissy kissed her, then darted down the steps and back into the car. The Range Rover roared to life, performed a U-turn in the middle of the road and accelerated away.

Jen unlocked the door and tapped in the alarm code. Somehow she managed to get Bella across the threshold and then shut the door with her foot. Glancing up the stairs she waited to see if Ewan would hear the slam and come out, but the house was silent. Even Teddy hadn't woken. Murmuring words of encouragement Jen inched Bella's dead weight down the hall and into the living room.

Manoeuvring her friend to the sofa, she laid her on her side, propped up with cushions so that if she was sick she would not choke on it. Then, to make her more comfortable, she pulled off Bella's jeans and folded them on a chair. Bella's hair spilled across the cushion, shining like tears. Jen bent to kiss her forehead. It was almost feverishly hot from the convulsions of crying.

'Poor baby,' Jen whispered. 'You don't deserve this, sweetheart.'

After tucking her in with the mohair throw from the back of the sofa she went to get a glass of water from the kitchen, then paused. There was a creaking overhead. Had Ewan got up?

Filling the glass, she brought it back to the coffee table. Bella was now breathing deeply, a thread of red-wine-coloured drool seeping from her lips onto the beige upholstery. She would regret that in the morning, but Jen wasn't about to move her. Taking out her phone, she took a photo, then attached it to a WhatsApp message and forwarded it to the mums.

Sleeping beauty.

Then she went back out to the kitchen.

25

The Mothers

4 December

Chrissy arrived first.

Before she had the chance to knock, Bella snatched the front door open and pulled her inside.

'What's happened?' Chrissy said, staring at her friend's white face. It looked dirty in the half-light, as if she'd smeared herself with wet mud.

Bella pointed.

Chrissy followed the direction of her finger, up the stairs into darkness. Stepping out onto the landing she listened for crying, but the silence of this floor was impenetrably dense, like smoke creeping down her throat, tightening her chest.

The door to Teddy's bedroom was shut, and with a sense of dread she walked towards it, stopping outside. She remembered the phone call from Ewan that day three years ago, to say that his wife had been hospitalised, to say that he had found her trying to smother their son with a pillow. That he had stopped her. That he hadn't told the authorities. At the time Chrissy had thought this was out of loyalty and love for his wife, but knowing Ewan better she understood now that he had just wanted her back at her post – looking after Teddy so he didn't have to.

She inhaled and pushed open the door.

The three-year-old lay on his back in his cot, perfectly still. The mobile dangling above his head whispered in the breeze from the open door, and coloured animals projected from the nightlight slowly circled the room. A red hare, a blue stag, a yellow owl. Chrissy stepped into the room.

Stumbling on a Duplo brick she automatically reached for the cot for support and it trembled under her grasp. Teddy sighed and turned over. She exhaled.

Electra arrived at the door a few minutes later, panting so hard she could barely speak when Bella let her in.

'Wha . . . what's going on?'

Bella pointed and Electra began climbing the stairs. When she got to the top Chrissy was coming out of Teddy's room and the two women looked at each other, then, as one, their heads turned to the only other door on this floor.

Skye came next.

When she stepped into the hall she could hear a voice coming from the floor above, low enough to be a man's, or perhaps a woman's deepened with shock. She began to climb. The smell that came to her nostrils as she did so made her gag. It jogged something in her memory. Queasy trips to the butcher's with her mother before she became vegan.

Emerging onto the landing she realised the voices were coming from an open door to her left.

Glancing back down she saw Bella's huge eyes gleaming in the darkness.

She walked into Bella and Ewan's bedroom.

Jen was last to arrive, her quiet tap loud in the utter silence of the house. Bella, who had been sitting on the lowest step rocking back and forth, got to her feet and opened it.

'Honey, what's happened?'

'I . . .' Bella stammered.

Chrissy appeared on the landing. 'Come up, Jen.'

The room was too small to accommodate them all comfortably and the women stood very close, sleeves rustling in the quiet.

Finally Electra broke the silence. 'We should call an ambulance.'

'Why?' Skye said. 'He's obviously dead.'

'We should call the police,' Chrissy said.

Ewan Upton lay on his back with his mouth open, arms spread across the mattress as if waiting for someone to embrace him. The duvet was pulled up to his chest. In the very centre of the expanse of white cotton was a stain, the shape of some vaguely familiar country. In the dark it would look brown or black, but the light pouring in from the en suite bathroom revealed it to be scarlet.

'Could it be suicide?' Skye said in a small voice.

'How many suicides choose the *stabbing yourself through the chest in bed* method?' Electra muttered.

'If it's murder,' Jen said, 'then I guess it could have been an intruder.'

None of them looked at her.

'I mean, that's feasible, in this area, right? That is possible.'

Nobody answered.

The clock in the corner made the tiniest electronic sputter as it flicked from 1.59 to 2 a.m.

'It . . . it was me.'

They all turned. Bella stood in the doorway, eyes starting from a face glistening with perspiration.

They took her back downstairs and led her to the sofa.

'With that.' Bella gestured to the fruit knife that lay on the carpet, its tip snapped off, its blade smeared with blood.

Sitting down beside her Jen took her hand. 'Bells, what happened? What did he do to you?'

Bella's face crumpled. 'Nothing. He didn't do anything. He was in bed. I just . . . I went upstairs and I stabbed him, and then I came back down here and went back to sleep.'

'You had an episode,' Chrissy said, standing in the middle of the room. 'A dissociative episode. It wasn't your fault.'

'I killed him,' Bella moaned. 'I killed Teddy's daddy. They're going to put me in prison. They're going to take Teddy away from me.'

Electra hushed her, pulling her into her shoulder.

Chrissy said, 'Jen, is there anything upstairs, any pills we can give her to calm her down?'

'I'll look.'

They waited, a still tableau, silent but for Bella's sobs, until Jen returned with two small brown bottles. 'These are her anti-psychotics. And it looks like these ones are sedatives.'

'Honey?' Chrissy went over and lifted Bella's chin. 'Take these for us, there's a good girl.' Jen handed her the glass of water from the coffee table and Bella meekly swallowed the tablets. 'Now, lie down here for a bit, have a little rest, just until you feel a bit better, okay?'

Bella nodded, lay back on the sofa and turned her face to the cushion. Chrissy stopped in the act of spreading the mohair throw across her. It was stained with blood. Folding it carefully, she laid it on the coffee table and covered Bella with her own grey cardigan.

The four of them went into the kitchen.

'Look,' Electra said softly. 'Shouldn't we call the police now? I mean, she won't go to prison, will she? Not if she pleads guilty by reason of insanity.'

'But what about Teddy?' Skye murmured. 'Wouldn't he have to go into care?'

In the silence a single car growled up the street, scrolling its headlights across the room. Interrogating each woman's face in turn.

Chrissy said, 'Maybe that's the right thing. If she's . . . dangerous.' Her voice was small with shame.

'She's only dangerous to arseholes,' Electra said.

'What, so he deserved it?' Chrissy said.

'No,' Electra said. 'He didn't deserve it, but it's done.'

'It's my fault,' Jen said.

All eyes turned to her.

'I knew she was getting sick again. I should have paid better attention. I should have seen what was coming.'

'No,' Chrissy said firmly. 'It wasn't your fault. You told us what was going on. We should have done something.'

Each woman experienced a lurch of guilt. They had been so wrapped up in their own problems they had not noticed Bella's suffering.

Bella, who had accompanied Chrissy to A&E when Russell was on a stag do, with a three-month-old Chloe running a temperature of 40 degrees.

Bella, who had looked after Juniper when Skye went to court as a character witness in the trial of the rapist teacher.

Bella, who had dropped everything and rushed to a sobbing Electra's side, bathed and fed the twins and put them to bed, before holding her friend's hand, reassuring her that she was coping brilliantly and that everything would get better.

Bella, who, shaky herself after the postpartum psychosis, had brought a home-cooked meal round to Jen's every night for two months following the stillbirth.

Their dear, kind, wonderful friend, who had never needed them more.

'It seems to me,' Chrissy said slowly, 'we have two options. One, we call the police. Teddy goes to the grandparents, or into care. I get her the best lawyer I can find, and we hope that after a few years they let her out, and maybe she'll get supervised visiting rights to Teddy.'

Nobody said anything.

'It's not fair!' Electra exploded. 'That bastard *did* deserve it for what he did to her. He ruined their lives. Surely that makes a difference!'

'It would still be manslaughter.'

'What's the other option?' Jen said.

There was a long pause.

'We don't,' Chrissy said finally. 'Call the police.'

The silence stretched, each woman as still as the body cooling in the bed upstairs.

'I started in criminal law,' Chrissy said. 'I know how the police work. An adult male goes missing, nobody's too worried about it, at least not for a while. Bella comes home from my place drunk. Wakes up tomorrow morning and he's not there. Assumes he's gone to work. Doesn't report him missing till tomorrow evening. For a while they do nothing. Then they do a little digging, find out he's embezzled from the company. There's his motive to flee.'

'What are you saying?' Electra said. 'That we cover this up? Get rid of the body somehow?'

'I've had plenty of clients who got away with murder.'

There were quiet intakes of breath.

'Say we get caught,' Skye said. 'What happens?'

'Assisting an offender. Three to ten years.'

'Oh my god,' Skye breathed. 'We'd lose our own kids.'

'We'd serve five, max,' Chrissy said. '*If* they solved the case.'

'But the crime scene,' Electra said. 'All they'd have to do would be to get forensics round here and it would be game over.'

Four pairs of eyes clicked to the ceiling, to the thin membrane of wood and plaster separating them from the bloodied corpse of their friend's husband, and a thrill ran down each woman's spine. The clock on the oven flashed to 2.07 a.m. Time seemed to have slowed to a crawl, or was it just that their racing hearts and racing thoughts had overtaken it?

'I think we can do this,' Jen said quietly. They looked at her. 'If we all work together.' She was breathing heavily, her black eyes bright. She still looked so fresh-faced. Unlike the rest of them, who'd been worn out by broken sleep and the drudgery of toddlers, Jen was still young. But at too high a cost. 'We've got Bella's life in our hands. Don't you remember what we said? What we promised?'

They did, of course they did. Three years and a lifetime ago, when they sat in Jen's hospital room – even poor, ill, heavily medicated Bella. Huddled in a closed circle around Jen, arms encircling her, heads touching, breath mingling, as she cried for her lost baby. And in the hushed gloom of a hospital night, frightened, lost and bewildered by the awful duty that had been entrusted to them, they had made a pledge. That they would be there for each other forever, whatever happened.

Jen reached out her hand and placed it palm down on the table. 'We have to help her.'

As one, each woman reached out her hand and placed it on top of the others.

Forever. Whatever.

26

Jen

The bloodstain on the carpet came out easily, leaving no trace, thanks to whatever protector had been sprayed on the wool. Of course a forensics team might find something, if they knew where to look, but hopefully Jen's plan might prevent that from happening.

She knelt down by the sofa. 'Bells.'

Her friend moaned and shifted.

'Bells, we need to get you cleaned up.'

She lifted Bella into a sitting position and held the glass of water to her lips. Bella blinked and opened her eyes. For a moment they were wide and innocent as a child's, then a cloud spread across her face.

'Jen?' Her voice quavered.

'It's okay,' Jen murmured, stroking her hair. 'You've got nothing to worry about, babe. We're sorting everything. I just need to get you washed.'

'Why?' Bella said stupidly, and Jen couldn't stop her eyes flicking down to the blood-spattered top.

Following her gaze Bella made a noise in her throat that Jen feared was the start of another bout of crying. She grasped the hem of the blouse and lifted it. 'Arms up. That's right. Good girl.' She took the top to the bin liner and bagged it, then returned to the sofa where Bella shivered in her bra and knickers.

As Ewan died he would have exhaled microscopic blood

particles. Jen knew this from the crime series she enjoyed so much. There would be blood in Bella's hair and all over her skin. They needed to shower it off, and then Jen would have to bleach the shower cubicle.

She helped Bella stand and led her to the stairs. Glancing back, she couldn't see any marks on the sofa, but she'd have a proper look later.

Laboriously they climbed the stairs. Stepping out onto the landing, Jen gripped Bella firmly by the elbow and led her towards the family bathroom. On the way past Teddy's room Bella whimpered and tried to pause, but Jen tugged her onwards.

'Not yet. When you're clean.'

The hot shower seemed to revive her and she followed Jen's instructions obediently, double-shampooing her hair and suffering the water to be so hot that her skin turned lobster red.

While she was drying off Jen bleached the cubicle and screen, then balled up Bella's underwear, the bath mat and the towels to put on a hot wash, before finally going to fetch clean underwear and a change of clothes from Bella's bedroom.

Jen was the first one to enter the room since they had all left it half an hour ago. The first thing she noticed was that the smell had started to dissipate as the blood dried. To speed up this process she opened the window, taking a moment to look out on the quiet street below. It was too late even for the junkies still to be shambling around. The perfect time to dispose of a body.

'What's happening?' Bella asked as Jen dressed her in the bathroom.

'It's all under control. Nothing for you to worry about.'

'I j-just can't remember.'

'Listen.' Jen took her face in her hands. 'He pushed you too far. That's it. End of story. You can't turn the clock back, so now we just have to move forward. We have to make sure you and Teddy are okay.'

'Teddy . . .' Bella murmured.

'You have to be strong for him. Can you do that?'

Bella's eyes searched Jen's and seemed to find some kind of strength there. 'Yes,' she whispered.

'You need to keep taking the pills – the sedatives, the antipsychs. You need to make sure you eat properly, and no alcohol, okay?'

Bella nodded.

'The police will want to speak to you. Can you manage that?'

'Yes.' Her voice was stronger now, her eyes brighter.

'Good, we'll go over everything you're going to say later on. But, in the meantime, go back downstairs, back to the sofa, because as far as the police are concerned that's where you spent the night. I've got things to do up here.'

The air in the bedroom smelled only of the city now, stale food and vehicle fumes. Jen inhaled and exhaled, steeling herself.

Then she went over to the bed and pulled back the duvet.

The familiar shape of him had taken on a strangeness in death. Though he must have been relaxed when he died his limbs lay awkwardly and his face was like something sculpted from wax, the eye sockets and cheeks pressed in too firmly by the sculptor. His skin was the colour of a winter sky, with patches of grey and purple, like sleet-heavy clouds.

She reached forward, unafraid, and poked him.

His flesh was firm and cool, but the dent her fingers made in his chest did not fill.

Opening the walk-in wardrobe, she slid the suitcase from the top shelf and began to fill it with Ewan's clothes.

27

Chrissy

Chrissy was waiting by the door when Jen came down with the case.

'The passports were in the pocket,' Jen said. 'I took Bella and Teddy's out.'

'Great,' Chrissy said, taking the case in a leather-gloved hand. 'Tell Electra so she can stop looking.' She opened the front door. 'I'll try and be as quick as I can.'

'Okay.' Jen closed the door behind her.

Glancing to her left and right Chrissy jogged down the steps and crossed the road to the car. There would be no CCTV on this street, but she would have to take the back routes home.

It was odd passing through the deserted city. There were a few people still out, some with hoods pulled low over their faces, walking quickly: she was perhaps not the only criminal abroad tonight. Others were drunk, rowing with companions or speaking urgently on their phones. One young woman, in a green sequinned party dress, lolled against a wall, eyes closed, as vulnerable as a sleeping hen in a city of foxes. But Chrissy could not stop to help her. All she could do was hope that each citizen was too wrapped up in their own cares tonight to mark the passing of one more black Range Rover.

It started to rain as she turned into Cheyne Walk. Tucking the case under the passenger seat, she got out and jogged across the road. The house was in darkness. Her heart lurched.

Had he already gone? Back to the flat he was renting in Earl's Court. If so, this part of the plan was in tatters.

She let herself in and listened. The house was silent. Even though she told herself it didn't matter so much, she experienced a moment of panic. Things were sliding out of her control. If this part of the plan went wrong, who was to say everything else wouldn't?

But then Atanis came out onto the landing.

'I thought you might have gone,' she said.

He came down the stairs. 'I would never leave your daughter alone.'

Then he stepped back and looked at her face. 'What has happened?'

Once she'd asked him, and he had agreed, there was no time to linger over goodbyes. He'd already given notice to his landlord, and though leaving a week early might cost him his deposit, he refused Chrissy's offer to reimburse him. Closing her hand over the wad of cash they always kept in a kitchen drawer to pay contractors, he said, 'I don't need your money. I am glad to have a chance to help you. To show how much you mean to me.'

Chrissy closed her hand over his. 'I'm sorry I can't tell you more.'

'It's okay. I trust you. And you can trust me.'

'We can't be in touch again.'

He nodded, then leaned forward and touched his forehead lightly to hers. She would never forget the soft creaking his leather jacket made as he moved, or the scent of his hair. If she had stayed where she grew up, got a job managing a local hairdresser or restaurant like her school friends, she would have married someone like Atanis. And perhaps she would have been happy.

He picked up the case and opened the door. Standing on the step, she had to lean on the door frame for support. She would never see him again. Perhaps it was not such big a deal – he had planned to leave anyway – but somehow this was too sudden a wrench, and too final. The other women would not understand, Skye particularly, but Chrissy felt at that moment that her sacrifice had been the greatest of all of them.

She watched him walk down the path and let himself out of the front gate. He paused for a moment on the pavement and raised his arm, his fair hair catching the light from the lamps lining the river's edge, and then he set off in the direction of the coach station.

Chrissy closed the door.

Chloe was almost too long for her cot now. She took after Russell's side of the family, who were all over six foot, even the women. She'd long since grown out of the largest Grobag available and now slept under a duvet in princess pyjamas, her bottom in the air, hair splayed out in a sunburst on the mattress.

Chrissy leaned down and kissed her daughter's fragrant head.

'I'm sorry, darling,' she breathed. 'I won't be long.'

Nothing would happen while she was gone. Chloe slept through the night and woke at seven on the dot every morning, but Chrissy couldn't suppress the sense of foreboding as she left her little girl's room and went downstairs.

The tarpaulin was rolled up in the summerhouse. It was surprisingly unwieldy to carry alone and she regretted not asking Atanis to help. By the time she'd dragged it through the basement and up the stairs she had to pause to catch her breath. Leaning against the banisters, she was unable to meet the eyes of the happy family smiling down at her from the wall. They were strangers to her.

When the buzzer went she started so hard she banged her head, then her heart set up a fast whirr. Had Atanis come back? Had he changed his mind about helping her? Or did he just want to see her one last time?

217

Christ, she wanted to see him too. Saying goodbye had been like watching a light go out.

Running down the hall she snatched open the front door.

'Mrs Welch?' The young man in policeman's uniform held out his badge.

28

Electra

The study smelled bad. A sweaty, greasy maleness that hinted at the desperate evenings Ewan spent blowing his family's future.

She had been tasked with finding his passport in order to sew the seed that he'd fled the country. A drowsy Bella had told them it was somewhere in here. Electra didn't see the point. Unless the police searched the house it would only be Bella's word that the passport was gone, and if they did search the house, they'd all be screwed anyway. Plus, there would be records at the borders if his passport had been used. But apparently Chrissy had a plan.

Electra wasn't optimistic. Master criminals they weren't. Panic-stricken and blundering they certainly were.

The chaos of the little room surprised her. She'd always had Ewan down as pretty anal, had wondered what Bella had seen in such a dour control freak, but getting to know Bella better over the years, she realised Bella thought she needed a man like Ewan. But bossy did not mean masterful, and joyless did not mean impressive. This was probably why she and Chrissy were so close: Bella just needed someone to tell her what to do. Electra had some sympathy for this. Being a grown-up was no fun.

She began with the desk drawers, raking through rolls of Sellotape and glue sticks and Post-its. There were a number of slips of paper that at first she thought were cab receipts, but closer inspection revealed them to be pawn tickets. One was described as being 'necklace – Tiffany'. Paperclipped to it were two tiny round pictures; one recognisably a childhood Bella, dumpling plump, the other a smiling grey-haired man. Her father. Ewan had pawned Bella's locket.

More pawn slips detailed a watch, a bike, a gold christening band, a set of silver cheese knives – wedding gifts, perhaps.

But no passport, so she turned her attention to the overflowing box of papers beneath the desk.

These were mostly bank statements. Long columns of transactions to companies with names like Game King, PokerStars, Spin to Win. Hundreds of pounds in each transaction. Sometimes he had lost thousands at a single sitting. Beneath the bank statements were letters from the mortgage company and various demands for payment from utility companies. Then she noticed, slipped down the side of the box, a manila envelope. Whatever it contained had been treated with a little more care, so she was optimistic it might be the passport – but on sliding out the contents she found only more bank statements.

She began idly flicking through them, then the yawn that had been brewing at the back of her skull vanished and her fingers began moving faster.

29

Chrissy

'We'll be having a word with Mr Mogg in the morning,' PC Franklin said as he climbed the stairs to the hall. 'The way he described it, you were having an all night rave. We were on the verge of sending a riot van.'

'He wasn't happy I got planning approval for my extension,' Chrissy said. 'I think he's looking for any excuse to get me into trouble.'

'Complaints about noise are not a police matter,' the young policeman said, stepping over the roll of tarpaulin. 'We've got better things to do than have our time wasted by some old sod moaning about a mums' dinner party.'

Chrissy chuckled ruefully.

'Excuse my French, Mrs Welch, but it's been a long night.'

'It has, indeed,' Chrissy said. 'I'd just finished clearing up when you arrived, and I'd quite like to go to bed now.'

'You do that, Mrs Welch. And apologies once more for disturbing you.'

'Not at all,' Chrissy said. 'I'm sorry your time was wasted.'

She maintained her smile until the door clicked shut, then dropped to her haunches and buried her head in her hands. 'Fuck fuck fuck fuck.'

*

She drove as fast as she could through the empty streets without letting the Range Rover's V8 engine carve up the silence with its characteristic snarl.

Surely that wasn't the first tendril of dawn creeping round the chimneys of the power station? Surely they had more time than this.

But as she turned left and started travelling parallel to the river, the moon emerged from behind a chimney, blade sharp, dappling the water with slivers of silver. Enough light to see by, but not enough to be seen by. There was still a chance, God help them.

The clock flicked to 3.30.

Fuck it. She put her foot down.

They were waiting for her in the kitchen, all four of them, faces drawn, expressions inscrutable.

Bella held a sheaf of papers to her chest. Her cheeks were flushed, almost feverish. What could have made enough of an impact to wake her from her shocked stupor?

Bella handed her the papers.

Sitting at the kitchen table, Chrissy looked at them for long moments, studying the numbers again and again, unable to quite believe what she read. Finally she raised her head.

'I think you're right. This is probably the money he said he'd taken from his company.'

'So he wasn't just saying that to frighten me,' Bella said softly. 'He really did steal from them.'

'It looks like he set up an offshore company to hide it. That *Hurgen* guy –' Chrissy pointed at a name on the top page '– is probably just an employee of the bank because an offshore bank needs a local director. Ewan clearly wanted it to be anonymous and untraceable, so his name won't feature anywhere on the paperwork, but he could access the money online using those login details.' She pointed at a series of figures scrawled in biro on the corner of the page.

Bella said, 'How do I pay it back to them before they find out it's missing?'

Chrissy opened her mouth to speak, but Jen interrupted her. 'Are you kidding?'

'But if I don't, the police will start investigating it and then . . .'

This time Jen laughed. 'We've just covered up a murder and you're worried about a poxy three hundred grand?'

'It's quite a lot of money,' Electra murmured.

'Not to the police. They're not going to give a shit when there's drug dealers raking in millions a month. Seriously. Not even the bank will miss it. Right, Chris?'

Chrissy shrugged.

'No, guys, this is good. It's a reason for Ewan to run.'

The women looked at one another with, for the first time that evening, a glimmer of hope in their eyes. This was a clear motive. Something had finally gone their way.

'Chris,' Skye said. 'If those are the login details, couldn't Bella just transfer the money to her own account?'

'She could. Yes. But, given the circumstances, the police might be checking her bank account.'

'*You* could take it, though – there's always clients giving you money, right? – then transfer it to her later?'

A pause. 'It would be a risk.'

Electra laughed quietly. 'And covering up a murder isn't?'

'Speaking of which.' Chrissy got up. 'Time is pressing on, ladies. Jen. Are you ready?'

They stood next to the bed and gazed down at the corpse of their friend's husband. It was cold in here and goosebumps had risen on their arms, but Ewan's flesh was smooth and grey as marble.

Jen bent down and moved Ewan's arms to his side, grunting a little with the effort. 'Rigor mortis is setting in,' she said. 'But I guess that might make him easier to handle. Ready?'

Chrissy swallowed.

'One. Two. Three.'

She forced herself not to flinch as her hands touched the chill curve of a dead shoulder. Grunting, they heaved him across the mattress and over the edge. He landed face down on the tarpaulin with a clump that could not, Chrissy thought, be mistaken for anything but the sound of a corpse hitting the floor. His buttocks had little dark circles in the centre, like rouge.

At the sight of them an explosion of laughter threatened to burst from her mouth. Although normally Jen was the first to be amused by such anatomical ridiculousness, she seemed to be concentrating on the job in hand, stripping the bed and depositing the soiled items unceremoniously on top of the body. It was a relief to Chrissy, no longer having to see the corpse, but Jen didn't seem to need a breather and was already folding the sides of the tarpaulin over the bundle.

After a lot of shunting and swearing and sweating they had him bound like a turkey joint on the bedroom floor.

She knew the package would be heavy and unwieldy, but not *how* heavy. Plus, there was resistance, as if, despite appearances, Ewan was not quite dead and was doing his best to thwart them.

In the end it was easiest just to slide the body down the stairs. Chrissy winced at each clunk, but though the head received a nasty bump against the banister, Ewan was well past the stage of bleeding.

The other women came out into the hall.

'We can't take that outside,' Electra said firmly. 'I've never seen a more obvious dead body in my life.'

'Got any better ideas?' Jen huffed, but Chrissy knew she was right. Anyone passing would certainly remember the sight of five women manoeuvring a human-shaped lump into the back of a car in the dead of night. But the sound of her friends arguing, even slightly, shredded Chrissy's nerves.

'I think she's right,' Skye said. 'It does look like a body.'

'It *is* a body,' Jen said. 'It's going to look like one whatever we do.'

The silence that followed made Chrissy's throat tighten. Had they gone too far to go back now? Bella was slumped at the kitchen table, head bowed. This was helping no one. Should she just suggest that they—

'Wait,' Electra said. 'It's a body, sure, but why can't it be a living one?'

'What, pretend he's just sleeping?' Jen snorted. 'If people see us with Ewan the police will be onto us straightaway.'

'Not Ewan. Bella. If anyone sees us, we're just helping our drunk friend.'

'Like before,' Chrissy said, looking at Jen. 'If someone reported it, we can admit to bringing Bella home drunk but claim they got the timing wrong.'

'We'll be getting her into the car, not out of it,' Skye said doubtfully.

'But anyone passing, particularly in a car,' Chrissy said, 'wouldn't have time to see that. They'd just see us supporting a drunk woman.'

Jen squatted down and began tugging at the ropes. 'Well, come on then.' She grinned up at them. 'We've got a makeover to do.'

Ewan was very difficult to dress, even in Bella's most elastic wardrobe items – leggings and a tunic – as his arms and legs were now almost rigid with rigor mortis. But eventually they managed it.

'It's pretty cold tonight,' Jen said, adding a bobble hat and scarf from the hooks by the door, 'and this should disguise him even more.'

They finished with Bella's long fuchsia coat, and the only footwear they could get his feet into – a pair of sheepskin slippers. The result was so comical, Chrissy could hold it in no longer. She began to laugh. That set Jen off. Electra looked at them incredulously.

'Are you kidding?' she said. 'Seriously, this is . . .'

225

Jen pointed, spluttered, then carried on laughing. By now, Chrissy was in physical pain. Electra shook her head, smiled, then she started laughing too.

Skye came out, her face white with shock. Jen made Ewan wave at her. Skye began to laugh. Even as Bella crept into the hall they couldn't stop, though they wanted to, and then even Bella relinquished her grip on reality and they all hooted and howled, just managing to cling to Ewan's stiff arms while the corpse's bobble hat jiggled.

Finally the laughter tailed off and they slumped against the walls and banisters.

Chrissy regained her composure first. 'I'm sorry, Bella. I think it's just nerves.' She felt as if she'd run a marathon.

'It's okay,' Bella said, and drifted back into the kitchen.

'Look,' Skye said suddenly, any vestige of amusement gone from her voice.

She was pointing at the rectangles of patterned glass in the front door. The sky outside was lightening.

Chrissy had parked the Range Rover right up against the steps so, unless anyone came out of the properties on either side, they should remain unobserved. After checking that the road was clear, she, Electra and Jen took hold of Ewan and began inching him out of the house.

It was almost impossible. The body was unbearably heavy and hindered them at every step. They grunted and puffed, staggering down one agonising step at a time. Finally, when Chrissy felt as if she had burst vital blood vessels, they reached the pavement.

The morning was clear and surreally silent. Her gaze flitted from house to house, alert to the slightest movement, but there was nothing. All was still and quiet.

She hit a button on her key fob and the Range Rover gave a shrill beep that made her wince. They had just begun walking the body across to the kerb when they heard the footsteps.

They froze.

The footsteps hesitated, then carried on. Then they hesitated again. A woman in high heels was stumbling up the middle of the street from the direction of the Kings Road. She had not yet noticed them.

As she came level with the car they stood perfectly still, waiting for her to pass.

But she did not.

She tottered straight towards them, even using the Range Rover's bonnet for support as she stepped unsteadily onto the pavement. Finally her head turned slowly.

'What are you looking at?' she slurred, her gaze unfocused.

It was the same sunken-cheeked woman they had seen when they brought Bella back earlier on. Her top was stained now and the heel of one of her snakeskin stilettos had snapped off.

Chrissy felt a moment's relief. The woman was wasted.

Out of the corner of her eye Chrissy saw Bella's front door quietly close.

'We're helping our friend inside,' Chrissy said. 'She's had too much to drink, that's all.'

That *was* what she'd said earlier, wasn't it?

The woman's head jerked and a frown creased her forehead. For a moment her eyes locked on to Chrissy's and Chrissy thought she saw something in them: suspicion? Fear? Did the woman think she was losing her mind? All the better.

'Silly bitch,' she muttered and then launched herself forward.

They watched her, a still tableau, as she hauled herself up the steps of the adjoining property, let herself in and disappeared into the darkness.

Without waiting to see if she would come to the window to spy on them some more, Chrissy opened the door of the Range Rover and, rather less ceremoniously than intended, they bundled Ewan inside.

'Good luck,' came a low voice from the top of the steps.

Electra and Bella stood hand in hand.

227

'Look after her,' Chrissy said. They had agreed that Electra would stay with Bella until she fell asleep.

'I'll be okay,' Bella said in a frail voice, 'I promise.' And Chrissy understood that what she meant was *I'll play my part, I won't let you down.*

She experienced another moment's dread that they had done the wrong thing: that in trying to help Bella they had doomed themselves to a life, if not of physical incarceration, then of the plaguing of conscience, until they all went mad.

Pushing the thought away she went round the side of the car and climbed into the driver's seat.

They'd come too far to turn back now.

30

Bella

Sitting at the kitchen table, drinking hot chocolate that she had managed to make herself, Bella felt oddly calm. Perhaps it was shock. Perhaps at the first sign of the police she would dissolve into a gibbering wreck and tell them everything.

But no, she didn't think so. Firstly, her brain felt back to normal. Someone – she couldn't recall who – had given her a double dose of her antipsychotics and they seemed to be working normally again. Even with the stress she had been under tonight, there were no tigers, no defaced pictures, no voices or delusions at all.

The reason she was calm, she suspected, was that all responsibility had been taken out of her hands. She was a child again. The mess she had created was simply being sorted out by the grown-ups. And Christ, was she grateful.

The picture of the five of them gazed at her from the radiator cabinet. They had been caught unawares by the automatic programme, she remembered, and their smiles were not quite ready. But knowing the secret they would all share, their enigmatic expressions seemed appropriate now.

When they had explained their plan to her, she hadn't been able to process it properly, but now, as she went over things in their mind, she felt a sense of relief. And hope.

'We don't want the police in here,' Chrissy had said to her, her voice slow and clear as if she were talking to a toddler.

'There's not much in the way of forensics, but there's probably enough, especially as we can't get rid of the mattress. We'll just have to turn it so a cursory glance around the room won't show anything.'

Bella had blanched at the idea of sleeping on that mattress, but she'd just nodded and let them carry on.

'Jen's got a plan to keep them out of here.'

Bella listened as Jen described what she was going to do, which sounded to Bella like the most stupid, reckless and courageous thing she had ever heard. Not for the first time she wondered if Jen was actually a psychopath.

'It should distract them long enough for the phone trace to come in from Poland and them to start thinking he's fled the country. They'll get the European police onto it, but the trail will be cold by then. They'll have to just file it away. Case closed.'

'Poland?' Bella frowned.

'My Polish builder is going to take Ewan's phone and passport with him when he goes back home tonight,' Chrissy said.

Bella gasped. 'You've told your builder?'

'I've asked him to do me this one small favour,' Chrissy said. 'He didn't ask what for.'

'For money? What if he tries to blackmail us later?'

'Not for money, no. And he doesn't know anything. Just that when he gets to Poland he needs to replace the battery in Ewan's phone – which we'll have taken out until that point so it can't be traced – and turn it on. That will flag its location to the police. He's also going to dispose of the passport somewhere it can be found later. It might make them think Ewan killed himself, or was murdered by people involved in the embezzlement. He'll throw the suitcase over the side of the boat into the sea.'

Why would your builder do that? Bella was going to say, but then she realised. So wrapped up in her own troubles had she been that she had forgotten her friends' lives were complicated too. It was simple enough. The builder was in love with Chrissy.

'What about . . .' She paused to inhale. 'The body?'

230

The women exchanged glances.

Chrissy said, 'It's all under control. You don't need to know the details.'

Bella was relieved. She was being protected from the truth. They had covered everything. All she would have to do was to play her part to the police. Then an unpleasant thought struck her.

'You're my friends,' she said. 'If the police question you they might suspect that you're lying.'

'Then we don't act like your friends,' Jen said. 'We're so different, right?'

The women looked at one another. It was certainly true. What did a dynamic editor have in common with a poorly educated childminder? Or a high-flying lawyer with a tattooed vegan?

'We act like backstabbing bitches. Slag each other off, make out that we're feuding and jealous, like not in a million years would we ever do anything to help each other. The perfect frenemies.'

Was it enough to outsmart the authorities? Bella didn't know, but it would have to be. And as terrifying as the position she found herself in was, it was better than the alternative.

She vowed then that she would do everything in her power to keep those women safe. She would play her part to the highest degree. She would protect them with her own sanity and self-control.

Footsteps crossed the ceiling above her head.

Ewan's up, she thought. Then her face crumpled. For the first time she felt the pain of his loss. The loss of the comfortable, routine lives they had lived for so long. The future felt daunting suddenly, as if the doors had been thrown open, letting in cold and wind and harsh daylight.

She and Teddy were alone now.

Electra came in to find her crying and the dismay on her friend's face brought her up sharp.

Wiping her eyes, she said, 'I'm okay. Really. Don't worry.'

Electra took her hand. 'Shall I take you up to bed?'

Bella nodded, then allowed herself to be led through the darkened hallway, up the stairs and along the landing to her bedroom door.

She paused at the threshold, trying to prepare herself.

Electra pushed open the door.

Her friend had found a duvet cover they hadn't used for years: Ewan said his toes got caught in the lace hem. It looked so pretty in the warm light from the bedside lamp. The corner had been turned back to reveal the soft, perfectly white sheet beneath. There was a glass of water on the bedside table and the air smelled of the lavender candle burning on the dressing table. The flame was reflected in the three rectangles of mirror so that there were four of them. Four little lights watching over her.

Like a ghost, she drifted into the room and lay down on the bed. Was this a dream? Would she wake up tomorrow and find herself lying in blood? She found she couldn't muster any reaction to this thought and it floated away, leaving only drowsiness. The pillow was soft and full.

Electra gently laid the duvet over her and bent to kiss her forehead. 'Goodnight, my darling.'

Moments later, despite everything that had happened that night, Bella was asleep.

31

Skye

As Chrissy drove, Skye anxiously scanned the horizon, but it was still only four, and the sky wouldn't get completely light for around two hours. There were cars on the road, but surprisingly few. Night-shift workers perhaps, or insomniacs.

Her legs were squashed by the bin liner in the footwell and she shifted to try and make them more comfortable.

It contained the bloodied throw and bedding, which would all have to be burned. While the others had been dressing the corpse, Skye had been cutting the material into little pieces to be disposed of in her stove. It wasn't a pleasant job. Some parts were still wet and she could smell the blood as she snipped. She had also brought Bella's whole knife block, containing the murder weapon, to swap with her own.

It was only when thinking about her kitchen, her little boat with its colourfully painted hull, its flowers and ornaments and pictures, its innocence, that Skye regretted what she had agreed to.

It wouldn't be forever, that's what she kept telling herself, but she couldn't help but feel that afterwards the boat would be tainted somehow.

The car slowed to turn onto the embankment road, and Skye's heart began to beat faster. If she was going to back out, now was the last possible moment.

She didn't believe in God or Jesus, or any other of the patriarchal monotheisms, but she did believe there was a balance to the universe. That evil deeds came back to you in the end. Look what had happened to her teacher. A fifteen-year prison sentence for statutory rape, and now he had cancer. He would die in prison.

But their deed hadn't been evil, had it?

Surely it was the opposite. In helping Bella they had been showing love and loyalty. And Bella's own crime had been an act of madness, not premeditated hate. Nature was full of instinctual violence and destruction. Any female deity would understand.

Closing her eyes, she murmured a few of the words she had learned during a brief flirtation with wicca.

Goddess of the moon . . . join with me . . . allow me to feel your presence within my heart . . .

The car slowed to a halt. 'We'll get him onto that bench.'

Skye opened her eyes.

'And then I'll park up over there.' Chrissy gestured to a nearby street. 'Can you wait with him for a minute or so?'

Skye nodded. She had no choice.

They managed to get him out of the car and onto the bench that was shielded from the road by trees. He was too stiff now to manipulate into position and anyone passing would think he was performing some kind of plank exercise against the bench slats.

But no one was passing.

Skye sat there, staring straight ahead of her, trying not to notice how the wind rustling Bella's scarf sounded like gentle breathing beside her.

A sliver of moon was now visible between the horns of the power station, silvering the ripples on the water.

Her little boat was slumbering there, between the bigger vessels of the bankers and software developers, many of whom moved out before winter bit. Though she'd often complained bitterly about these fair-weather houseboaters, tonight it was a definite advantage. As soon as they'd lugged Ewan down the gangplank, low in the water now that the tide was out, their journey along the pier would be concealed from the road by the empty boats.

A breathless Chrissy returned, and without a word they heaved Ewan upright and dragged him across the pavement towards the pier gate. They were now exposed to the road, and to any passing road or river traffic. Skye was almost hoping to hear a voice, a slowing engine. To have this awful responsibility taken out of her hands.

But none came. She tapped in her code and the gate swung open. A moment later they were through and dragging the body, now concealed by the fretwork balustrade, towards the pier. After that it was easy. The wooden pier was smooth and the toes of Ewan's furry slippers slid easily across the damp slats.

Now they were hidden from all but the residents of the boats themselves and anyone peering across from the darkened park on the other side of the river.

They came to the familiar gangplank, with its sentry ponytail palms in terracotta pots, and laid down their burden.

After pausing a moment to roll out her shoulders, Skye crossed the gangplank and collected the skein of rope that hung by the cabin window. She'd just got back to Chrissy's side when there came a sound like a distant chainsaw. For a while Skye tried to figure out what it was, then with a lurch of the heart, she knew.

A police boat was approaching from the west, very fast.

They threw themselves onto the deck as the engine slowed. Glancing at her friend she saw that Chrissy was paralysed with terror, eyes starting from her head. Skye squeezed her own eyes shut and prayed.

The sound of the engine became a roar that vibrated through the slats of the pier. Water splashed against the supports, stirring up the rich green perfume of the river.

The boat was passing under Albert Bridge and now the engine slowed to a growl. Skye could hear voices coming from the vessel, quiet pop music echoing against the brickwork of the bridge struts.

At that moment a scrap of cloud blew across the moon, plunging the pier into darkness. The goddess had blinked her eye.

The vessel came level with them, the engine a low mutter. Through the pier slats Skye could see the lights from the boat dancing on the tips of the waves it had thrown up. Would they be bright enough to pick out the three shapes lying on the bridge, and if so, was there any chance they might take them to be piles of rope or tarpaulin?

A sharp laugh came from the boat. Then the engine roared. It sped away.

Skye exhaled. The goddess was with them.

'What the fuck?' Chrissy breathed when the engine had faded to silence. 'I thought we were dead.'

'They can't have seen us,' Skye whispered. 'They just slowed down so as not to rock the boats.'

They got to their knees and began to tie the body.

Then Skye's hands abruptly stopped moving. 'He's going to float.'

'No,' Chrissy said. 'No, the gases won't start forming for a while and by then we'll have got him away.'

'He didn't drown, so his lungs will still be full of air. He'll float.'

They stared at each other.

Chrissy said, 'I could go home and get something, a bike lock or . . .'

But there was no time. The glow of dawn had made silhouettes of the trees in the park opposite.

'The knife block,' Chrissy said. 'That's heavy. We'll weight him down.'

'But how do we attach it to him? It'll just slip off if we tie it.'

Chrissy blinked quickly, as if she was thinking, her mouth open, ready to save them. But nothing came.

'The anchor,' Skye said suddenly.

Chrissy stared. 'You have an actual anchor?'

'Yes, of course. But hang on . . .' Her heart sank. 'We'll have to move the boat to raise it. That would take a while, and the sound of the engine—'

'Oh, God . . .' Chrissy sank down, her head dropping to her

knees, in an aspect of surrender.

But Skye scrambled to her feet.

She had a special anchor for light mooring, on silt or mud. She'd never used it, it had come with the boat. But where was it?

Running across the ramp and down the steps she began opening cupboards. At some point Chrissy was standing beside her, asking what they were looking for, and soon the floor space was completely filled with the detritus they had yanked from the cupboards. Long-lost photograph albums and deflated yoga balls. Winter jumpers she'd forgotten she owned, baby toys and power tools. Books and pans and paint pots.

'Is this it?'

Skye turned. Chrissy was cradling a large red lump of metal topped with a broad cap. If there had been time, Skye would have hugged her. Instead she bolted back up on deck and began to make a reef knot with the end of the rope that bound Ewan.

When she had finished, when he was bound and weighted, the rope attached to a rowlock at the end of the stern, they stood beside one another and gazed down at the rather pathetic form, in its grubby fuchsia coat and furry slippers. It was oddly satisfying having complete control over him. Was this what those men had felt when they had her so subdued and powerless that they could do whatever they wanted to her? She nudged him with her foot and the bobble on the woolly hat jiggled.

A bitter wind had blown up, and the river was choppy, the boats clunking together bad-temperedly. Down in the small gully between the edge of the boat and the pier, the surface of the water was black and impenetrable.

'Ready?' Skye said.

Chrissy nodded. They bent and tucked their hands under Ewan's back and hip.

'One . . . two . . . three . . .'

It wasn't far to fall and he made barely a noise as he hit the water, sinking immediately, the ripples closing over his head and then fading away.

And that was it. It was done.

They straightened up.

A rim of the sun peeped over the trees in the park, turning the canopy blood red. Skye glanced at her watch. It was almost six. In an hour Pedro would be dropping Juniper back. Not long to clear up the devastation downstairs.

'Good morning,'

They turned sharply.

The software CEO stood on his deck in a dressing gown, nursing a steaming mug. 'Bit bracing today, isn't it?'

'Certainly is,' Chrissy said.

'I do like to watch the sun rise when I'm in London, though.'

'Yes,' said Chrissy. 'It's beautiful.'

They all stood there, watching the red sliver fatten and burnish. From the road behind them came the grumble of a bus. London was waking up.

'Right,' Chrissy said briskly. 'Home for a steaming bowl of porridge, I think.'

'Jolly good idea!' the CEO called.

'See you later, Skye.'

'Yes, see you soon.'

They embraced and Skye felt she might never let go.

32

Jen

'Jen's got a plan to keep them out of here,' Chrissy said.

Bella had looked at her with those wide, brown, trusting eyes, and for a moment that sense of power over another person gave Jen a head rush.

'We're going to make another crime scene.'

They had doubted her, she knew, all of them had. They didn't think she could pull it off. Deep down they were all certain they would get caught. Only Jen had faith. Chrissy was right, you *could* get away with murder. It wasn't hard to outsmart the police, whose imagination only stretched to the most basic of methods and motive. A robbery gone wrong, a gangland hit, domestic violence, child abuse. It wasn't their fault. Most criminals were as dull-witted as they were.

But not Jen.

There were so many forks in the path she had devised, so many tangling branches, that the poor stupid plod would get hopelessly snarled up.

And now, standing in the middle of the room, she surveyed her work, and was satisfied. It all worked perfectly. From the single black hair coiled like a taunting question mark, to the cereal bowl left on the side. Nice touch that, if she said so herself. No one left Weetabix to dry, it set like rock.

She had to admit that the unwashed sheets were down to slovenliness as opposed to cunning. But it was the perfect way to kill two birds with one stone: throw suspicion, however briefly, onto Eliot, while simultaneously scaring the crap out of him badly enough that he would never defy her again.

The lily-livered shit hadn't even bothered to try and call her, even though he knew she'd been ill. Not that she would have taken the call. He should have known better than to take her on in a power struggle. His mother was a slightly more formidable opponent, but she wouldn't be for much longer. It would be two against one when it came to loyalty, and the poor cow had no hope against those odds.

The blood had soaked through the kitchen roll now, so she went for another strip, carefully pocketing the wet one. It had taken several attempts to smash the glass of the table, and when her fist didn't work, she'd had to resort to bashing it with the marble mortar Eliot had got her for her birthday.

Then, and this was the hardest part of the whole night, she'd had to shred her hand with the zester of the cheese grater. It made her feel faint just thinking about it, but it had produced enough blood to liberally decorate the table and the kitchen floor.

The hand bandaged, it was time to go.

She took one last look round the flat, wondering when she would see it again, and let herself out into the darkened hall.

33

Iona

Present

It had taken a frustratingly long time to get the chief to sign off the warrant to search Bella Upton's property and it was mid-afternoon by the time they pulled up outside.

So that she could sit with Bella Upton, Iona had brought Yannis along to conduct the search, accompanied by a recent transfer to the department, Sami Hajjar. Absurdly tall, Sami would be able to see into the highest of cupboards and above all the wardrobes, but Iona found him mildly irritating.

'Come on then,' she said and got out.

Sami clambered out of the back seat, slamming the door too hard, and she and Yannis exchanged a glance.

With heavy feet she trudged up the steps to Bella Upton's front door. This would not be fun. Bella was bound to cry and comforting the distressed was not one of Iona's talents. Yannis would be far better at that part, but a couple of hours with Sami was a worse fate, as far as Iona was concerned.

Bella opened the door and her brown eyes widened.

'Hello, Mrs Upton. In light of our ongoing investigation into the disappearance of your husband and Jennifer Baptiste, we have a warrant to search your property.'

With a shaking hand Bella took the papers Yannis held out to her.

'These are details of your rights as occupier of the property and an address to send a request for compensation for any damage done.'

Bella's face crumpled and she began to cry. Iona's heart sank.

With his usual charm, Sami pushed past her into the house. She and Yannis followed, heading into the living room as a weeping Bella closed the door and crept in behind them.

'I d-don't understand,' she said. 'What am I supposed to have done?'

'It's just routine,' Iona said.

'You're entitled to have a friend or neighbour come in and witness the search,' Yannis said gently. 'Is there anyone you can call?'

'Chrissy,' Bella gasped and snatched the phone from her pocket.

She went out into the hall, but they all heard her end of the conversation.

'The police are here. They've got a warrant to search the house.'

Silence as the other woman spoke.

'They say I'm entitled to have someone witness the search. Can you come over?'

Silence again.

'How long will it take you? Okay, see you then.'

The other woman must have been at work, Iona thought, glancing at her watch. It was good of her to come, considering this friendship did not appear to be particularly important to her.

Bella came back into the room.

'She has to come from Blackfriars, so can you wait twenty minutes or so?'

Iona thought that twenty minutes was optimistic, but Yannis said of course they would wait and could he make everyone a cup of tea.

It had been half an hour. Sami was becoming restive. He had commenced his irritating habit of cracking his knuckles.

'I'm afraid, Mrs Upton,' Iona said, laying down her mug, 'that we are legally entitled to commence the search without a witness being present, in the event of an unreasonable delay.'

'Please,' Bella said. 'Just a few minutes more.'

Iona got up and wandered over to the window.

The street was deserted. A crow was tearing at a black bin bag on the opposite pavement and the litter spilling out was caught by the breeze and somersaulted along the pavement.

White flakes fell gently against the window. At first Iona though it was soot, but then, with a skip of the heart, she realised it was snowing. She only just managed to repress a childish urge to announce the fact. Christmas was coming. Again that childish sense of delight, before the reality set in that she would be spending it with her dreadful sister-in-law, and that she still hadn't got Maya's Secret Santa present.

Her scar started to itch as soon as she began to ponder what the hell to buy her colleague. Everything had some kind of dangerous connotation. It was a bloody minefield. The only consolation about the whole business, she thought, gazing out at the thick white sky, was that her roof might finally stop leaking.

'That's her!' Bella cried, for the third time, as an engine grew louder. She seemed to think that every passing vehicle contained her friend.

Yannis wandered up to join Iona at the window. 'We should just get on with it,' he murmured.

'It's not a Range Rover,' Iona said.

The car pulled in directly outside the house.

'See!' Bella cried.

Well, perhaps she was right this time. The neighbour on the left lived abroad and any friends of Marta the junkie would probably use public transport. This could be Chrissy.

The back door of the car opened and the passenger got out.

'What the fuck?' Yannis breathed.

It was Jennifer Baptiste.

243

34

Iona

Present

'Do you know how much time we wasted looking for you?'

'It's not my fault you let your imagination run away with you,' Jennifer Baptiste snapped.

Iona felt Yannis's gaze on her, but she didn't return it. They could have had this conversation back at Bella Upton's house, but Iona, incensed at the prospect of the humiliation this reappearance was going to cause her, had made Baptiste come into the station. The search had been promptly abandoned, and Sami had sniggered all the way back in the squad car. It must be all round the building by now, and to think she'd almost asked for forensics to attend. The chief would be booking her place on the diversity forum right now.

'Please tell me –' she was trying to maintain an air of authority but could tell the young woman was laughing at her '– where you spent the seven days from the fourth of December to the present.'

'The Hilton,' Jen said. 'In Islington.'

'The hotel?'

'Thought I deserved a bit of pampering.'

'That must have set you back. How did you pay for it, seeing as you left your wallet at home?'

'I took my credit card, didn't I? I ain't stupid.' She laughed.

Iona briefly closed her eyes. 'And may I ask why you left your phone at home?'

'Because me and my boyfriend had a row and I didn't want him pestering me. It was a last-minute thing. I was hungover and I just wanted to get away and detox before Christmas.'

'We found blood in your flat and signs of a struggle.'

'Like I said, we had a row.' She held up her hand to reveal lacerations that had scabbed over but must have been painful at the time.

Yannis sat straighter in his chair. 'Did he do that to you?'

Jennifer laughed. 'No. I did it myself thumping the table. He was really pissing me off.'

'Were you arguing about Ewan Upton?'

'Ewan Upton?' Jen raised her eyebrows. 'Er, *no*, why?'

'Because he's missing too.'

She waggled her finger. 'Ain't no *too* about it. I never went missing.'

'How well did you know Ewan Upton?'

'He's my boss.'

'Were you friendly?'

'Not particularly.'

'You see, that surprises me, because there were a number of calls between the two of you in the weeks before his disappearance.'

For the first time Jennifer Baptiste looked uncomfortable. 'Yeah, well, I was worried about Bella. We had a few conversations about it.'

'Why worried?'

'I thought she might be . . . depressed.'

'Were you worried about Teddy's safety?'

'Not at all, no. She would never do anything to hurt him. She just seemed a bit down.'

'What did Ewan say when you spoke to him about this.'

Jen snorted. 'Not much.'

'Did anything of a romantic nature happen between the two of you?'

Jen grimaced. 'You *seen* Ewan? I got better taste than that.'

It was perfectly true that, though she might not fancy Eliot herself, Iona could tell that he was attractive. Ewan, on the other hand, looked, from the photographs, as if he was settling into middle age the same way most straight men seemed to: hair thinning, waist thickening. For a woman as interested in appearances as Baptiste clearly was, it was an unlikely pairing.

'Do you have any idea where he might have gone?'

'France? Bolivia? Kazakhstan? Why the hell would I know?'

Iona's eyes narrowed. Baptiste might play the mouthy-girl card, but she was clearly clever. 'Please don't be flippant, Miss Baptiste. Just answer my questions.'

The young woman looked at her steadily and Iona felt a strange stirring of desire mixed with unease. Jennifer Baptiste was formidable. A good friend, perhaps, but certainly a dangerous enemy.

'A significant amount was taken from the accounts of some of Ewan Upton's clients. Do you have any idea what happened to the money?'

'Look, I'm their childminder, that's all.'

'And Bella's friend.'

'Not especially.'

'Friend enough to be worried about her. Friend enough to come straight round as soon as you got back from your little jolly.'

'Yes. When I heard about what happened with Ewan, I came straight round. Like anyone would. The poor cow's having a nightmare.'

'But you haven't been back to your flat, yet, have you? You got the Uber straight from the Hilton. So who told you?'

'I saw it on Facebook.'

Iona glanced at Yannis. The women's social media pages had very high privacy settings and it was impossible to see who had posted what and when.

Iona sat back in the chair. She'd run out of questions. They would have to let this woman go. Apparently Eliot Goulding was already waiting for her at the front desk. When they'd released her stuff back to her she'd called him straightaway.

'Are we done?' Jennifer said.

Underneath the heavy make-up and street style she was a beautiful young woman. Iona could picture how she would look first thing in the morning, long black eyelashes resting on her clear cheek, dark hair spread across the pillow. But she could never be in love with this woman. She was too hard, too calculating. The way she was looking at Iona now, cool and totally unruffled, suggested she could read Iona's mind, scent out the weakness and doubt.

'Yes,' Iona said softly. 'We are. Thank you for your time.'

Jennifer got up and, as Yannis opened the door, swept out of the interview room.

He held the door open for Iona too, but she didn't follow, just leaned back in her chair and tipped her head back.

This whole thing had been a total waste of time. Her first unsolved case. A blot on an otherwise unblemished record. She knew most police officers had at least a dozen failures in the course of their careers, but this was a first, and it hurt.

She'd been so sure there was more to the disappearance of Upton than met the eye. The motives were all there: jealousy, fear, rage. A cast of characters with ambivalent feelings for one another. Opportunity. Means.

But she had been wrong.

'Well,' Yannis said quietly, sitting down at the chair Jen had just vacated. 'I guess the Baptiste murder case is closed.'

'Don't.'

'Ah, don't worry about it. There was definitely something funny about it all. I reckon she set the whole thing up to get back at her boyfriend. Poor bastard.'

'Do you think they did row about Ewan Upton?'

Yannis shrugged. 'Maybe. But if there was anything going on he'd have been in touch with her by now, wouldn't he?'

'Unless she took a burner phone with her to the hotel and spoke to him from there. We could check all the calls she made and received on the hotel phone, and whether or not she had any visitors. He might have gone there before he left the country. And we could organise a surveillance team to watch her.'

Yannis sighed. 'Okay, boss.'

'Don't sound so enthusiastic,' she snapped.

'Look, why don't we just hand it over to Fraud? They'll be pissed off enough already that we left it so long.'

Iona understood how he felt. It was nearly Christmas, and there would be more than enough to occupy their time in silly season. Besides, the whole thing had become a complete embarrassment. She would need a swift and dramatic success in the near future to regain her former esteem in the office.

'Boss?'

Dogging the heels of middle-class mothers for no other reason than an old-fashioned hunch was, frankly, old-fashioned and in the modern force there wasn't the luxury for that romantic style of policing.

From the offices beyond came an extremely loud burst of 'All I want for Christmas is You'. Iona had always liked that song. The young Mariah Carey had been her first real crush. No doubt they would be playing it, and all the other cheesy classics, *ad nauseam*, tonight, until everyone was up and dancing. They'd booked the room above the Paxton's Head. The office Christmas party always took place in this small rather atmosphereless pub round the back of the Kings Road. The proprietors were prepared to put up with the raucous behaviour of the local constabulary in return for the blind eye that was turned to after-hours drinking the rest of the year. It would be hot and cramped and with a bit of luck no one would notice her absence.

'Iona?'

'Okay,' Iona sighed. 'Can it.'

'Right.' Yannis jumped up and bounded out of the room.

248

Iona followed with slower steps and wandered through the rapidly emptying offices. Most people were already in the pub. On the carpet were stray ribbons of tinsel and little sprinklings of glitter. She passed Maya's desk. In the bin was the cheap paper she'd used to wrap the Secret Santa present she'd asked Darcy to buy for her on the way back from the Uptons'. She felt a moment's guilt at the thoughtlessness of the gift, but pushed it away. Maya wouldn't care. She was probably planning to get off with Yannis tonight.

Walking up to the window she saw a red Toyota parked on the double yellows directly outside the station. A man got out of the driver's door. She was about to rap on the glass to tell him to move when he raised his head and she saw it was Eliot Goulding. He was frowning anxiously, his gaze fixed on the reception area of the station.

And then suddenly his face lit up. There was no other word to describe it. It may have been the lights on the wet road, or the general Christmas sparkle radiating from every window, but she could see his eyes shining from up here.

Jennifer Baptiste skipped down the steps towards him.

Placing a palm against the cold glass, Iona wondered if anyone would ever look at her that way.

The young couple clashed into one another and clung there. Iona could see, even from up here, the way Eliot's biceps tightened as he held her, their heads pressed together.

Her breath misted the glass and for a moment they disappeared. She wiped it with her sleeve.

Now Eliot was holding Jen at arm's length, looking at her with something like consternation. Then a grin spread across his handsome face and, pulling her back into his arms, he swung her around and around and around.

Iona went back to her desk and started drafting her report for Fraud.

*

249

The phone rang just after nine. It was the chief. She could barely hear him for the music and bellowing.

'Sorry? I didn't catch—'

'WHERE THE FUCK ARE YOU?'

'Just finishing up the Baptiste case, sir.'

'There is no Baptiste case. I expect to see you walking into this bar in the next fifteen minutes or you really will be doing the diversity forum.'

'I thought I was anyway.' She winced at a particularly loud burst of masculine braying.

'Maya beat you to it, I'm afraid. Triply diverse that one: woman, black *and* gay. All she needs is a disability for a full house.'

'Maya?' Iona repeated. 'Maya Wierucki?'

'Yes, that one. She's been asking where you are, so show your face, the troops like it.'

'On my way, sir.'

The room was hot and smelly and pounded like the ventricle of a heart. She almost turned round on the threshold, but then someone coming in behind her propelled her forwards and into the sweating throng. Sami was dancing slackly, arms raised to reveal huge wet patches on his shirt. The chief was having a heated discussion with one of the junior officers who apparently *reminded him of himself at that age*, so would certainly be fast-tracked for promotion. The narcissism of the old boys' network. She couldn't think of anything worse than being reminded of herself at a young age: intense, humourless, self-righteous.

She spotted Yannis, laughing with a group of lads in the corner. Where the others looked as drunk as they were, their eyes hooded and their movements blurred, Yannis glowed. He was the one, she thought, who should go all the way to the top. He knew when to stop, where she would waste all her energy and resources chasing some gut feeling. It had always been so. She was the girl who had worked until 3 a.m. revising for

A-levels, had fundraised so tirelessly for Shelter one Christmas that she'd collapsed, had trained for weeks for the bleep test. It was a gift, knowing when you were beaten. One she wasn't blessed with. But tonight she would try and forget the Baptiste/ Upton case. She would have a few drinks with Yannis and talk about the football or the price of beer.

But then Yannis was blocked from her view.

Maya was coming towards her, her skin burnished by the Christmas lights, her tight curls woven with the translucent wrappers from a tin of Quality Street, like bright jewels.

Iona went to meet her.

35

The Mothers

After

It was warm enough to sit out on the deck while the boat chugged upriver. They had already passed out of the environs of the city, past Twickenham and Hampton, Walton and Staines, to Runnymede, where the river was bounded by quiet water meadows and woodland.

Eight hundred years ago this was the place another contract, another promise of loyalty, had been made and kept.

The sky above was cloudless blue except for a few fine plane trails. The trees were bursting with pink and white blossom like confetti ready to fall, and the air was scented with honeysuckle.

Jen and Electra lay on towels on the deck in their bikinis, while Chrissy sat with Skye at the tiller, sipping gin and tonic. It had taken a long time to get here, with one of the anchors dragging along behind. But they were making faster progress now that they'd dropped Bella off, at a waterside pub a mile or so previously.

The boat made a slow turn around a bow in the river and at once the current slackened.

Chrissy leaned over the railing. The water must be deep. The riverbed was out of sight, even in the full glare of the sunlight.

'Here?' she said.

Skye nodded and chugged the boat to the inner edge of the bend, where the water would be at its deepest. The bank was undercut here, where the flow had eroded it. If they were very lucky a section might soon collapse, burying whatever rested on the riverbed beneath.

Skye went to the cleat at the prow and began unwinding the wet rope, lowering it back into the water. After a moment, the line went slack and she felt, through its vibrations, the anchor thud onto the riverbed.

It was time.

Electra got to her feet, taking a moment to admire the tanned concavity of her stomach. She was back to her pre-baby weight, so perhaps it had all been worth it after all. Ho ho.

Zack claimed not to like her new boniness and insisted on bringing home the unsold cakes from the university café where he worked between lectures: made her hot chocolate with double cream and marshmallows before bed.

Walking over to the railing she gazed down into the dark water. A face she no longer recognised looked back at her. It had been a long time since she had been that troubled, despairing woman who had told Zack she no longer loved him, but the memory of the pain she caused them both drew her face back into the old lines that were still there in her muscle memory.

He'd cried when she told him that she'd made a terrible mistake, the worst of her life, in letting him go. He'd been calling Thea's number to end their burgeoning relationship even before she had stopped speaking, but she stayed his hand. There was a condition and it was a big one. Firstly, he had to go back to university.

They couldn't afford it, and besides, he was happy with his job and his family. Maybe they could even have another?

No, he was going to be a journalist, like he always wanted, and now they *could* afford it.

How?

253

That was the condition. She could not tell him.

But they were always honest with one another, weren't they?

Not this time. This one time it had to stay her secret. The promise she had made wasn't just hers to keep.

Had there been someone else? It didn't matter, he forgave her, but was there some rich Daddy she'd managed to screw the money out of?

No.

Eventually he'd agreed to abide by the rule. Thea had been duly called, and apologised to, and her pain would be added to the burden of Electra's guilt, but she was young, she would get over it.

'Lec?' She turned. Chrissy was waiting for her. Smiling, she slipped on her flip-flops and headed for the ramp.

Skye stripped off on the deck. Her tattooed body never felt exposed, not like before, when it was baby pink and so deliciously easy to bruise and redden. She was tempted, for a moment, to send a picture to Mort. He was in an important pitch today and she loved the idea of him opening up a shot of her pierced labia right in the middle of the CEO's speech. But she'd pretended she was having a quiet day at home and didn't want him asking too many questions. He was smart and perceptive enough to be hard to lie to.

It was one of the many reasons, alongside his gentleness, his humour and his selfless lovemaking, that she loved him. She was deciding whether or not to tell him. It wouldn't make any difference: she would not invite him to live with her, suggest they had a child, or ask to meet his parents. It would just be another nice thing they shared, like the Netflix access code and the two-seater kayak they sometimes took up to Greenwich.

She would never tell him what she had done, however, not just because the fates of other people rested on her silence, but because she had seen what men who professed to love you, who you trusted implicitly, were capable of. She would love Mort at a distance she was comfortable with, until the weather turned, and then she would move on. Raise anchor and sail away with her daughter. It was high time they adventured beyond London, England, maybe even Europe, and for that reason she'd decided to home-educate Juniper. There was a big wide world out there and it was fast becoming a woman's one. She'd thought she wanted money to settle down, but it turned out to be the opposite: money meant freedom. It meant not having to rent out her womb to Pedro and Felippe. It meant that she could teach her daughter, with no hint of hypocrisy, that a woman's body, like her life, was entirely her own.

Pulling on her tankini, she went to join the others.

Chrissy stared at herself for a long time in Skye's bedroom mirror and tried to remember what she had looked like when Atanis had last held her. She'd cut her hair since then, deciding that forty-five was high time to lose the shoulder-blade-length curtain she'd had since childhood. Her new sharp crop made her look suitably formidable and she'd noticed a distinct change in the behaviour of men towards her. They were deferential rather than flirtatious. As a consequence, she smiled less. Russell, on the other hand, seemed happier than he had ever been, thrilled perhaps by the fact that his wife could no longer command male attention, that she had become just another decaying middle-aged woman, while he remained as attractive as ever. He teased her about the lone black hair that sprouted on her chin.

It was this, this weakness, that had finally ended her feelings for him. Next year, when Chloe started school, she would set in motion her plans to divorce him.

Chrissy pulled on the frumpy Boden swimsuit Russell had bought her for her birthday and went back up.

In the fields that bordered the river, the wheat had already grown tall and was starting to turn from green to gold. It was high enough that they wouldn't be able to see anyone coming

255

along the bank, but neither could they be seen: someone would have to come right around the bend. Jen and Electra had drawn the long straws and would keep watch at either end of the bank while the other two did the dirty work.

They parted. Jen walking towards the western edge of the bend, Electra walking east. The white disc of the sun was still low in the sky. By midday it would be blisteringly hot.

Skye and Chrissy stood on the bank, preparing themselves for the plunge into the dark water.

The green rope hanging from the cleat at the stern thrummed gently, as if bony fingers were plucking at it.

Skye handed Chrissy a mask. The sight of one another's noses squashed against the glass made them laugh and they had to force themselves to repress it. A fit of the giggles would impact their ability to hold their breath, and they wanted to get this over quickly. On a day like this there would be dog-walkers and hikers about.

'Ready?' Skye said nasally.

'Ready.' Chrissy took her hand.

They jumped.

The shock of the cold took their breaths away and they surfaced, gasping, kicking out at anything that might seek to grasp their ankles and pull them down into the weed that tickled the soles of their feet.

'Weed,' Chrissy gasped. 'That's good. It'll hold it down.'

As the cold seeped into their flesh, cooling their blood, their hearts settled. They trod water, heads bobbing in the warm air, the sun glinting off the water droplets that jewelled their hair, while their bodies floated in darkness, watched by eyes they could not see.

And yet, the water was not as opaque as it had looked from above. It was possible to see a foot or so in front of your face, but even so, each woman felt vulnerable, glad that the other was within touching distance. Two were not really needed for the job in hand, but they were both there 'just in case'.

In case the cold gets to you.

Or you get cramp.

Or you need to fight off a vengeful corpse.

They held hands, their body warmth passing between them, like a promise, then, kicking off the sandy bank, they swam out into the deeper water where the rope disappeared. The skin of their submerged arms was green and each woman thought for a moment about her own death and the decay of her body.

Inhaling, they dived into the dark.

Chrissy immediately lost her sense of direction and blundered about in a brown fog of panic, unable to tell up from down. Then she felt Skye's hand reaching for hers.

She grasped it. And knew at once she'd made a terrible mistake.

Her kicking feet brought her exploding to the surface with a scream.

The bones had been as soft as the cartilage of a roast chicken. The flesh pulpy and so cold.

'You all right?' Electra called from the bank.

'Y-yes,' she stammered.

She was in danger of hyperventilating. But Skye was still down there. Alone in the dark with the corpse. Chrissy couldn't just abandon her. Swallowing down the surge of vomit that burned her throat, she took a breath and went back down.

Skye knew how to untie a reef knot, so this task would be hers alone.

The weight of Ewan's body pulling the rope taut made it more difficult, but she could not bear to clamp him under her arm, and prayed that as she jerked and tugged, his dead face wouldn't come swimming from the gloom. She wasn't sure she could handle that.

The rope was slippery with algae and once or twice she despaired. And then suddenly her forefinger found a tiny loop.

She worked it in, digging and pulling until the loop became wider and the knot became looser. And then suddenly it gave. The rope slackened, Ewan rolled away and she was left holding the mushroom anchor.

She kicked to the surface and Chrissy burst out beside her.

'I did it,' Skye panted. 'Are we done?'

'We should strip him,' Chrissy said. 'Otherwise, if they find him, it'll look suspicious. Let the clothes just drift.'

Skye felt like crying.

Electra had googled *Bodies decomposing in water* on one of the work computers (frequently used for such searches to check the veracity of plotlines), and had discovered that after a few weeks submerged a body could only be recognised by DNA and dental records. With most of the soft tissue in an advanced state of decay it would not even be possible to tell how the victim had died, and without any obvious head injuries it would look like suicide.

But Chrissy was right. A fuchsia coat might make the authorities think twice.

Electra, who had read a great many thriller submissions, had also informed them that because the water here was deep, slow-moving and very cold under a canopy of trees, the gases formed by the bacterial decomposition of his tissues would take far longer to bring the body to the surface. By then Ewan would be unrecognisable, and almost certainly in bits. As this stretch of river was rich in wildlife such as pike and otter, he may even have been eaten. If they were really lucky, his teeth and smaller bones would be spirited away by helpful weasels.

Jen whistled sharply.

A couple was strolling along the bank.

Jen engaged them in conversation, keeping their backs to the water while Chrissy and Skye swam around to the other side of the boat. Jen managed to keep them talking even as they walked on and, listening carefully to the voices, Skye and Chrissy edged themselves around the hull until they heard Electra call a cheery goodbye.

'Right.' Chrissy smiled wanly, her teeth chattering. 'My turn.'
'Wait. I'll get you a knife.'

Against every human instinct – of disgust, fear, dread and self-preservation – Chrissy went back down. She had no real idea where the body had ended up and had to resurface several times before finally locating it, wedged tightly against the vertical side of the bank, beneath the overhang. When she felt along its length the water clouded with sediment, like a ghost looming from the depths. He was already being buried.

The hat and scarf and slippers were long gone and the coat was ragged. But before she could take it off she would have to cut the ropes that bound him.

For one terrifying moment, as she sawed away with the bluntest knife she had ever used, she was sure that his legs twitched. But that only happened in horror films, and this wasn't a horror film. It was a lovely day out in the countryside. *Five Women and a Boat.*

Finally the rope frayed and broke. As it unravelled she felt his arms sigh out from his sides, as if to embrace her. Biting down the urge to kick away, she grasped the collar of the coat and pulled. Something stuck. Something pulled away. The water became cloudy with white matter, and then the coat was free.

She swam towards the other bank, where the current was faster, and let the coat and the rope be taken by the stream.

Then she resurfaced.

The sun glinted on the water. Iridescent dragonflies bobbed over it in pursuit of the flies dancing in the reflections. In the distance, a tractor engine growled cheerfully.

Skye was beside her, her tanned face glittering with water droplets.

'Done,' she panted. 'We're done.'

*

'The chicken burger for me,' said Jen, 'with sweet potato fries and no onion.'

'Beetroot risotto, please,' said Skye.

'Sea bass,' said Electra, 'but salad instead of the veg.' The teenage waitress dutifully noted it.

'I'll have the battered cod,' said Bella. 'And so will my friend. She's just freshening up.' She smiled up into the waitress's face, but the girl did not glance at her. Poor frumpy Bella who nobody ever noticed, who was capable of nothing but being slightly pitiful. Her smiled broadened. This morning Chrissy had transferred sixty-two thousand pounds into her bank account. The plan was to use most of it to pay off the mortgage arrears, but she had her eye on a little yellow Triumph Spitfire she'd seen in the back pages of the *Chelsea Times*.

She felt an optimism about the future that she hadn't experienced for years, though she would keep taking the tablets.

The delusions had stopped after Ewan's death. There were no more butterfly wings or bloody eggs or defaced pictures. Nothing else materialised on her Kindle, and the tiger never made another appearance.

This left her with an uncomfortable dilemma, because there were two possibilities as far as she could tell. The first was that she had imagined it all because her subconscious felt threatened by him. But the second was more troubling.

What if Ewan had been *trying* to send her crazy?

Perhaps he'd wanted to get her sectioned, out of his hair so she couldn't complain about how much time he spent 'working', or make any inconvenient discoveries about their finances. But there was an even worse option. During that first bout of illness she had, once, tried to take her life, in the hospital with a broken tooth glass. She'd been discovered immediately and fixed up, but once that door had been opened there was always the possibility that she might try again. Her stepfather always insisted on reminding Ewan to 'keep an eye on her'. Ewan would roll his eyes, but perhaps he had absorbed the suggestion, and as the money ran out and he started to hate her, 'suicide' could have seemed like an attractive idea. Maybe he'd even insured her life. It was an outlandish theory, but she couldn't seem to shake it, and perhaps she shouldn't, since, instead of guilt and grief about her husband's demise, it left her with a sense of grim satisfaction – a battle won. She'd got there before he did.

Chrissy came back, her hands and forearms scrubbed red.

Bella looked down at her friend's hands and wondered at the dark matter in the corner of her little fingernail. But before her brain could bloom into imaginings, she snapped the mental elastic-band and thought of the way Teddy would look standing on the side of the pool at the Greek villa she'd booked for the summer. Her parents and her sister and brother-in-law would be there. The first family holiday they'd had since her marriage.

The champagne arrived. Chrissy opened it deftly and started pouring the glasses. It sparkled in the sunlight filtering through the old glass in the windows.

It was an old pub, the original building dating back to just a hundred years after the Magna Carta was signed. The walls were covered with the inevitable Magna-Carta-themed curios: a copy of the original signed document, paintings of the king being forced to sign by the rebel barons, a wax replica of the king's seal used to ratify the pledge, red as a splodge of fresh blood.

'Not for me.' Jen put her hand over her glass.

They looked at her in consternation.

'But this is a celebration,' Skye said.

Jen smiled. Then she patted her stomach. 'A double celebration.'

At the shriek from their table, all the other pub-goers turned round.

'I thought you were just getting fat!' Electra squealed.

'How far gone are you?' Chrissy said.

'Four months,' Jen grinned. 'And he's fine. Perfectly fine. This time I managed to cross the threshold of the hospital and get scanned.'

Once the excitement had died down and a lemonade had been ordered for Jen, the women settled themselves and a hush descended. Even the toddlers at the large table in the corner seemed to sense that something important was happening because they stopped fighting over their father's mobile phone and turned back to their food.

At the table by the window, the women raised their glasses. Their eyes passed over one another in turn, catching and holding before moving on. The chav. The media-twat. The hippy. The Sloane. The frump. Nothing in common whatsoever. Nothing but the only thing in the world that could ever matter or have meaning. Life and love.

Forever.

Whatever.

They drank and put their glasses down. And then the food arrived.

36

Jen

He was such a strong little boy. She'd laughed when he said he could carry her that first day, then shrieked as he lifted her off her feet and she almost toppled head first over him onto the sofa. After that difficult birth, when he'd almost died, it was as if his subconscious had seized life with an iron will to survive and thrive. Other than an early bout of chickenpox that had imprinted a single perfect circle on his round tummy, Bella told her he'd never had a day's sickness. He was allergic to nothing, and ate whatever was put in front of him. At first, Jen had been bitterly jealous – how could this frumpy, middle-aged woman have created such a robust child when she, ten years younger and kickboxing-fit, could not? But as time went on and she noticed more of his father's characteristics – the sturdy frame, heavy brow, large and powerful hands, she began to wonder. Did those fighting genes come from Ewan?

Sometimes he was there when she arrived in the morning, power-gulping a coffee in the kitchen while Bella was upstairs getting ready for work. Regarding him in his Lycra cycling gear, back hair tufting up from his collar, love handles quivering above the waistband of his shorts, she wondered at how Bella could bring herself to sleep with him. If Eliot ever let himself go like that he'd be out the door.

'I brought some pastries from GAIL's,' she said. 'Want one?'

He turned and gave her a smug smile. 'Would kind of make cycling to work pointless, wouldn't it?'

'A lifetime on the hips, eh?' she said, grinning through her distaste.

'Exactly. You've gotta work harder at it at my age. Your time will come.'

She leaned back against the worktop and pushed out her new breasts. 'Not me. I'll still have it at ninety.'

'I don't doubt it,' Ewan said, looking her up and down in a manner that was, frankly, creepy. 'Right, I'm off,' he said.

'I'll tell Bella you said goodbye, shall I?'

'If you like.'

She watched him leave with a mixture of contempt and pity for her friend. And something else. The tight green bud of an idea.

The following morning she brought him a wheatgrass smoothie and giggled delightedly as he winced his way through it. Afterwards, he said, 'Thanks . . . I think,' which was one of the most predictable pieces of banter she'd ever heard.

'You're welcome. Now I'd like one of those posh coffees, please.'

She watched him as he made it, whacking levers on and off, twisting dials, banging metal implements into the sink, clearly loving the way the machine whirred and hissed under his manly touch.

When he finally handed it to her she knew she had to make a big deal out of it.

'Mmmmmmm,' she said, closing her eyes and licking the froth off her lips. Then she added, 'It's as good as Starbucks.'

This set him off, droning on and on about the perfect temperature above which the milk would scald, where to get the best beans. How the *general public* didn't deserve decent coffee.

'Oh, I don't, do I?' she said archly.

'I didn't say you.'

'So, I'm special?'

'Oh, absolutely.'

There was a pause. He couldn't think of a way to continue the flirtation, so she stepped in.

'Think you'd better educate my amateur tongue, then?'

He swallowed. Grinned. Said, 'Okay,' then tossed the dregs of his coffee in the sink and scampered out.

It had been easy after that. A few more mornings sipping coffee, standing ever closer, while Bella banged around upstairs, flushing the toilet and running the electric toothbrush. Then one morning he came down later, took longer to get ready, and Bella left before he did.

They fucked in the hall while Teddy watched TV. Ewan came quickly, grunting like a pig, while she pretended to, pushing him away afterwards, laughing breathlessly as if in surprised delight. 'Oh my *God!*'

He gave this slick smirk then, as if he'd done something really clever, arched an eyebrow and said, 'See you later.'

She showered off his stickiness and rinsed out her knickers, drying them with Bella's hairdryer before making Teddy his mid-morning snack. Whatever the others thought, that was the first time she'd ever been unfaithful to Eliot. But it had been for a good cause, and conscience had never been much of a problem to her.

It was a fortnight, supposedly, until you could do a test. She let Ewan fuck her every day for that two-week period, sometimes in the morning, sometimes at lunchtime when he popped back from work. Once in the evening, when she stayed late so that Bella could fill in forms for the HR department. That was the time she felt sorriest for her friend. Leaning across the kitchen table while Ewan shunted her from behind, mouth-breathing, biting his lower lip in some toe-curling impression of a rock star, as the lasagne cheese burned under the grill. She could see his buttocks juddering in the microwave's black door.

It was starting to make her nauseous, his raggedy foreskin, the

265

ingrowing hairs that pimpled his pasty flesh, the tongue probing her mouth like a questing grub. She had been with Eliot so long she took for granted his delicate features, his smooth, caramel skin and the definition of his body: thought it was nothing special. But now she knew different. For the first time in her life she'd even had to resort to lube. If only it could have been Joe. But even Eliot might notice if his baby was mixed-race.

He came quickly that evening, then went off to his study to catch up on the 'work' that Jen had been convinced was kiddie porn, until his request that she wore crotchless panties convinced her that his libido was as conventional as the rest of him.

When she was completely sure – even though it was still early she trusted to the fact that all his cells would be as robust as the rest of him – she ended it.

She tried to do it as nicely as possible, after Bella had gone to work one day, telling him she just couldn't do it to her friend any more, that she fancied him but she loved Eliot. That he would always be special to her. All the bullshit.

But he wouldn't take no for an answer. He started calling her four or five times a day, sending texts at times he must have known Eliot would be around, claiming he just wanted to talk. Afraid Eliot's curiosity would be piqued by these late-night notifications, she started distancing herself from him, making up excuses not to see him. Until he decided that he was being taken for granted and flounced off back to his mum's.

That was the final straw. She called Ewan and agreed to discuss things the following morning while Teddy napped. She was prepared for one final goodbye fuck, *no hard feelings, Ewan*. What she wasn't prepared for was what he said, quite calmly, over artisan coffees at the kitchen table, surrounded by the crumbs of Bella's toast.

'I'll tell all of them. Eliot, Bella, all your friends. You'll lose everything.'

'You wouldn't,' she said. 'You'd lose everything too.'

'See, that's what I've got on you, *babe*.'

266

She winced.

'I don't have anything to lose. There is literally fuck all in my life that I care about.'

'Well, that must include me then, so let me go, Ewan, please.'

She wasn't really expecting it to work.

He sat back in his seat and folded his arms, the twist of his mouth making him ugly. 'You are not going anywhere, unless you want to end up with no friends, no career – clients don't much like childminders shagging Daddy – and no precious Eliot.'

She pressed her lips together. Would he really go through with this? If so, he'd lose her anyway, and Bella would divorce him. No. No, she wouldn't. She would forgive him. He must know that.

But she wouldn't forgive Jen. It would be all her fault for 'seducing' him. The other mums would feel the same way, scared that she might move on to one of theirs.

And what about Eliot? Could she tell him the truth? Would he understand that she'd done it for the two of them? Would he ever love her again the same way?

'I know you're pregnant.'

She froze. 'H-how . . . ?

Ewan started to laugh. 'Well, I only suspected actually, because of all that puking the other morning, but *now* I know. And I know you'll want to keep it too. *Poor Jen and her poor dead baby.*'

She almost snatched up the breadknife from the breadboard and plunged it into his stomach.

'You're a single parent, and everyone knows your relationship is *fiery*, which is just code for violent. If it went to court, who do you think would get custody of the baby? The middle-class professional with the stable home – or you?' He looked her up and down with disdain and she realised that all these weeks he'd just been hate-fucking her. As much as she despised him, he despised her more.

Hatred swelled in her skull, making the silence between them hiss, but when she finally spoke her voice remained steady. 'Give me time to think what to say to Eliot.'

'You've got a week.'

'Two. Please.'

'It'll cost you.'

While Teddy played with his train set, she gave Ewan a blowjob, kneeling on the cold tiles of the kitchen floor. His stubby cock triggered her gag reflex at every thrust. After a few minutes, she looked up to see if he was nearly done. His nostrils were flared, his lips parted and moist, his eyes closed. What was he fantasising about? she wondered. That he was raping her? That she was crying and begging him to stop?

As he grunted to climax, holding her head in place, she hated him more then than she'd ever hated anything or anyone in her whole life. And that was when the plan bloomed black and brilliant in her mind.

Jen had often wondered if she had been born without an empathy gene. Sometimes she thought she might be the *psycho* Eliot always said she was. Certainly she felt no guilt about what she decided to do. The one thing that gave her hope – no, not hope: she didn't really care either way – the one thing that was *evidence* she might be a normal person after all was that she was capable of love. She loved Eliot, always would, with a flaming passion that was sometimes blind hatred, till the day she died. She had loved her daughter as she held her limp in her arms for the few moments she allowed herself before pushing the baby, and all her feelings for her, away. And she loved her friends. Including Bella. But however bad it felt at the time, this would be good for Bella in the long term.

She began by replacing Bella's medication.

The white oval risperidone tablets were almost identical to paracetamol. You were not supposed to come off antipsychotic medication suddenly, and if you did there was a serious risk of experiencing a psychotic episode. But apart from a general increase in Bella's anxiety there didn't seem to be any noticeable effects, at least at first. It didn't really matter, though. Jen had other plans.

She started small. A few words here and there, some comments that would throw a normal person, let alone someone with doubts about their sanity. Then she moved on to bigger things. Watching the family closely enough to be able to choose just what would push Bella's buttons. With free reign of the empty house while Teddy napped, the ideas tumbled into her mind like confetti and it was a job to restrain herself. *Keep it small*, she told herself. Enough to make Bella uneasy but not to seek medical help. On Skye's boat she had flicked through the pages of her spirituality books, learned about the concept of the soul, stuff normal kids who went to decent schools probably knew about anyway. She'd been particularly proud of the egg. Carefully blowing it like her grandmother had shown her, then injecting blood into it with a Calpol syringe, before sealing it with wax. There was a chance Ewan wouldn't break it in Bella's presence, but even the description would freak her out.

It was six days before Ewan's deadline when Bella came home from a particularly enjoyable day at work. Jen made herself laugh at all the silly anecdotes about her gay work colleague, upon whom she clearly had a pointless crush. She wanted Bella to feel good for as long as possible. It might be a long time before her friend felt happy again.

Mothers Club was at Chrissy's that night, and Jen was determined that Bella would have a nice time. But Bella arrived at Chrissy's sobbing.

Jen was frozen to the spot as Bella choked out that she had had a row with Ewan.

'What about?' Chrissy had said gently, and Jen had held her breath.

'He's been g-gambling,' Bella stuttered. 'We've lost everything.'

Baby or no baby, Jen had to have a drink to calm her nerves. It could so easily have been a different admission. Bella said he had stolen money from his work too. Now that his life was unravelling, might he want to bring Jen down with him? Surely it was only a question of time.

No one noticed what they were drinking, so engrossed were they with comforting Bella. Jen made cocktails in Chrissy's kitchen, keeping every glass refreshed, giving Bella twice as much vodka as everyone else, until she was slurring and lolling on the sofa. The gathering broke up unhappily, everyone concerned that this added stress might make their fragile friend do something stupid.

As Chrissy drove them back through the rain-glossed street, Jen felt excitement blooming in her chest. An excitement she had only felt once before, when the same promise of freedom from tyranny had come into her reach.

Chrissy helped her get Bella up the steps, but there was clearly somewhere else she wanted to be, which worked just fine for Jen. A little bit of extra guilt from Chrissy would be useful. Chrissy was a doer.

Jen told her she would make sure Bella got to bed, and they said goodbye.

After she'd settled Bella on the sofa under the turquoise throw, Jen got out her phone, took a photo, attached it to a WhatsApp message and forwarded it to the mums.

Sleeping beauty.

Then she went into the kitchen.

It didn't take long to find gloves. The fuchsia coat hanging from a hook in the hall had a pair in the pocket. Fortuitously, they were mauve leather, and so would not shed fibres. They looked expensive and Bella would probably miss them at some point, but by then there would be more important things on her mind.

As she climbed the stairs the glowing animals from Teddy's nightlight danced slowly across the walls.

From downstairs she could hear Bella's slack snoring, but up here all was silent.

Stepping out onto the landing the hare moved across her body, casting her gloved hands in its red glow, turning the mauve crimson, then it danced on, to Ewan's bedroom door, leaping over the threshold, as if to mark it out for a sacrifice.

Jen walked on, through the blue and yellow light, until she came to the doorway.

Ewan lay on his back, and now that she was close she could hear him breathing, deeply and regularly. He was a good sleeper then. With a bit of luck his child would take after him. Stepping into the room she held her breath for a squeaky floorboard or any other giveaway. Eliot was sometimes woken by her mere presence entering the bedroom.

But Ewan didn't stir.

She drew closer.

The little fruit knife with the snapped point was about four inches long. That was enough, if she aimed well. She would have to apply a lot of force, but a more easily fatal strike to the throat would produce much, much more blood, which might alert a forensics team to her presence at the scene.

Easing herself onto the bed she straddled him. She didn't have much time to get this right. Deep sleeper as he was, even he would be roused by her thighs pressing against his hips. Sure enough, his breathing caught and his eyeballs twitched under the lids.

She positioned the knife carefully, in the small runnel between his fourth and fifth rib.

He opened his eyes.

Thrusting her whole weight forward she drove the knife into his chest.

He bucked once, like a defective fairground Buckaroo, then was still.

She waited a moment, then felt for a pulse at his wrist. There was nothing. She climbed off him. If a forensics team chose to investigate there was no way of expunging every trace of her presence in the room, but she worked there after all, so it wouldn't be so strange.

She went downstairs.

Her friend was still sleeping peacefully, her snores like the contented grunts of a pig.

Poor Bella, who had been driven to the edge by her husband's emotional cruelty, which they would all attest to, in addition to her already documented psychosis, had simply snapped. During an acute psychotic episode she'd murdered her husband and then simply forgotten about it.

There was a risk Teddy would be taken away, at least temporarily. This was unfortunate, but hopefully he would go to Bella's parents and she would get plenty of supervised visiting rights.

Jen laid the bloodied knife on the turquoise throw, then eased the mauve gloves off inside out and pocketed them to dispose of later.

Then she quietly let herself out of the house.

There was a spring in her step as she walked back to the estate, a certainty that everything was going to work out perfectly.

The best bit by far would be running rings around the police. Those ineffectual muppets who had let her dad beat seven bells out of her mum every Saturday, who had filed away her report when she went to them with her own bruises, and who never even bothered getting the forensics team in when, coming home from The Dog on that last Saturday night, her father 'fell' down the flight of concrete steps to his death. No, the police deserved everything they got.

It had been such a surprise when Chrissy suggested covering up the murder to protect Bella. All the time they were discussing it she had felt like laughing. The offer to create a second crime scene was in hindsight perhaps an act of hubris too far, but it looked very much like they had got away with it. She had replaced the correct medication that same night, and she was glad that Bella didn't seem to have suffered too much. In fact, Bella seemed happier than she had ever been. She still had Teddy, she was slimmer, wealthier and very much enjoying her job as assistant manager of Menswear.

It had all worked out beautifully.

Jen raised her glass of lemonade and drank, feeling the cool liquid pass down her chest and into her stomach. She imagined it percolating through the umbilical cord to the baby slumbering there. That healthy baby with Ewan's flawless genes. It was slightly troubling to think he might inherit Ewan's looks, but Teddy seemed to have taken after his mum, so maybe this one would too.

Her chicken burger arrived and she slathered it with more ketchup than she ever normally used, liberally coating each of the sweet potato fries, calling the waitress back to ask for honey dressing for the salad.

The boy had a sweet tooth, like his mummy. What else would he inherit from her? Her brains, hopefully, though she wouldn't let him get away with half the stuff she did when she was growing up.

What was it her granny had said to her mum after some new teenage outrage, like nicking money out of her purse, or staying out all night? *You let her get away with murder.* Well, yes, her mum had. She knew full well what Jen had been doing when she burst back into the flat breathlessly that Saturday evening long ago as the shouts drifted up from the concrete stairwell. She'd got away with it then because the police were too lazy and corrupt to bother questioning the 'accident'. They had better things to do, like selling off the drugs they confiscated from the estate's dealers, than conduct a proper investigation, and Jen had been expecting the same half-hearted approach to the investigation into Ewan's disappearance. But these detectives had been a surprise, and not a pleasant one.

Jen's disappointment that the investigation was being run by a woman, and thus immune to her flirtation, had turned to consternation when she received Chrissy's Facebook message that the police were at Bella's, ready to conduct a search. The poor Uber driver had got an earful all the way back from Islington: he was going too slow, taking all the wrong roads, was he stupid or something? When they brought her into the station, for the first time in her life she'd felt something akin to fear. But she'd stuck to her story, and eventually they had to let her go. The detective was clearly pissed off – she knew something was up – and even the good-looking black guy seemed immune to Jen's charms. Maybe she was getting old. Time to settle down.

The baby kicked as the first hit of sugar stimulated his growing brain, firing up the synapses and nerve endings. She could almost imagine the delicate thoughts blooming in his head like droplets of milk in water. *I am. I feel.*

She held her stomach and murmured softly and a moment later she felt what might be a little hand push up to touch her own. Her breath caught.

Tomorrow she would go shopping, for all the stuff she'd seen in the others' houses when theirs were babies: the black and white flashcards, Baby Bach CDs, the endless books. She would breastfeed him for the whole six months you were supposed to. And he wouldn't be going to the local sink school that taught kids like Eliot to keep their sights firmly fixed on mechanics and plumbing and building. This boy would attend the school Chloe and Teddy went to. She knew how to work the system. She'd sort it somehow.

Yes, he would be clever, she was determined on it.

Clever enough to get away with murder.

Acknowledgements

First and foremost, as ever, thanks to my lovely agent Eve White and Ludo Cinelli for their unwavering support and advice. To Sam Eades and Katie Brown at Trapeze for their incisive editorial talents, and the rest of the team at Trapeze for really getting behind this book: for mean attention to detail and general handholding, Jennifer Kerslake, for copy-editing, Jo Gledhill, and proofreading, Jade Craddock.

Since I became a mother myself, I've made some great mum friends, and our shared experiences and tribulations have informed many of the incidents in this book. So, in no particular order, thanks and love to Wendy, Shelley, Alison, Donna, Laura, Rhian, Lynne, Sofia, Sue, Louise and Betina.

Just say the word and I will dispose of your husbands.

Newport Community
Learning & Libraries

Newport Community
Learning & Library

Credits

Trapeze would like to thank everyone at Orion who worked on the publication of *The Mothers*.

Editor
Katie Brown

Copy-editor
Joanne Gledhill

Proofreader
Jade Craddock

Editorial Management
Jennifer Kerslake
Isabelle Everington
Charlie Panayiotou
Jane Hughes
Alice Davis
Claire Boyle

Audio
Paul Stark
Amber Bates

Contracts
Anne Goddard
Paul Bulos
Jake Alderson

Design
Lucie Stericker
Joanna Ridley
Nick May
Clare Sivell
Helen Ewing
Charlotte Abrams-Simpson

Finance
Jennifer Muchan
Jasdip Nandra
Afeera Ahmed
Elizabeth Beaumont
Sue Baker
Victor Falola

ST Julians
15│09│20

Marketing
Tom Noble
Lucy Cameron
Jess Tackie

Production
Claire Keep
Fiona McIntosh

Publicity
Alainna Hadjigeorgiou

Sales
Jen Wilson
Victoria Laws
Esther Waters
Frances Doyle
Ben Goddard
Georgina Cutler
Jack Hallam
Barbara Ronan
Andrew Hally
Dominic Smith
Maggy Park
Linda McGregor

Sinead White
Jemimah James
Rachel Jones
Jack Dennison
Nigel Andrews
Ian Williamson
Julia Benson
Declan Kyle
Robert Mackenzie
Ellie Kyrke-Smith
Rachael Hum

Operations
Jo Jacobs
Sharon Willis
Lisa Pryde
Lucy Brem

Rights
Susan Howe
Richard King
Krystyna Kujawinska
Jessica Purdue
Hannah Stokes